DEVIL MAY CARE

VEGAS SLAYERS - BOOK 4

CHRISTINE POPE

DEVIL MAY CARE

Copyright © 2026 by Christine Pope

ISBN: 978-1-946435-90-3

Published by Dark Valentine Press

Cover design by Indie Author Services

Ebook formatting by Indie Author Services

Chapter One

———·‹‹‹‹·۞·››››·———

"...AND LUXURY VINYL PLANK throughout, with carpet only in the bedrooms," Delia was saying as she walked out of the living room of Caleb Lockwood's latest acquisition and headed into the kitchen.

He nodded, even though he knew only a portion of his brain was absorbing her comments.

A much larger part was preoccupied with watching the swing of her long red hair as she moved, the gorgeous shape of her long, slender legs as highlighted by the dark gray pencil skirt she wore. She'd come straight here after leaving the real estate agency she ran with her mother, so she had on her usual work uniform of slim skirt and silk blouse and high heels. Now that May was just about to flow into June, that blouse was sleeveless, and she'd abandoned the jackets she wore during the cooler months here in Las Vegas, but she looked as elegant as ever.

"Um...sure," he said, and she paused and looked across the Formica-topped peninsula—an element in the kitchen he knew was slated for the chopping block, since Delia wanted to tear it out and replace it with an island—and set her hands on her hips.

"Earth to Caleb," she said, and he couldn't help grinning.

"Sorry," he told her. "I trust you on all this. I don't have to know every single detail."

Her brows lifted. They were a dark russet, several shades deeper than her coppery hair, and a perfect frame for the cool, gray-blue eyes he never tired of looking into.

"Even if I go crazy and decide to install marble in the bathrooms and herringbone hardwood floors in the rest of the house?"

Although she had far more real estate experience than he did, even Caleb knew you didn't put costly materials like that in a flip that at most was going to sell in the mid to upper $400,000 range. "Well, okay," he said. "I'd probably have a few questions about that kind of stuff before I signed off on those invoices."

"Good to know you plan to pay a little attention," she remarked, then turned back to the kitchen as though to give it another once-over.

Why she needed to look at it again, he wasn't sure, since he already knew that she planned to rip out everything, just as she intended to similarly gut the master bath and the hall bath that serviced the two secondary bedrooms. The house—which he'd snagged in an online auction after the demon-backed Aegis Holdings collapsed, thanks to their utter defeat at a poker tournament designed to conjure all sorts of diabolical energies—was your basic three-bedroom, two-bath model, measuring a little over 1,700 square feet and located in a neighborhood of equally modest, vaguely Mediterranean-style homes.

Delia estimated they'd probably be able to make around $40-50K on the flip as long as they were careful about the improvements they implemented. Maybe it wasn't quite as quick a way to earn a buck as his time working the various casinos around town, influencing a card turn here and a dice toss there to ensure he won far more than was statistically likely, but he had to admit that flipping houses was a whole lot more honest.

And he wanted to be honest. He wanted to be the man Delia thought he was, the man she'd told she loved only three weeks ago.

He wanted to be worthy of her, despite lineage on his father's side that went straight back to a Prince of Hell.

They'd kissed that day, a kiss that had been

everything he hoped for and much, much more. And there had been plenty of other kisses after that, including a few sessions on the couch at his place or the sofa at her house, passionate interludes that he'd hoped might lead straight into the bedroom.

But they hadn't. Was she taking things slow because that was how she approached all intimate relationships...or was she holding back because she was worried he would bust out with some demon horns and a tail at an inappropriate moment?

Caleb knew that would never happen. Far more human blood than demon ran in his veins, and although that blood gave him some handy powers like being able to teleport or conjure flames —or make sure the cards went in his favor whenever he wanted—he didn't have an alternate, demonic form. He wasn't like the demons who'd taken on human bodies to be able to conceal their true natures. Those bodies had been nothing more than suits, while he knew his biology was no different from Delia's or any other mortal.

Or rather, while there might have been a few genetic markers to prove his grandfather hadn't exactly been the guy next door, it wasn't the sort of thing that would show up in a simple blood test. You'd have to analyze his DNA with an electron microscope to find anything at all out of the ordinary.

And even though he understood that Delia was holding back for her own reasons, he knew he'd wait for her as long as necessary. When he'd met her back in January, something within his soul had understood that no other woman could ever be the one for him.

She came out of the kitchen and glanced over at the fireplace in the living room. One could argue that such a feature wasn't really necessary in a place with the kind of climate Las Vegas enjoyed, but it did add to the value of a property. This one wasn't terribly prepossessing, with its '90s-vintage brass hardware and ceramic tile surround that looked suspiciously like the same tile on the kitchen floor.

"I do want to spend some money to fix that up," she said, and Caleb tilted his head at her, brow raised slightly.

"I thought we were trying to watch our costs on this project."

"We are," she replied, looking utterly unconcerned. "But I have a stucco guy who can cover all that up and make the fireplace look more Mediterranean, which will fit better with the style of the house. It should be less than a grand, and it'll make a real statement."

All right, that didn't sound so bad. He knew the soapstone slabs on the floor-to-ceiling fireplace in his recently remodeled home had cost four times the amount, but it seemed clear that Delia was doing her best to get the most visual bang for their modest bucks.

"Sounds good," he said. He'd never intended to scrutinize every line item on the budget for the remodel, and he knew that if Delia said something would cost a certain amount, then it would.

"But," she went on, "everything here looks cosmetic, just as we'd hoped, so I think it will go fast. We should be able to get this thing done and on the market in about six weeks."

"Great," he said. "Then I guess there isn't anything else we need to do here. Meet you at your place?"

She nodded. They'd fallen into a routine of alternating whose home would be their evening hangout—well, during those times when they wanted to stay in rather than go out to eat or maybe catch a movie or whatever—and since they'd been at his house the night before, they'd already agreed to go to her place.

"I'll lock up here," he added. They both had keys to the flip property, and he figured that would give Delia time to get home first and pull into the garage, maybe take off those stilettos she was wearing. He noticed she tended to ditch them each night as soon as she could.

"Thanks."

A quick flash of a smile—one that made him warm a little, even though he guessed they wouldn't share anything more than kisses tonight, either.

Then again, kissing Delia was plenty exciting all on its own.

She paused to press her lips against his cheek as she went past, and he reached over to squeeze her hand before she made her way to the tiny foyer and let herself out the front door.

The house felt much smaller with her gone. But that was all right; he'd be over at her place soon enough, and besides, this wasn't anyplace where either of them intended to live.

No, the flip property was just a way of keeping himself occupied and making a little extra cash in the bargain.

Well, that and ensuring he and Delia would have a reason to see each other pretty much every day...not that he thought he needed to worry about that. She might not have given any signs that she was ready to jump into bed with him, but at least she'd made it obvious enough that she enjoyed spending as much time in his company as possible.

And he was okay with that.

Delia's home wasn't as big as his, but it was still a good thousand square feet larger than the house they were currently flipping. As always, he found himself relaxing almost as soon as he walked in the door; the decor had a sort of eclectic farm-house/coastal vibe, very different from the stark black and white splendor of his thoroughly remodeled mid-century home.

Not for the first time, he wondered where the two of them would live if they ever formalized their relationship. He felt at home in Delia's house, but he would have preferred something larger, and definitely a backyard with a pool. And although she'd had a lot of input in the design of his house, Caleb knew she'd mostly gone along with his wishes when it came to the decor and that it was probably a little too modern for her.

Most likely, they'd need to meet somewhere in the middle. Which was fine; he really liked his house and felt at home there...but he knew he'd also make a mint if he decided to sell it.

Win/win.

Of course, he knew he was getting a little ahead of himself. He and Delia might have known each other for almost six months now, but they'd only taken that real quantum leap in their relationship three weeks ago. He guessed it was going to require a decent chunk of time before they started seriously talking about any possible futures together.

As he'd guessed, Delia was already barefoot by the time he got to her house. Not that he had a problem with that; she always kept her toenails polished, unlike her fingernails, and she had very pretty feet.

It looked as if she'd been sorting through that day's mail when he arrived, because she had two small stacks sitting on the kitchen island in front of her, probably separated into what she wanted to keep and what she could go ahead and toss. Caleb didn't get nearly as much mail, but he'd been trying to keep a somewhat low profile ever since he got to Las Vegas. Also, he'd only been in his current house for a few weeks, whereas he knew Delia had owned this place for going on three years.

A bottle of pinot noir also sat on the island, and she picked it up and poured some into a stemless wine glass that waited nearby, then handed it over to him.

"What're you in the mood for tonight?"

He could think of a whole lot of things, although he knew she was only asking about what he wanted to order in. Delia Dunne had many sterling qualities, but being a good cook wasn't one of them. It made sense; she lived alone and worked long hours, and whipping up a gourmet meal every night wasn't very practical.

"Whatever sounds good to you," he said. By that point, he'd sampled most of the nearby places that delivered or that DoorDash would fetch, and they were all decent. For him, it was more about being there with her than what they were having for dinner.

Her mouth pursed. Whatever gloss she'd been wearing for most of the day had worn off by now, but her lips were full and rosy without it.

And he knew all too well how luscious those lips felt when they were placed against his.

She picked up a small, somewhat crumpled envelope and frowned as she opened it and gazed down at its contents.

"What is it?" he asked, hoping it wasn't bad news.

But no, that wasn't a standard business-size envelope, but more the kind used for invitations and that sort of thing. God knows he'd seen plenty of them while he was growing up, since his parents were active socially and always seemed to be attending charity banquets and balls and golf tournaments.

All part of the façade his father had worked very hard to maintain. No, nothing to see there, only a prosperous upper-class family like thousands of others.

Well, except for the part where Daniel Lockwood was half demon and possessed a set of powers that most mortals couldn't begin to dream of.

Delia smiled at him at once, as though she guessed she needed to reassure Caleb that the envelope hadn't contained anything compromising.

"It's a wedding invitation from one of my cousins in Chicago. I sort of vaguely remember my mother saying something about Olivia getting engaged a while back."

"Olivia's your cousin?"

"Yes—my aunt Vicky's youngest daughter."

Now that they had that straightened out, Caleb couldn't help asking, "So...you're going to Chicago for the wedding?"

He'd thought he'd kept his tone carefully neutral, but some sort of edge must have slipped through because a smile flickered at the edges of Delia's mouth.

"No, they're getting married here in Las Vegas," she replied. "My mother also mentioned that her fiancé recently bought a house in Henderson. I guess he and Olivia decided they would rather have a kind of destination wedding since he already owns property in the area and they'll have a place to stay for as long as they like."

Caleb supposed that the plan made some sense. Growing up in Indiana, he'd been to Chicago enough times to know that it could be a soupy mess in the summer. Sure, Vegas was hot, but the humidity was usually down in the teens or twenties, which meant it was a lot more comfortable.

"When's the wedding?"

Now Delia frowned. "That's the weird thing... they're getting married on the thirtieth."

"Of *this* month?" he asked, eyebrows lifting again.

Maybe he didn't know a whole lot about weddings and wedding planning, but he thought that sounded like pretty short notice.

"That's only a few days from now," he added.

"I know," Delia said, and turned the wrinkled envelope over in her hand, expression still a little perplexed. "It sure looks like the invitation got misdirected, judging by the condition it's in. It's kind of strange that my mother didn't mention it to me, since I know my parents would have been invited, too—Vicky is my father's younger sister."

Caleb had to admit that did seem a little odd, since what he'd seen of Delia's and her mother's interactions indicated they were fairly close. "Maybe she assumed there wasn't much to talk about, since you're just attending and not actually in the wedding party."

"Maybe. And since she was out of town at that conference in L.A. last week and also had two properties fall out of escrow this month, she's been kind of preoccupied." Delia's frown morphed into an amused little smile. "Will you be my plus-one?"

He blinked at her. "You want me to go to the wedding with you?"

The smile didn't budge. "Do you see me dating anyone else?"

He supposed not. Still, inviting him to a family

event like this seemed like kind of a big step. He'd met Delia's mother only because the two of them worked together, and he'd spent enough time at Dunne & Dunne handling real estate business that he'd bumped into Linda on several occasions.

However, he'd never met Delia's father or anyone else in the family. That wasn't so strange, not with her father's relatives in Chicago and her mother's family in Seattle, but Caleb had just assumed that Delia had held off introducing him to her father because she still wasn't completely sure where things were heading with the two of them.

"No," he allowed. "And I think it would be fun. Where's the ceremony being held?"

She picked up the invitation and scanned it briefly. "Something called 'The Angel's Dream Wedding Chapel,'" she replied, then grinned. "Sounds appropriately cheesey and Vegas-y."

About the same notion had passed through his mind. Was that on purpose? Was part of the reason Delia's cousin and her fiancé had decided to tie the knot here in Las Vegas that they didn't want to take the whole thing too seriously?

A sudden thought occurred to him. "Hey, we should go check out the chapel."

Delia appeared dubious, to say the least. Brow lifting slightly, she asked, "Why?"

"I've never been to a Vegas wedding," he told

her, which was only the truth. "I want to know what I'm walking into so I'll know how to dress."

Still looking a bit skeptical, Delia glanced down at the invitation again. "It just says 'dressy casual.' I don't think she's expecting the male guests to dress like Elvis or anything."

"Maybe not, but it couldn't hurt to take a look anyway," he said, trying to sound as persuasive as possible. While he'd been all right with staying at her house and ordering in, going out on an exploratory mission and grabbing something to eat nearby felt like much more of an adventure.

For a moment, Delia hesitated, but then she took another look at his face and seemed to understand he was more in the mood to go out than have another quiet evening in. "Okay," she said at length. "But give me a minute to change. I don't feel like putting those stilettos back on."

"Not a problem," he replied. "I'll check out restaurants in the area and make sure I pick something casual."

"Almost everything in Las Vegas is casual," she said with a chuckle.

True enough, unless you were going out to one of the top-tier places. And while Caleb appreciated fine dining, he was much happier finding someplace that had great food and not a lot of pretension. The buttoned-up shirts and suit jackets and hoity-toity country club fare had always been his father's kind of thing, not his.

"True," he allowed. "So I'll scope things out, and you can get changed."

She nodded, paused to take a sip of pinot noir, then leaned over to give him a quick kiss before she headed out of the kitchen and down the hall where the main suite was located. "I won't be too long."

No, she wouldn't. While she always looked put together—probably because she never knew when she might run into a potential client, and therefore even her casual outfits were stylish and attractive—she also knew how to get ready fast. Caleb still wasn't entirely sure how she did it...some magic of her own, he supposed, something separate from her ghost-whispering talents and her newly developed ability to see into people's thoughts.

Not everyone's thoughts, thank God, and apparently not his. At least, not all the time. Their minds had connected a couple of times when she was under severe duress, but it wasn't as if she could dip into his brain whenever she felt like it. He didn't know whether that was because his demon blood made him just enough different that her gift wouldn't allow her to see into his mind, or simply because the talent was very new to her and she still didn't have much control over it.

Either way, he was glad his brain mostly seemed to be opaque to Delia Dunne. While he'd been on his best behavior ever since he'd met her, Caleb knew there were quite a few incidents in his past he'd prefer not to explain.

Not right now, anyway. He knew at some point he'd need to come clean with her, but he preferred to put off that dreaded moment for as long as possible.

The last thing he wanted was to see the disappointment in her eyes when she realized he hadn't always been quite as laid-back and friendly as he appeared to be now.

Instead of allowing his thoughts to dwell on that uncomfortable moment in the future, he got out his phone, found where the Angel's Dream Wedding Chapel was located, and did a quick search for nearby eating establishments. The chapel seemed to be downtown, within walking distance of the Clark County Marriage Licensing Bureau— made sense—and therefore was also a quick walk or even shorter drive away from at least ten restaurants.

He narrowed it down to a Mexican place, a Greek restaurant, and a spot that seemed to specialize in Cornish pasties, and figured he'd let Delia choose from those options. As far as he was concerned, he didn't really care where they went as long as it meant they were going out and exploring.

Just as he was returning his phone to his pocket, she came back to the kitchen, now wearing skinny jeans, some leather thongs, and a sleeveless embroidered top that looked vaguely ethnic to him. A pair of silver hoops hung from her ears, and again, he couldn't help being struck by how absolutely gorgeous she was.

"Ever had a Cornish pasty?" he asked, and she blinked.

"No," she replied. "Are pasties in our future?"

"They can be," he said. "There's a place about a five-minute walk from the chapel. Or there's also a Greek and a Mexican restaurant nearby if that's more your speed."

"Pasties sound good," she said at once. "Might as well do something different, right?"

Yet another thing he loved about her. She was almost always up for an adventure, and she never seemed to complain or try to poke holes in his ideas. Sure, if she disagreed with one of his suggestions, she'd tell him exactly why—and could produce the charts and graphs to prove her point—but she was one of the least "my way or the highway" people he'd ever met.

"Then let's go check it out."

***

He drove while she played navigator from the passenger seat. The Mercedes had a perfectly adequate navigation system, but Caleb still preferred to have Delia guide them in. She was the Las Vegas native, after all, and although she'd told him the Angel's Dream chapel was fairly new and not a landmark like some of the other wedding venues in town, she still knew exactly where they were going.

There had always been the possibility that someone would be getting married right then, since weddings happened every day of the week and pretty much twenty-four hours a day in Las Vegas, but the parking lot looked relatively empty when they arrived. He had to admit the place seemed fairly low-key in person compared to the neon-lit kitsch his mind had conjured up, and was instead a simple, pretty building, all white with a small steeple and a cross on top.

The website had said the chapel was open from nine in the morning until nine at night, and in fact, the door to the lobby stood open to the warm evening air as they got out of the car.

"We'll just peek inside," he told Delia.

"Don't you think the people working there will want to know why we're doing that?" she asked.

"Probably," he responded, choosing to ignore the dubious expression she continued to wear. "But that's simple enough. You can just explain that Olivia is your cousin and she asked you to stop by and take a look at the venue in person for her since she's doing all this remotely from Chicago."

This utter lie made Delia's lips pull into a reluctant smile. "You think of everything, don't you?"

He could only grin in reply. "Just call me the king of bullshit."

She chuckled then, although she appeared serious enough once they reached the front door and stepped inside. Cool air surrounded them, doing its best to combat the warm breeze coming in from the parking lot.

Once again, he was surprised to see that there didn't seem to be anything overtly "Las Vegas" and over the top inside. Pale travertine beneath his feet, an electric fireplace surrounded by off-white stacked stone on the other side of the lobby, a couple of tastefully spare crystal chandeliers overhead.

A woman who'd been sitting on the other side of a white wooden reception desk near the front door stood as soon as they entered. "Can I help you?" she asked. She didn't seem too surprised to have a couple of strangers come in off the street, and Caleb reminded himself that a lot of chapels in Vegas allowed walk-ins, even though he wasn't sure if Angel's Dream was one of them. "Are you interested in having a wedding here?"

"Oh, no," Delia said hastily, then paused and sent an apologetic glance over at Caleb, as if realizing that she might have offended him by sounding so opposed to marriage. "That is, my cousin, Olivia Gunderson, is getting married here on the thirtieth. She asked me to stop by and check out a few things in person, since I live here in Las Vegas."

"Of course," the woman said. "We have a wedding scheduled for eight o'clock, but the chapel is empty right now. Go ahead and take a look around—just make sure you don't take too long, since the wedding party for that group should be arriving in about twenty minutes or so."

"We won't take long at all," Delia assured the woman. "Thank you."

And then she looped her arm around Caleb's and guided him out of the office/reception area and into the chapel itself. He would be the first to admit that churches weren't really his thing, but a wedding venue like this didn't have any overtly Christian iconography in its decor, just a few tall, stained-glass windows depicting stylized angels done in subtle pastels.

Once they were alone, Delia glanced around and then back over at him. "So...what exactly are we looking for?"

"Nothing in particular," he said. "I just wanted to get the vibe of the place. It's definitely not all Elvisified, so I guess I don't have to worry about dressing like the King or anything."

"No," Delia replied, lips now twitching in

amusement. "I think a nice suit should be fine. You might not need to wear a tie, though."

That would be good. Temperatures had been inching up, and although they hadn't hit triple digits yet, he was sure the local weather would be kissing the nineties in a few days. Not being strangled by a tie could only be a good thing.

"I wonder why they chose this place," he commented, and Delia shrugged.

"It's pretty," she said. "And that part of the extended family is big. I think Olivia probably wanted to have her wedding someplace that was classy enough that it wouldn't upset my Aunt Vicky, but was also out of the way enough that she wouldn't have to worry about inviting the entire family. Otherwise, she would've probably had at least three hundred people attending."

Caleb had to admit that sounded like a pretty big crowd. No wonder Olivia wanted to duck out and have a destination wedding. Sure, some of the family would be there—it looked as if the chapel could hold about a hundred guests—but having the ceremony here in Las Vegas seemed to guarantee that she wouldn't have to worry about pissing off Great-Aunt Edna or long-lost cousin Eddie if they were somehow not included in the guest list.

While he and Delia were talking, they'd been slowly moving down one of the outer aisles toward the dais at the front, which held a white lectern and several white wooden planters filled with white rose trees. Although nothing about the setup looked at all out of the ordinary, a certain tension began to grow in Caleb's midsection, a knowing without understanding how he knew that something wasn't quite right about this place.

Just as they reached the dais, the temperature in the room seemed to drop at least ten degrees. He looked up, wondering if they'd just paused under an especially industrial-sized air conditioning vent, and that was the reason for the suddenly icy breeze that seemed to blow past his face.

However, no vent was anywhere close to the spot where they stood.

Caleb had grown up with cold weather, but the skin along his forearms prickled anyway. He looked over at Delia, whose expression seemed serene enough.

It sure didn't look to him as if she'd felt the odd shift in temperature.

And then the whispers began, at first so soft that again he wondered if they came from the ventilation system, just like the frigid air that seemed to have descended on him. They grew louder, though, surrounding him in waves of sibilant sound, of words he couldn't quite catch.

In that same moment, Delia reached over and

took his hand, fingers tight on his. "Do you hear that?" she murmured.

So he wasn't imagining things. "Yes," he said in a similar undertone, even as he kept his hand firmly wrapped around hers, making sure she knew he was there for her no matter what was going on. "Can you understand anything of what they're saying?"

Face paler than it had been a moment earlier, she stood quietly and appeared to listen to the whispery voices surrounding them. "No," she said after a moment or two. "Every once in a while, I'm able to catch just a syllable here and there, but none of it makes any sense."

"Whatever it is, it's not natural," Caleb replied, and she nodded, fingers still clinging to his.

"No," she said. Voice more strained than ever, she added, "Can we please get out of here?"

He didn't even have to pause to consider her question. "Absolutely."

Still holding hands, they walked away from the dais and toward the entrance to the chapel. As they went, the whispers died down and had dwindled to nothing by the time they stepped out into the lobby.

What the hell was going on here?

The woman behind the desk gave them a pleasant nod, but since she was on the phone with someone, it didn't seem as if she was inclined to engage them in conversation.

Good thing, too. Caleb really didn't want to try explaining to her that her chapel might be haunted.

He and Delia emerged into the warm evening air. The sun hadn't quite set and cast a baleful orange light across the city's hotels and casinos, their many windows glowing like charged citrine.

By some unspoken agreement, neither of them said anything until they were safely inside his Mercedes and he'd begun to back out of his parking space. Once they were out on Las Vegas Boulevard and heading south toward the Cornish Pasty, though, Delia looked over at him, wide-eyed.

"Just what the hell was *that?*"

Chapter Two

—·‹‹‹·۞·›››·—

CALEB'S JAW WAS SET, AND DELIA COULD tell he wasn't any happier about the supernatural phenomenon they'd just experienced than she was.

"I don't know," he said as he guided the E-Class toward their destination, which luckily was only a few blocks away.

After an experience like that, she knew she could use a drink.

And she also had absolutely no idea what was going on. As she'd told him just a moment earlier, she thought she'd picked up a syllable here and there from those weird whispers in the chapel, but certainly not enough to even piece together a complete word, let alone a sentence.

The sign for the Cornish Pasty Company appeared on their left, lit up by some neon but not too much by Vegas standards. Caleb pulled into the parking lot out back and put the car in park, although he didn't turn off the engine. Cool air continued to stream into the cabin.

"Did you know we were going to encounter something like that?" she asked next, and now the look he shot her seemed startled.

"Why would you think that?"

She shrugged. "Well, it was your idea to go check out the chapel."

"Just so I'd know what I was walking into," he replied, expression still troubled. "Believe me, a by-the-hour wedding chapel in Las Vegas is just about the last place where I'd expect to run into anything like what we just experienced."

His words had the ring of truth, so she didn't bother to press him on the subject. Delia doubted he had anything to do with this.

Well, except for the part where weird happenings seemed to follow Caleb Lockwood around like a bunch of baby ducklings trailing after their mother.

"But let's go inside," he went on. "The place doesn't look too crowded, so hopefully, we can find a table in a corner and continue this discussion over drinks and some food."

That sounded like a great idea, so she didn't bother to protest. Instead, she slung the strap of her purse over her shoulder and opened the passenger-side door, then climbed out.

On the other side of the vehicle, Caleb did the same. Although he didn't take her by the hand when he came over to join her, Delia noticed that he stood fairly close, as if he wanted to make sure he would be right there in case he needed to leap to her defense.

She sort of doubted anything was going to go down at the Cornish Pasty Company, but then again, she hadn't thought they would be dealing with anything supernatural at the Angel's Dream Wedding Chapel, either.

When he opened the door to the restaurant for her and she went inside, she saw the place had a sort of warm industrial vibe, with exposed brick on one wall and the air conditioning ducts doubling as a design element on the high ceilings. As she'd thought, the restaurant didn't seem too crowded, and when Caleb requested a quiet table off in one corner, the college-age girl working as hostess only nodded and guided them right over.

She asked if they wanted drinks, and they both ordered beer—Guinness for Caleb and some Voodoo Brewing brown ale for Delia, since it didn't seem like the sort of place to get wine—and once the hostess was gone, they both settled against the backs of their chairs. However, she couldn't help noticing the way his gaze slowly traveled across the interior of the restaurant, appearing to catalog all the patrons. There was one group of college kids at a bigger table on the other side of the space, and a family not too far away from them, but other than a man and woman drinking beers at the bar, those were the only people eating there that night.

"So...." he said, and Delia couldn't help smiling a little.

Obviously, he was just as much at a loss as she was.

"That's probably a good way to sum it up," she said, even as she reached for a menu. She didn't know when their server was going to appear, but she figured she might as well be ready for whenever they did.

Caleb took the hint and picked up a menu as well. Good timing, because the waiter—a guy who looked like he was probably around Caleb's age of thirty, although with night-dark hair and the kind of warm-toned skin that told her he was probably Native American—came over with their beers and asked them what they wanted to eat.

Since Delia had never been here before, she went ahead and got the original pasty, while Caleb seemed as if he wanted to take a walk on the wild side and got the lamb vindaloo. Their waiter told them their food would be out shortly, and then he headed back to the kitchen, leaving them alone.

"I assume you've never encountered anything like that before," Caleb ventured, and Delia shook her head, then reached for her pint glass.

"Not really," she replied. "I mean, I've encountered temperature drops in some haunted houses, so that part wasn't so odd, but all those voices at once?" About all she could do was lift her shoulders. "That was a new one."

"Same here." He picked up his Guinness and took a long pull. When he set the glass back down again, he had a bit of foam on his upper lip, and despite the possible direness of the situation, Delia found herself wishing they were someplace more private so she could lean over and lick it off.

And that, she thought, was the sort of impulse she would never have experienced before meeting Caleb Lockwood.

No, their chemistry wasn't the problem. It was just...everything else.

"Should I say something to Olivia?" Delia asked then, and Caleb frowned.

"I was wondering that, too."

Of course he was. He might have been a quarter demon, and he might have only been in her life for barely six months, but their thoughts seemed to run along the same lines more often than not.

She still wasn't sure what to make of that.

"I mean, all my instincts are telling me to warn her," Delia said. "But it's not like we're close. I'm not even sure if she knows about the ghost-whispering stuff I do on the side. If I try to tell her the wedding chapel she chose might be haunted, there's a good chance she's going to think I've lost my ever-loving mind."

Caleb tilted his head, eyes narrowing somewhat. "Your extended family doesn't know about your abilities?"

"Well, my parents don't shout it from the rooftops, if that's what you mean," she replied, even as she realized her answer might have sounded somewhat defensive. But it was true; if her aunts and uncles and cousins had lived in Las Vegas as well, then it probably would have been a lot harder to hide her extracurricular activities, so to speak. Since they all lived thousands of miles away, though, and none of them was all that involved in her life, the topic basically had never come up.

Caleb's lips parted, and Delia wondered if he was going to press the issue. However, something in her expression must have told him she didn't want to pursue that particular topic, so instead of speaking, he only reached for his pint of Guinness and sipped from it again.

"Maybe we should check the place out again, just to confirm what we experienced," he suggested.

While on the surface, Delia supposed that was a sensible enough suggestion, she wasn't sure what it would prove. "What...you think if we go back, we might not sense anything at all?"

"I'm not sure," he said. Nothing in his expression or tone seemed to indicate he was particularly invested in the idea, but she had a feeling he was right. No scientist worth his salt would ever publish his findings with only one data point, and although neither she nor Caleb were scientists, it just made sense that they should try to re-create the circumstances surrounding the phenomena they'd experienced a few minutes earlier.

And that meant they needed to go back to Angel's Dream and see if the same thing happened.

However....

"The woman at the front desk said they were having a wedding at eight," she pointed out, and Caleb only shrugged.

"Yeah, but those places are basically like conveyor belts, right? You come in, get the hour you paid for, and then have to move on."

That was true. Delia had gone to a couple of quickie weddings of friends or clients over the years, and you paid your five hundred bucks or whatever your particular package cost, had the ceremony, took the photos, and then got out. Any receptions or other gatherings afterward had to take place in an entirely different venue—often the banquet room of a local restaurant or hotel.

"So we go back at nine after the eight o'clock ceremony is clearing out and see if we can find anything?" she asked, and Caleb nodded.

"That seems like the simplest plan to me."

Since Delia couldn't think of any better options, she said, "Okay, we'll try that."

It seemed they had a plan. Whether it would prove anything was an entirely different matter.

The manager—or whoever the woman working the front desk at Angel's Dream was—looked startled to see the two of them reappear a few minutes after nine. They'd gotten there just in time to see a stretch Mercedes limo whisk away the happy couple, which made Delia think they must have paid for one of the deluxe packages.

The wedding guests had already headed out to their cars, so no one else appeared to be in the building except a cranky-looking guy in coveralls, probably someone on the staff tasked with going into the chapel and cleaning up whatever detritus people might have left behind.

"We wanted to take a look at the chapel again, if you don't mind," Caleb said easily, accompanying the request with one of his patented thousand-watt smiles.

So far, Delia hadn't met many straight females who were immune to that smile, and it seemed the manager of Angel's Dream was no exception.

"Oh, of course," she said, smiling in return.

"We have one of our staff in there cleaning up and getting ready for our first ceremony tomorrow morning, but you're welcome to go in. Just know that he and I both leave at nine-thirty, so don't stay any longer than that."

"We'll only need a minute," Caleb assured her.

He looped his arm in Delia's, and they headed into the chapel. The custodian was over on the other side of the room, bending down to pick up what looked like a dropped program. However, as soon as he caught sight of them, he sent them an annoyed look and disappeared through another door, one Delia guessed probably led into a supply closet or something similar.

Well, at least they wouldn't have to worry about him interfering with the vibes in the space.

Still arm in arm, the two of them moved toward the dais. She could feel herself tensing as they approached, even though everything now felt utterly neutral, with no repeats of the strange, almost buzzing sensation she'd experienced when she'd first walked into the room.

And definitely no temperature drops...and no strange chorus of unseen voices.

Caleb's brows drew together. "I'm not getting anything."

"Neither am I."

Still frowning, he gently released her arm and stepped onto the dais, then moved behind the lectern. Delia wasn't sure what that was supposed to prove, although she thought maybe he was trying to provoke whatever spirits might be lurking in the place. After all, that was where the officiant was supposed to stand, not a quarter-demon interloper.

"Nothing," he told her, then came down off the dais to join her.

"So, what...did we hallucinate the whole thing?"

An amused light flickered in his warm brown eyes. "I doubt it. But whatever's here, it seems to be lying low for the moment. I assume you're not hearing anything, either?"

"Not even a single whisper," Delia replied. While she supposed some people might have been relieved by the utter lack of anything supernatural going on, she couldn't help thinking something was seriously wrong here.

Caleb glanced up at the twenty-foot ceiling with its white-painted beams and smooth plaster, and shrugged. "Well, we weren't able to duplicate what we first sensed here, so we might as well get going."

Fine by her. Maybe if they'd hung around long enough, the whispers would have started up again, but she didn't think so.

"All right," she said. "Let's get out of here."

Caleb drove her home. When they got there, she invited him in, guessing that their conversation wasn't over.

"Some water?" she asked. The one beer with dinner had been enough for her, and she didn't see the point in drinking anything else, especially when she had an early house showing the next morning.

"Sure," he replied.

She went into the kitchen, and he followed her, then leaned up against the black granite counter as she poured water from the pitcher in the fridge and handed over a glass.

"So," he said after he'd taken a sip, "either we both had the same hallucination, or whatever's hanging out in that chapel got a whiff of your psychic powers and decided to lie low."

"Or maybe it was your demon blood," Delia suggested, and his shoulders lifted a fraction.

"It's possible," he said. Something flickered in his eyes, and she wondered if she should have even mentioned his demonic heritage. Although he'd always been honest with her about it, she knew he didn't like to discuss the inhuman blood that flowed through his veins unless he absolutely couldn't avoid doing so. "Or...."

"Or what?"

For a second or two, he didn't answer, and instead remained leaning against the counter, fingers tapping against the glass of water he held. It was in still moments like this that Delia was struck again by how really handsome he was, how sculpted his expressive mouth, how the sweep of his dark brows contrasted with his sandy blond hair.

Maybe someday she'd get tired of looking at him, but that day definitely wasn't now.

"The atmosphere in a place like that must be pretty charged," he said after a pause. "All those hopes and dreams, all those people gathering to wish their loved ones well. Do you think it's possible that all we picked up was some sort of emotional residue and not anything ghostly?"

Delia found herself frowning. It was an angle to the situation she might not have even thought of, but she supposed Caleb had a point.

Except....

"I've been in places like that before and never sensed anything odd," she told him.

He didn't look too fazed by that revelation. "Maybe not," he replied. "But have you been in one since your powers really started to wake up?"

No, she hadn't. The last quickie wedding she'd attended in a place like that had been her college friend Suki's, who'd wisely decided that it would be much smarter to put all the money she and her fiancé might have spent on a much more lavish ceremony toward a down payment on a house instead. That had been more than two years ago, and in fact, Suki and Zack had bought a house about a year after their wedding, so going the budget route had obviously been a smart choice.

Anyway, back then, Delia had thought her "psychic" gifts extended to ghost whispering and nothing else. She hadn't been able to communicate with her mind or close down interdimensional portals or do much of anything except sense whether a house was haunted and figure out the best way to let a resident ghost know it was time to move on to the next world.

"I haven't," she admitted. "So you could be right. In which case, there's no reason in the world to tell Olivia that something might be iffy about the chapel she chose for her wedding."

"Probably not," Caleb said. "Still, I might try to slip back in there at some point and see if I notice anything. If it still feels fine, then I guess we'll just have to chalk it up to being a psychically charged atmosphere and call it a day."

"All right."

She knew she sounded far less than certain, and he seemed to realize she needed a little reassurance. He set his glass down on the counter and came over to her, wrapping his arms around her waist and pulling her close. At once, her body responded to his proximity, the usual warmth flooding through her as she looked up so their mouths could meet.

Ah, those lips, so warm and welcome, so strong. Not for the first time, Delia wondered why she couldn't seem to allow things to go any further than this, why she didn't seem to have the inner will to take his hand in hers and lead him down the hall to her bedroom.

But she didn't. No, she allowed the kiss to linger, and eventually she pulled away.

"Thanks for making me feel better about all this."

If he was at all disappointed that she'd ended the kiss...and had given no indication that she wanted things to proceed further...she couldn't see any evidence of it in his face. Instead, he smiled a little as he reached down to push a strand of hair away from her cheek.

"Just doing my job, ma'am."

In response, she grinned, and knew the moment had safely passed.

"Well, you're damn good at it."

They agreed to meet at the flip house the next day to go over some flooring samples, and then she walked him to the door and waited there as he got into his charcoal-hued Mercedes and backed out of the driveway. Once he'd turned the corner, she shook her head at herself.

Coward.

The next morning, she had to be up earlier than usual, since the client she was meeting at a prospective property couldn't be there at any other time except eight in the morning. Although Delia hadn't been up particularly late, she was still a little annoyed by the disruption to her regular routine, since normally, she didn't get to the office until around nine.

Or maybe she was just irritated with herself because of the way she'd allowed things to end the night before.

Of course, she'd been a real estate agent long enough that she would never allow any of her inner turmoil to reveal itself to a client, and was briskly cheerful as she showed the house to the prospective buyer, a single man who'd told her he worked in security. It would be a cash transaction, making her wonder exactly what kind of "security" he was talking about, but long ago she'd learned not to ask too many questions. The provenance of people's funds only mattered if they were selling their house and the transaction was dependent on those funds for escrow to close.

Once she was done with the showing—the man said he was interested but needed some time to think things over—she headed back to the office. Her mother probably wouldn't be in for at least another half hour or so, giving Delia some necessary space to get her head together and try to figure out if it really was wise not to say anything to Olivia about the chapel. Sure, the wedding was less than a week away, but wedding chapels were pretty thick on the ground in Las Vegas. Her cousin could probably find another venue without too much trouble if Delia decided to stick her nose in it and issue a few warnings.

On the other hand, neither she nor Caleb had sensed anything strange when they checked out the place a second time. Which was the true impression? Those odd whispers and the other phenomena associated with them, or the serene quiet they'd experienced during their last visit?

No way of knowing, of course, which tended to be the problem when dealing with anything supernatural. There were always so many variables involved, many of which didn't even reveal themselves right away.

It's going to be fine, Delia told herself. *That chapel probably hosts seven or eight weddings a day, maybe more. If there was anything weird going on, don't you think someone would've noticed something by now?*

Maybe. However, she'd already learned that there were huge chunks of the population who didn't have a psychic bone in their bodies. And even if someone had a tendency to be sensitive, it was very likely that they'd push aside any feelings of foreboding or odd flashes, believing them to be something their own minds had conjured up rather than being caused by some sort of external phenomenon.

Also, even if everything was just hunky-dory with the chapel, and she and Caleb had picked up on psychic emotional residue and nothing more, there was also the teeny little wrinkle of her asking him to be her plus-one.

Smooth move, Delia.

Not that she would have gone with anyone else, but she could have attended the wedding alone. She'd been single since she and her ex-fiancé Bill had broken up several years ago, so it wouldn't have looked too strange.

But she knew things were getting serious with Caleb, and not inviting him would have been even more awkward. Her mother already knew they were seeing each other, and Delia assumed Linda must have passed that information on to Delia's father at some point, although in general, he tried to stay out of his daughter's personal life.

They probably would have asked if she'd shown up alone.

No, it would be fine.

For now, anyway. Delia knew that if she and Caleb continued to see each other...if their relationship continued to progress...then at some point, she'd have to tell them the truth about him.

With his permission, of course, but since he'd told her from the beginning who and what he was, she sort of doubted he would want her to withhold that information from her parents. After all, if the relationship progressed to its logical conclusion, then at some point, they'd be his parents, too.

God knows he could use connections like that in his life. Although he hadn't talked about them very much, Delia got the impression that his mother was a cold woman, more concerned with appearances than providing any real emotional support to her son, and Caleb's father?

Well, it sure seemed as if everyone was better off with him safely banished to Hell.

One step at a time, Delia told herself. From what she'd been able to tell, her mother already liked Caleb a lot, and she had no reason to believe her father wouldn't like him, too. Once he'd been established in her life and her parents had gotten to know him better...well, maybe that would be the time to reveal the truth.

However, that was all far off in the future, and Olivia's wedding was only a few days away. While Delia was more and more inclined to believe what Caleb had said about psychic residue, she also thought it couldn't hurt to reach out to the one person who could do a little digging and maybe see if there was some reason to believe things at the Angel's Dream Wedding Chapel weren't exactly what they seemed.

She reached for her phone and went over to the messages, then looked up the text thread with her best friend Pru, who just happened to be a private detective and was great at this sort of thing.

Pru? If you have some time, could you look into the Angel's Dream Wedding Chapel for me? Who owns it and for how long, that kind of stuff.

Because it was so early in the morning, Delia doubted she'd hear from her night owl friend until closer to noon.

That was all right, though.

When Prudence Nelson was on a case, the truth always came to light.

Chapter Three

———·‹‹‹·☾·›››·———

Delia seemed tense the next afternoon. Not that Caleb could really blame her after the strange but utterly inconclusive goings-on at the Angel's Dream chapel the night before, but he couldn't help thinking something else must be weighing on her mind.

"I don't have to go to your cousin's wedding if you don't want me to," he said. All morning, he'd been wondering if Delia had invited him out of obligation and not because she really wanted him there, and he figured he might as well give her an easy out in case she was having second thoughts.

She'd been studying samples of luxury vinyl plank, all of which were currently laid out on the carpeted floor of the house he'd bought a few weeks earlier. Now she looked up at him and blinked, her expression mystified.

"Why in the world would you say that?"

He hitched his shoulders. "Just a feeling. I don't want to make things uncomfortable for you."

At once, she stepped away from the sliding glass window—she'd placed the samples near it because she wanted to see what they looked like in natural light—and came over and slid her arms around his waist.

"Have I told you lately that you're the nicest quarter demon I've ever met?"

He couldn't help smiling. "Well, that's kind of a low bar."

"Maybe, but I meant it." She paused there, her lovely face now very serious. "And I wouldn't have asked you to go if I hadn't wanted you to be my date."

That was what he'd been hoping to hear. Still, the expression in her eyes seemed almost wary, and he guessed there was more she wanted to say.

"Is something else going on?"

Delia's mouth tightened for a fraction of a second, and she took a step back, ending their embrace. However, she remained close enough that Caleb couldn't take her shift in position as a rejection, more just a quiet acknowledgment that she'd given him a reassuring hug, but now it was time to get down to business. "This morning, I asked Pru to look into the chapel. Just in case."

Clearly, she was worried that she might have

overstepped by doing so, even though it was her cousin's wedding and some might have said she had a familial duty to make sure the place wasn't owned by the Mob or something.

Or worse. Aegis Holdings might have fallen apart, but they had only been a subsidiary of the Styx Group, the shadowy company that seemed to have been in cahoots with Calach, the original demon Caleb and Delia had tangled with back in January. He knew Pru had been investigating Styx as best she could, although it sure seemed as if she hadn't done much more than run into repeated brick walls in her search for who...or what...ultimately controlled the corporation.

"That was a good idea," he said, gratified by the way Delia's expression brightened at once upon hearing his words. "Has she found anything?"

"Not a whole lot, but to be fair, she only started her research about an hour ago. But she also said she was glad I'd gotten in touch because she wanted to get together with the two of us and talk about what she found regarding the Styx Group."

Caleb found himself frowning. "I thought she wasn't having any real luck with that."

"That was my impression, too, but it sounds like she has something she wants to discuss." Delia paused there. "Is it okay to meet at my place around six, or would you rather get together at your house?"

"Your place is fine," he said at once. True, his house was bigger, but Pru and Delia had been friends long before he came along, so it just seemed more logical to have their meeting someplace where Pru was more comfortable.

Although Delia didn't come right out and say she was glad they'd decided on her house for the little get-together, something about the way her posture seemed to relax told him she'd been hoping for the same thing.

"Great," she said. "Then I'll go ahead and text her."

She went over to the kitchen peninsula, where she'd left her purse, and picked up her phone and tapped out a quick message. Once that was done, she returned to the flooring samples and set her hands on her hips, frowning slightly as she stared down at them.

"I think Nordic Oak is the way to go," she said at length. "Having lighter flooring will make the house look bigger. Does that sound okay to you?"

The question was a courtesy, nothing more. Or rather, while Caleb realized she wouldn't make those sorts of decisions unilaterally, he also understood that Delia knew way more about this stuff than he did, and it was better to go with the flow unless he was violently opposed to one of her choices.

"It sounds great," he said. "I like what you've chosen for the house."

Which wasn't a lie. He could tell she was doing whatever she could to make the little tract home feel light and bright and airy, choosing finishes that looked much more expensive than they actually were. Whoever ended up buying the place was going to get a great deal.

"Then I'll go ahead and place all the orders," Delia responded. "I'm pretty sure everything is in stock, but I'll double-check that to make sure. No point in having this project hang on any longer than it needs to, not when you have a bunch of cash wrapped up in it."

Like he cared about that. Yes, he'd rolled a decent chunk of the profits from the sale of his previous home into buying this one, but he had many times that stashed in various accounts around town. His finance guy had recommended a broker, and early earnings on his stock portfolio looked promising, giving him yet another source of income. Caleb wasn't quite sure why he hadn't wanted to be more hands-on about the stock market stuff—it was gambling in its own way, he supposed—and yet he honestly didn't care what was happening with his portfolio as long as he wasn't losing money.

Maybe investing in the stock market wasn't immediate enough for him. After all, it wasn't as if he was sitting down at a blackjack table with a bunch of other investors and trying to see who would come out on top.

Delia's phone pinged, and she picked it up. "Okay, we're good for six o'clock at my place," she said after taking a quick look at the screen. "And I have just enough time before my three-thirty client to swing by the flooring warehouse and get this order taken care of." A pause, and she slanted Caleb a glance from under her eyelashes. "Can you manage to stay out of trouble until six?"

"I'll do my best," he drawled, even as he wondered exactly what he would do with himself until then. Even though Las Vegas appeared to have been swept clean of demonic influences, he hadn't had much appetite for gambling after that mess with the tournament at the Desert Paradise casino, and even though his house backed up to a golf course, he still didn't have the slightest desire to take up the game.

Well, he could always have a swim when he got home, maybe take a look online to see if any other promising properties had popped up. Although he would prefer not to buy another flip until this one was finished and on the market, if the right house came along, he might go ahead and pick it up anyway.

Delia came over to him and gave him a quick

kiss, nothing too lingering, since he knew she was strapped for time. And honestly, he wouldn't have wanted to get too hot and heavy here anyway, not when there wasn't a stick of furniture in the place and the air seemed just slightly stale from the house being closed up for so long.

He preferred to wait for better things.

"See you at six," he said.

A swim had helped to clear his head a little, and he'd showered afterward to get the chlorine off and prep for the meeting at Delia's house. Not that he expected anything to happen between Delia and him, not when Pru would be there as well, but Caleb supposed that his mother's impressing on him the need to look presentable at all times was still buried deeply enough in his psyche that he really couldn't do anything else.

When he pulled into the driveway, he noted that Pru's little green Mini Cooper was parked at the curb already. Since he was right on time, he guessed she must have been eager to get over to the house and share her findings.

If she was that Johnny on the spot, Caleb had a feeling that what she'd wanted to share couldn't wait.

Steeling himself for whatever might lie ahead, he went to the front door and rang the bell. It was way too early in their relationship for Delia to have given him a key, but he kind of wished he had one anyway. He didn't like things being so formal between the two of them.

She answered the door in skinny jeans and a loose, sleeveless blouse, so he knew she'd given herself enough time to change before their "meeting" started. Also, while he knew she had a fairly extensive wardrobe and was always the height of professionalism when she was at work, he guessed she wasn't really a fan of those clothes, since she always did her best to get out of them almost as soon as she could once she was off the clock.

Once a punk rock chick, always a punk rock chick, he supposed.

"Hey, Caleb," she said, and stepped out of the way to allow him inside.

The foyer was just barely visible from the living room, but that didn't stop him from bending down to place a quick kiss on her lips. It wasn't as if Delia was trying to hide her relationship from Pru or anyone else, so he didn't see the need to change the way they usually greeted one another.

"Hope I didn't miss anything," he said, and Delia smiled.

"No, although Pru's champing at the bit to

share what she's found out. Let's go sit down—I already have some munchies and a pitcher of iced tea ready to go."

Caleb would have preferred a pitcher of beer or maybe margaritas, although he also understood that it probably wasn't a good idea to muddle his wits too much if they had serious topics they needed to discuss. He followed Delia into the living room, where Prudence Nelson was sitting in one of the club chairs. Her hair was still the same dark emerald green it had been during their adventures in Laughlin a few weeks earlier, which surprised him a little. From what he'd been able to tell, she tended to change it with almost bewildering frequency.

Maybe her hairstylist had told her to cool her jets for a while to avoid damaging her shoulder-length locks beyond repair.

"Hi, Pru," he said as he settled himself on the sofa.

"Hi, Caleb," she responded. She had a glass of iced tea and a plate of munchies—stuff he thought was from Trader Joe's, mini quiches and a section of a small pepperoni pizza—sitting on the coffee table in front of her. "Glad you could make it."

Something in her tone almost made it sound as if they'd been waiting on him to get started. In a way, he supposed that was true...although only because Pru had been early, and not because he was running late or anything.

"Well, my calendar had an opening," he quipped.

Delia grinned, although Pru only shook her head.

Caleb went ahead and got himself some iced tea and a few snacks as Delia sat down next to him on the couch. He wondered if she'd put something together that was a little more substantial than just chips or cheese and crackers because she intended this to substitute for their dinner, and thought they'd probably still need to order some takeout after they were done talking with Prudence.

"Okay, so Delia asked me to look into the Angel's Dream Wedding Chapel," she said, obviously deciding there had been enough chitchat and now it was time to get down to business. "And almost at once, I found some kind of sketchy stuff."

"Such as?" Caleb asked, then drank some iced tea.

Next to him, Delia sat up a little straighter, her expression immediately concerned. "What, is it owned by the Mob or something?"

Pru shot her a crooked smile. In contrast to the green hair, she had dark eyes and pale skin, and was pretty enough in a sort of French street urchin sort of way. "No, not as far as I've been able to tell. But it was purchased recently by a shell company that looks like it's the same outfit that has been buying a bunch of other wedding chapels across Las Vegas."

Delia was frowning, although that didn't stop her from putting a few morsels on one of the plates she'd stacked on the coffee table. "Why would anyone want to buy a bunch of Vegas wedding chapels?"

"I have a theory." Pru set down her iced tea and then reached for the satchel she had sitting on the floor next to the club chair she currently occupied. Caleb knew she carried her laptop and various other odds and ends in the thing—and that she never seemed to leave the house without it—but this time, rather than her computer, she pulled out a large paper map of Las Vegas, one that had circles around what he assumed were the properties in question, along with a series of lines connecting them.

Lines whose pattern looked ominously familiar.

Delia asked the question first. "Are those...?"

"Yep," Pru responded. "Ley lines. We already knew that they crisscross the city, and it turns out all the recently purchased chapels are arranged along them...except for Angel's Dream. That place sits right where two of the lines intersect."

Making its location extremely powerful. Two such ley lines had connected under Rubel Castle in

Glendora, where Caleb's father and the rest of the part demons had attempted to open a gate that would allow their master Belial to return to this world. The plan had been foiled, which was why Caleb had spent two endless years cooling his heels in Hell before he had a chance to return to the mortal plane...and why all the other members of the Greencastle group were still stuck down there.

"No wonder it felt so off," Delia murmured. She'd paled a little, and Caleb reached over to give her fingers a reassuring squeeze.

Pru sat up a little straighter. "You went there?"

"Yes," Delia replied. "Caleb thought we should check it out, so we popped in there yesterday. And when we were there, we experienced weirdnesses like the temperature dropping and hearing voices that shouldn't have been there, so we thought something must be up."

"Although we went back a little while later, and everything seemed quiet enough," Caleb put in. "So we weren't sure what to think."

Pru listened to all this with narrowed eyes. Although she'd been around plenty of supernatural activity when they went on their rescue mission to Laughlin only a few weeks earlier, he got the impression that she would still prefer to take all this with a grain of salt.

Even though the evidence of her eyes and ears was kind of hard to ignore.

"Why do you think you didn't notice anything during your second visit?" she asked then, and he shrugged.

"I have no idea," he said. "Just because I'm part demon doesn't mean I have the answers to all this stuff. It's not like I took a class called 'Paranormal Activity 101' or something."

That comment made Prudence chuckle, although he thought he detected something almost uneasy about the sound, as if she knew deep down there wasn't anything remotely funny about any of this.

"Point taken," she replied. "I was also able to trace a couple of the Styx Group's financials. Maybe they're getting sloppy. Anyway, I'm about ninety percent sure they're the ones behind the shell company that's buying the wedding chapels."

"First investment properties when masquerading as the Aegis Group, and now chapels," Delia murmured. Her slender form seemed very tense as she sat upright next to him on the couch, and Caleb wished he could pull her close and give her some much-needed comfort.

With Pru Nelson sitting across the coffee table from them, he guessed that probably wasn't a very wise thing to do. Not that she would say anything, of course, but he guessed an eye roll would be all she needed to communicate her annoyance with such public displays of emotion.

"Everything under the guise of some other company making those deals," Prudence said. "I'm not sure what Styx's game is, though."

Delia's fingers tightened on the knees of her jeans. However, she sounded calm enough as she responded, "Well, in Laughlin, the demon August Sellers was clearly trying to use my power and the power of the Colorado River to open a gate to the underworld. And even though we still don't have all the details of what was going on during that tournament at the Desert Paradise casino, it sure looks like they were trying to do about the same thing."

"That's what demons always try to do," Caleb said frankly, and both women fastened him with gazes that were a little too sharp. "I mean, besides the ones who come here just to indulge in some petty mischief. But higher-level demons—the ones who can plan this kind of stuff and attempt to carry it out—they're always looking for a way to unleash Hell on Earth. They're still angry about being cast out of Heaven millennia ago."

"That's a long time to hold a grudge," Pru said, and he couldn't help smiling a little.

"True, but that's how demons are. So when they fail with one scheme, they move on to the next." He kind of thought Prudence had buried the lede on this one, considering how they'd been spending months trying to get more information about the Styx Group. Then again, he supposed he could see why she thought the issue with the wedding chapels was a little more pressing, since Delia's cousin was supposed to get married at one in just a couple of days.

"So...they're going to try to do something with ley line energy again?" Delia asked. A faint crease had appeared between her brows, the one that told Caleb she was wrestling with a problem she didn't quite understand. "It didn't work last time, so what's the point?"

No, it hadn't, thanks to his intervention. True, he hadn't even known exactly what he was doing at the time, only that the demons controlling things during the tournament were summoning up the kind of dark magic that could have laid Las Vegas waste. The only thing he'd truly understood was that it needed to be stopped.

And it had, thank God.

"Demons don't really follow that whole idea of the definition of insanity being something you do over and over again, expecting to get a different result." Caleb knew he sounded dry, but doing what he could to detach himself from the situation was the easiest way for him to focus and attempt to discover what was really going on here. "And, to be honest, ley lines are the best way to summon the kind of energy they need for that kind of massive magic. They don't possess it themselves, which is why they have to work with the natural energies in this world."

"And the wedding chapels?" Pru asked. She also seemed a little puzzled, and he couldn't blame her. "What's the point of using those?"

"They're places where a lot of emotional energy has been focused," he replied. "So I suppose if you put that on top of the energy already in place from the ley lines, then they're going to pack an additional punch. The wedding vows and commitment ceremonies create a specific *type* of emotional resonance—hope mixed with permanence—that demons can twist into binding energy for their rituals. Other emotional nodes, like funeral homes or hospitals, have strong energy, but it's the wrong 'flavor' for creating stable gateways. These are all just educated guesses, though—it's not as if there's any real science to back it up."

That was for sure. Magic and science were pretty much the opposite of one another, so you couldn't use science to explain anything that happened in the magical realm...or the world of angels and demons.

"I'd say you still have a unique perspective on the situation, though," Delia told him, and again he shrugged.

For all he knew, he could have been making shots in the dark and nothing else. He didn't want her—and Pru—to think he had all the answers.

Just about the opposite, actually.

Before he could reply, someone knocked at the door. Caleb immediately tensed, while Delia only looked puzzled.

"Were you expecting someone?" he asked, knowing he sounded a little too tense.

"No," she replied, even as she set down her glass of iced tea and rose from the couch. "But we still get people going door to door here, even though there are 'No Soliciting' signs all over the neighborhood. Let me take care of it."

She headed over to the door and opened it. A moment later, her startled voice traveled back to Caleb and Pru in the living room.

"Ty?"

Ty Carter, the half angel who'd first made an appearance during the Desert Paradise poker tournament and had proved to be a valuable ally during the mission to rescue Delia down in Laughlin. Although Caleb had warmed to the guy somewhat over the past few weeks, he still couldn't prevent an unwelcome thought from passing through his mind.

Had Ty been surveilling them somehow, waiting for the right moment to appear?

Over in her club chair, Pru raised a hand to smooth her hair—an unconscious gesture, Caleb guessed. Still, he couldn't help being a little amused. He hadn't missed some of the glances she'd sent toward Ty during their adventure in Laughlin...or the way he'd seemed almost admiring of Delia's best friend during a few stray moments.

Get a room, you crazy kids, Caleb thought then, although he knew the pair were a long way from getting there.

Or anywhere at all, to be honest. Fraternizing with green-haired cuties probably wasn't part of the half angel's mission.

Delia came back into the living room, with Ty a few feet behind her. As always, he wore a T-shirt and faded jeans and boots, his dark hair pulled back into a ponytail. His cover while living here in Las Vegas was supposedly as a tennis pro at the DragonRidge Country Club, but he dressed more like a motorcycle mechanic during his downtime.

"Ty," Caleb said, his tone purposely wry, "what a lovely surprise."

As usual, the man didn't bother to take the bait. "It's not a surprise, and you know it. I needed to talk to you once you were all together—and once some of my suspicions were confirmed."

"Suspicions about the wedding chapel acquisitions?" Pru asked, and the half angel immediately looked over at her.

"Yes," he said. "So, you already know about it."

"We know a couple of things," Delia said. "The rest is just guesswork. But please, go ahead and sit down. I'll grab a glass from the kitchen so you can have some iced tea."

For just a moment, Ty looked as if he might protest, to say he hadn't come over here for a social call. But then he seemed to realize doing so would waste more time than simply going with the flow, so he nodded and said, "Thanks. I appreciate it."

She headed into the kitchen while he took a seat in the empty club chair next to Prudence. The map she'd produced earlier was still laid out on the coffee table, probably a little too close to the tray of TJ's goodies, now slowly getting lukewarm.

Ty's gaze sharpened as he looked down at the map. "So...you've already tracked all of them."

A slight hint of pink touched Pru's cheeks. "Well, these were the ones whose sales I was able to locate. I wasn't totally sure whether this was everything, though."

"It is," Ty said, then paused as Delia returned with a glass and handed it over to him. He thanked her and poured himself some iced tea from the pitcher before continuing. "There are some chapels here in Las Vegas that have so much history and are such landmarks that the owners weren't willing to give them up at any price."

Nice to hear that sometimes integrity won out over cold, hard cash. "We were talking about the chapels' position on the ley lines that cross Las Vegas," Caleb said.

"Yes, that's why the buyers wanted them," Ty replied.

By that point, Delia had sat back down next to Caleb. "So...the buyers are more demons?"

"Most likely," Ty said.

"We're pretty sure the Styx Group is behind all this," Prudence remarked, and both Ty's eyebrows lifted.

It seemed the all-knowing half angel didn't know everything after all.

"You're sure of that?"

She shifted in her chair so she was facing him a little more directly. "Yeah, it seems as if Styx has its fingers in all this. I haven't been able to find out much more than that, though. They're pretty good at covering their tracks."

"Yes, they are," Ty said, now looking grim. "They've hidden the information about who's running things so well that we haven't been able to learn very much, either."

Not for the first time, Caleb wondered who that "we" referred to exactly. When Ty had first appeared at the Desert Paradise poker tournament, he'd been working with two other men, but they hadn't been a factor during the rescue mission to Laughlin, or in the weeks since. Had they been reassigned, or had someone farther up the food chain decided that Ty could handle all this on his own?

He had a feeling that if he asked, he wouldn't get a straight answer. The half angel only told them what he absolutely had to, and even then, getting information out of him could be like pulling teeth.

"Why not?" Pru asked.

For a moment, Ty looked almost uncomfortable. Did he not like admitting that the side of the angels wasn't as omniscient as it seemed, that maybe demons were still able to pull a trick or two on them?

But then he said, "Whoever's in charge at the Styx Group, they're very good at obfuscation. Our best guess is that the company has all sorts of subtle wards running, the sort of thing that makes it impossible to pierce the corporate veil, so to speak, and get a real glimpse of what's going on there. So you being able to discover that the shell company buying properties here in Las Vegas is connected to them is something of a feat."

Pru didn't exactly squirm in delight, but Caleb could tell she was pleased by this praise. "Well," she said, her tone now deprecating, "I think they got a little sloppy. Most likely, they probably didn't think anyone would be able to put two and two together this quickly."

"We were thinking that maybe the other reason the chapels were a target is because of the emotional energy that concentrates in those kinds of spaces," Delia put in, and Ty immediately inclined his head toward her in agreement.

"That's exactly why," he said. "The demons will be able to turbocharge the energy they're summoning, for lack of a better word. And the Angel's Dream chapel sits right at the intersection of two lines, so it's probably their primary focus."

Caleb had to admit it was sort of ironic to think that a place with such a name might be the location of a hellmouth opening in the middle of the city.

"So...what can we do about it?" he asked. Theories and speculation were great, but if they couldn't come up with a plan to keep the demons from harnessing all that energy, then they—and everyone else in Las Vegas—were going to be in a world of hurt.

"My cousin is getting married at that chapel," Delia said. Although she sounded brisk enough, Caleb thought he caught just the slightest waver at the edge of her voice. True, it didn't seem as if the two women were very close, but most people probably wouldn't be too happy at the prospect of one of their relatives getting trampled by demons as they were exchanging vows.

Ty didn't seem too startled by that revelation, seeming to signal that he already knew Olivia Gunderson was in harm's way. "You need to find a way to get her to change her plans," he said. "There are other chapels in the city that are safe, so all you have to do is convince her that she needs a venue change."

This admonition obviously didn't sit very well with Delia, since she crossed her arms and sent the half angel a flat stare. "And can you tell me exactly how I'm supposed to do that? It's only a few days until the wedding, and I assume I can't just come right out and tell Olivia that she needs to go else-where because a bunch of demons want to open a gateway to Hell in that particular location."

"You're a persuasive woman, Delia," Ty replied, unperturbed. "I'm sure you'll think of something. In the meantime, about all we can do is monitor the situation and do our best to keep as many people out of harm's way as we can."

"There must be something else," Pru protested. "Sitting around on our hands isn't going to help anyone."

"I didn't say we should just 'sit around,'" he returned calmly. "But without a few more facts in our pocket, I don't know what else to do."

"Are the other people getting married in those chapels in any danger right now?" Caleb asked, and Ty frowned.

"I'm not sure...but I don't think so. May thir-tieth is a full moon, one that takes place while Mercury is retrograde, and I think that's why that particular day is going to be the most dangerous."

Delia's cousin had definitely picked a doozy of a date for her wedding ceremony.

Next to him, Delia sat up a little straighter, chin lifted in a position he knew all too well.

Maybe the odds were stacked against them, but Caleb knew she would do whatever it took to keep her family safe...and the rest of Las Vegas as well.

Chapter Four

—·‹‹‹·◌·›››·—

THERE DIDN'T SEEM TO BE MUCH TO discuss after that. They all agreed to meet back at her house when they came up with some actionable information, and then Delia walked Ty and Pru to the door. She halfway wondered if the two of them were going to go somewhere together after this.

Apparently not, though, since Prudence got in her beloved Mini Cooper and Ty climbed into a white pickup truck parked at the curb, and they headed off in opposite directions.

Oh, well. Delia couldn't help thinking there was a spark of attraction between the two, but she sure wasn't going to play matchmaker.

At the moment, she had plenty of other drama to keep her busy.

She returned to the living room, where Caleb was waiting for her on the couch.

"Not very welcome news, huh?" he said, and she allowed herself a sigh.

"Not really," she replied, then sat down next to him. By that point, it was nearly seven, and she supposed they should be thinking about dinner. The snacks she'd put out had helped a little, but she knew she needed something a bit more substantial to eat than a couple of mini quiches and half a slice of pizza no bigger than her hand.

Most likely, she was thinking about food because that was easier than trying to figure out how she could possibly tell her cousin Olivia that she needed to change wedding venues.

"What do you want to order in?" Caleb asked, and she wanted to hug him.

How did he always seem to know what was going on in her mind?

"Something horribly fattening," she replied.

"Fettuccine alfredo from Tortellini?" he suggested.

That was her favorite local Italian restaurant. Most of the time, she tried to avoid the dish affectionately referred to as "heart attack on a plate," but right then, she just wanted the comfortiest comfort food she could find.

"I love you," she said simply, and he grinned

and then leaned over so he could press a kiss against her cheek.

"I'll call in the order."

He got his phone out of his pocket and placed an order for a family-size alfredo, along with a house salad and an order of garlic bread. Probably the bread was redundant, considering all they'd be eating was pasta heaped with cream sauce, but that was all right.

Still, she guessed she should send any leftovers home with him. Being part demon seemed to have given Caleb the metabolism of the gods, considering he could eat pretty much anything he wanted and never gain weight. She tended to be okay at that sort of thing, too, although she knew a meal like this would probably require an additional half hour on the treadmill tomorrow morning.

That was all right, though. Maybe the mindless exercise would give her the time she needed to think of some convincing arguments as to why Olivia needed to move her wedding to a location that wasn't quite so spiritually fraught.

"It's going to be okay," Caleb said as he rose from the couch, extending a hand to help Delia up as well. "After all, it's not as if the Styx Group has bought up every wedding chapel in Las Vegas. There are other places where your cousin can have her ceremony."

"Easy for you to say," Delia replied wearily as

she headed into the dining room to set the table. Tortellini's tended to be pretty prompt with their deliveries, which meant they didn't have a lot of time to get things prepped before the food arrived.

"I do like to look on the bright side," he agreed.

She couldn't help smiling as she got out some placemats and napkins, then made a side trip into the kitchen to fetch plates and glasses and flatware. Or rather, she got the plates out of the cupboard and handed them over to Caleb so he could take them into the dining room.

Not a moment too soon, because the doorbell rang just a bit after that. He hurried to get it, obviously wanting to be the one who paid for the meal and tipped the driver. As harrowed as she was in her mind right then, Delia decided she wouldn't waste any energy on protesting.

If nothing else, he had a lot more money in the bank than she did.

He brought the bags of food into the dining room just as she was setting a bottle of Montepulciano on the table. "Good choice," he commented, eyeing the bottle of wine.

"Glad you approve," she said with a smile.

They sat and were quiet for a moment as they portioned out the food, and Caleb uncorked the wine and poured some for both of them. Delia had to admit it all smelled delicious, and her outlook on life improved further as she took a swallow of wine and let its friendly warmth course down her throat.

A piece of garlic bread helped as well...but not so much that she could completely ignore the reason why she'd needed this calorie-fest in the first place.

"I keep racking my brains, trying to come up with a totally logical reason why Olivia should move her wedding somewhere else," Delia said as she set down her wine glass and reached for her fork. "But so far, I can't come up with anything."

Caleb twirled some fettuccine around his fork, his brows pulling together as he appeared to ponder their current quandary. "What would make someone change wedding plans at the last minute?" he asked. "I mean, normal people reasons."

She couldn't help teasing him a little. "Are you saying you don't know what 'normal people reasons' might be?"

That question got her a smile, as she'd hoped it would. "Well, considering I was raised by a half demon and the frostiest bitch east of the Mississippi, there's a whole lot I don't know about 'normal.'"

Delia set down her fork and reached over so she could lay her hand on top of his where it rested on the table. Although his tone had been light enough, real pain had underlaid those words. He'd spent his whole life having to pretend to be something he wasn't, and even though he'd had other quarter demons as his friends, they'd all been pretending as well, hiding the truth of their natures from everyone else in the small Indiana town where they lived.

It must have been a hell of a way to grow up.

"I think you're doing pretty well at it," she told him, and the tense set of his jaw seemed to relax slightly.

"Well, it helps that I can be myself around you," he replied, and the simple, matter-of-fact way he said those words made her heart ache for him that much more.

"Yes, you can," she said.

Their gazes held for a moment. Then he shifted in his chair and reached over to pick up his glass of wine, and she realized he wanted to move on. Maybe someday she could get him to truly open up about his past and his childhood, but she knew that time wasn't now.

No, right now they needed to deal with the matter at hand.

What could they come up with to convince Olivia that Angel's Dream was the absolute last place she should be getting married?

"Venue double-booking, maybe?" Delia said, then immediately shot that idea down without even waiting for Caleb to respond. "No, she's probably already signed a contract, and I doubt they're that sloppy at the chapel."

"I have a feeling you might be right about that." He sipped some wine and swirled the Montepulciano in his glass as he appeared to think it over. "Maybe health code violations? I mean, the place looked clean, but...."

Delia pursed her lips. Would health code violations even be a thing in a place that didn't serve food? Honestly, she couldn't say for sure.

"I suppose that might work." She popped some fettuccine alfredo into her mouth, giving herself a moment to savor the rich, comforting flavor. Maybe the indulgence wouldn't solve anything, but it sure tasted good. "Or possibly a scheduling conflict with the officiant or something."

Caleb set down his wine glass and reached across the table to twine her fingers with his. The subtle strength in that touch reassured her just a little. "You know what?" he said. "Maybe you're overthinking this. Sometimes people just need to hear that you're worried about them."

Still holding his hand—she knew she wouldn't let go right away, would continue to take comfort from that grasp for as long as possible—she asked, "You think I should just call Olivia and be honest? She's going to think I'm nuts if I start talking about ley lines and portals to the otherworld."

That familiar glint entered his warm brown

eyes, but his tone was surprisingly serious when he spoke. "Feel out the situation first," he told her, then gently let go of her hand so he could reach for his glass of wine again. "See what her state of mind is like. You might be surprised."

Maybe some people were capable of believing six impossible things before breakfast, but from what she knew of her cousin, Delia kind of doubted Olivia was one of them. "I don't even know how to open a conversation like that."

Before he could respond, his phone sent a ping from inside his jeans pocket. Shooting her an apologetic glance, he pulled it out so he could glance down at the screen. At once, his expression grew troubled.

"What is it?" she asked.

He held up the phone so she could see the alert that had flashed up on his home screen. She guessed he must have set it up so he'd get notified anytime something weird happened at one of the chapels in town.

Electrical Issues Force Closure of Three Vegas Wedding Venues.

Cold moved down Delia's spine as she read the words. Now seemed like a really good time for another swallow of wine. Once she'd fortified herself, she said, "It's already starting, isn't it?"

Being Caleb, he didn't bother to waste time by making light of the situation.

"We may have less time than we thought," he replied grimly.

They cleared the table soon after that, both of their appetites effectively dampened by the unnerving news, and then moved to the living room with the remainder of their wine and settled on the couch to strategize.

"Okay," Delia said as she tucked her legs under her and turned to face him. "I think maybe I'll call my Aunt Vicky first—she's Olivia's mother. I hope a talk with her might give me some insight into Olivia's state of mind and how set she is on using Angel's Dream as her wedding venue. Maybe Olivia just landed on that place because it seemed convenient and not because she was totally in love with it or anything."

"Good idea," Caleb agreed. "And after you talk to her mother, then you can approach Olivia as the concerned cousin who wants to help with the Vegas arrangements."

"Exactly. And if she won't budge...." Delia let the words trail off, since she really didn't want to finish the sentence. Although neither Caleb nor Ty had gone into any great detail about what might happen to the people in the chapel when all that energy was directed through it to open the demons' hellmouth, she doubted it would be anything pleasant.

"And if she won't budge, then we'll just have to find ways to protect the wedding guests," Caleb finished for her. "Holy water in the champagne fountain, salt around the perimeter, whatever it takes."

She couldn't help but smile at those suggestions. "The reception dinner is being held at the Anthem Country Club, so there won't be a champagne fountain at the chapel."

"Point taken," he said, and the amused light returned to his dark eyes. "But I'm not going to let anything happen to your family. You know that."

He'd been holding his wine glass as he spoke, but now he set it down so he could reach over and take both her hands in his. Delia gazed back at him, noting the stern set of his jaw, the way he'd made that statement with complete sincerity.

Caleb Lockwood might have been part demon, but he was also a man of his word. If he said he was going to do something, he did it, whether that was buying a new investment property or coming to her rescue when a demon tried to use her as a sort of psychic battery to open a portal to the underworld.

"Yes," she said softly. "I do."

After that seemed to be settled, Caleb got up from the couch, telling her she needed to get some rest. She walked him to the front door, even though she wished he would stay longer.

If she hadn't been holding back...if they'd already taken the next step in their relationship... then maybe he wouldn't have needed to leave at all.

Maybe he could have spent the night here, been a comforting presence when she woke up in the middle of the night and stared into the darkness, worried about what might be coming next.

Unfortunately, that wasn't going to happen. Not tonight, anyway.

"Thank you," she said. "For...well, just everything, I guess."

"You know we're in this together," he replied before pulling her into an embrace that lasted a good bit longer than their usual goodnight hug. It was so good to lean her head against the solid warmth of his chest, to smell the faint scent of his cologne mixed with something that was purely him, warm and friendly and not the slightest bit demonic.

When they finally separated, she felt a little steadier. This was all one big mess, but Caleb was right.

They were going to face it together. She didn't have to do this by herself.

"I'll call my aunt tomorrow morning as soon as it's a decent time," she said.

"Good. And Delia?" He paused with his hand on the doorknob. "It's okay to trust your gut. You've got this."

She only nodded. After he pressed a soft kiss against her lips, he turned and headed outside.

Once he was gone, Delia locked the door, even as she realized that a locked door wasn't much protection against demons...or whatever else might be out there. As she passed the window in the living room, she noticed that the porch light was flickering strangely—not with the steady on-and-off of a dying bulb, but in an erratic pattern that made another of those creepy-crawly sensations that felt like an icy little spider working its way down her back.

She pulled the curtains closed. No energy left to worry about what it all might mean, although she knew she needed to bring it up with Caleb tomorrow.

Right then, she just hoped she'd be able to get a decent night's sleep.

The next morning, Delia made herself get up and head into the kitchen as though this was just another perfectly normal day, pausing as she went to flip on the TV in the living room, another part of her morning ritual. Most of what the news had to say didn't interest her that much, but she liked to hear the weather and traffic reports, just in case some unexpected showers might pop up or there was a massive traffic jam she would have to avoid on her way to work.

As she got out her favorite mug, she pondered for what felt like the umpteenth time what she planned to say to her aunt. She'd rehearsed those words before falling asleep, and now she ran through the little speech again, hoping it wouldn't sound as awkward out loud as it did in her head.

Just checking in, wanted to hear how the wedding planning is going, oh, remember that I'm local, so if Olivia needs any help with the Vegas details....

But then her ears perked up. From the other room, she could hear one of the morning anchors reporting on overnight "power grid anomalies" that seemed to have affected a number of businesses downtown.

That same sensation of icy cold made a return visit, only this time it was also accompanied by an uneasy rumble in the pit of her stomach. The man on the news hadn't mentioned any specific businesses, but he hadn't needed to. Most of the quickie chapels Delia knew of were located near downtown, simply because it was smart to be in close proximity to the hotels and the casinos and the restaurants, along with the Clark County office where people had to obtain their wedding licenses.

And she'd bet the fifty-seven dollars currently residing in her wallet that a little digging would prove all the businesses affected by the power grid issues were those same chapels.

This wasn't good.

But it was still way too early to call Caleb. He might not have been an utter night owl like Pru, but he also tended to sleep in because he didn't have to get up and go to work.

Delia, on the other hand, needed to be in the office by nine. Luckily, she didn't have any early clients like she had the day before, but she still couldn't lounge around and wait for it to be a decent hour so she could call him and ask him what this latest news report meant.

If he would even have any real idea. He certainly possessed far more knowledge about the world of the demonic than she did, but he'd also admitted that he didn't know everything.

Like her, he was probably flying blind...and praying they wouldn't slam into an unseen obstacle in the fog.

Delia had to wait until her mother was safely out of the office for a house showing before she could make the call to her aunt. While she wasn't necessarily trying to hide anything, she also didn't want her mother wondering why her daughter was calling Vicky Gunderson out of the blue like this. As far as Delia had been able to tell, the two women got along fine, something that didn't always happen with sisters-in-law, but they weren't terribly close, either, thanks to the geographic separation in the family. All the same, Linda would know that her daughter pretty much limited her communication with her extended family to Christmas cards and birthday cards, and phone calls were basically a non-starter.

But once the coast was clear, Delia got out her phone and headed over to her contacts list. Thank God she had everyone's number in there, mostly because she always figured it was better to keep as much contact information as possible on hand, just in case.

Well, this was definitely a "case."

"Delia!" Vicky sounded cheerful enough when she answered the phone, but also a little startled, as if she couldn't quite figure out why her niece would be calling her out of the blue. "This is a surprise. How are you?"

"Oh, I'm fine," Delia replied as she settled back

in her chair. Luckily, she didn't have any appointments until after lunch, so she wasn't too worried about being interrupted. "Busy, but good. How's Chicago?"

For a few minutes, they chatted about the weather and family news before Delia managed to steer the conversation toward her real reason for making the call.

Doing her best to sound casual, she asked, "So...how's Olivia doing with all the wedding planning? She must be pretty excited, considering how close it's getting."

A slight pause followed her comment, and when Vicky spoke again, Delia thought she could detect an edge of concern in her aunt's tone. "She's excited...but she's also stressed about keeping track of all the details, even though she's been trying to keep things simple. In fact, she told me she's been having trouble sleeping this past week or so. It sounds like she keeps having weird dreams about the wedding."

Once upon a time, Delia would have dismissed odd dreams as nothing more than the subconscious manifesting stress in strange and sometimes uncomfortable ways. Now, though, she knew that dreams could have a meaning of their own and weren't something to be dismissed out of hand. "Dreams?" she repeated, hoping she didn't sound too eager.

"She hasn't told me anything specific," her aunt replied. "But she did say yesterday that she keeps waking up feeling like something terrible is going to happen. I told her it's just normal pre-wedding jitters, but...."

She didn't complete the sentence, as if something in her own subconscious was doing its best to send out warnings, and she wasn't sure whether she wanted to acknowledge those signals.

"But you're not sure," Delia said, even as hope stirred within her. If both her cousin and her aunt were having misgivings, maybe this might not be as difficult as she'd feared.

"Exactly. Olivia is usually so sure about what she wants. It's just not like her to be this anxious." A sigh came through the iPhone's speaker, and Vicky went on, "Actually, since you're local, would you mind checking on some of the venue details for her? I think it would help put her mind at ease to know someone she trusts has eyeballed everything before she and Alec arrive."

Talk about getting permission in advance. Not that Delia and Caleb hadn't already inspected the chapel, but if they needed to go back, then no one should bat an eyelid at any return trips. "Of course," she replied at once. "I'm happy to help. In fact, why don't I give Olivia a call this afternoon and see if there's anything specific she wants me to check on?"

"Oh, she'd love that," Vicky said, relief clear in her voice. "Thanks, sweetie. You're a lifesaver."

If only you knew, passed through Delia's mind as they ended the call. *If you had all the facts in hand, you'd move heaven and earth to make sure this destination wedding was relocated to someplace much safer.*

Like maybe an erupting Kilauea, or possibly an ice floe somewhere near the South Pole.

But since her aunt currently occupied a place of blissful ignorance, Delia knew she and Caleb would have to work behind the scenes to make sure she remained that way.

Almost as soon as she set down the phone, it buzzed again.

Caleb.

Did you see the news?

I did. I'm stuck here at the office, though.

That's all right. I think I'll head out and poke around, see if I can sense anything off.

Any problems with your own power?

No, everything was fine over here.

Delia wondered if she should mention the odd flickering of the porch light at her house, then decided she could leave that aside for now. Nothing had acted up since then, and she supposed it could have been the bulb. LED lights were supposed to be extremely stable, but maybe she'd gotten a dud or something.

Well, be careful. I'll go straight over to your place when I'm off work.

I'm always careful.

Delia wasn't so sure about that, but she couldn't help smiling a little as she ended the convo. If nothing else, Caleb Lockwood had been in some pretty tight spaces and had managed to wriggle out of them anyway, so she wouldn't let herself be too worried.

All the same, she couldn't wait for this day to be over so she could see him in person and reassure herself that any "poking" he'd done had been relatively harmless.

No sign yet of her mother, so Delia decided she might as well go ahead and call Olivia. Her cousin had her own graphic design business and worked from home, so she didn't think such a call would be too much of an interruption.

Besides, she'd gotten past the first hurdle of the conversation with Vicky, so she figured she'd better strike while the iron was hot.

"Hi, Delia." Olivia didn't sound especially surprised to hear from her, a reaction explained by her next words. "My mother texted me and said you might call. How are you?"

"I'm fine," Delia replied. "But how are you?

Your mother said you've been a little stressed about the wedding planning."

A long pause on the other end of the line, and when Olivia spoke again, her voice sounded somehow smaller, not nearly as sure of herself. "God, is it that obvious? I've been trying not to worry everyone, but...." Another pause, followed by an audible sigh. "I don't know. Ever since Alec and I booked the chapel last month, I've just had this weird feeling about it."

"What kind of weird feeling?" Delia asked carefully. The last thing she wanted was to allow any of her own misgivings to seep into the conversation. No, she needed to hear what her cousin had been experiencing without any outside responses possibly coloring her account.

"This is going to sound kind of crazy," Olivia said, then gave a shaky laugh. Delia didn't know her cousin all that well, hadn't seen her in several years, but she could tell right away that laugh had been a complete fake. "But every time I think about walking down the aisle at that chapel, I get this overwhelming sense of...dread, I guess. Like something terrible is waiting for me."

"That doesn't sound crazy at all," Delia said, doing her best to sound soothing. "Have you told Alec how you're feeling?"

"A little," her cousin replied. "He just thinks

it's cold feet, and maybe he's right. But the dreams are so vivid—way more vivid than any other dreams I've ever had. Most of the time, I can't even remember what I've dreamed, but with these dreams, I can see every awful detail as soon as I open my eyes in the morning. People screaming and running and trampling each other, the chapel filling with smoke and flames...."

That did sound pretty awful. No wonder her cousin was so hag-ridden.

Was her subconscious trying to protect her? Did she also have some spark of psychic powers hidden somewhere inside?

Impossible to say. Both of Delia's parents had already said flat out that no one else on either side of the family had any kind of psychic gifts, so they had no idea where her ghost-whispering talent had come from.

Which didn't mean a whole hell of a lot. Most people worked very hard to hide anything about themselves that invited too many questions.

Especially back in the day, when claiming you were telepathic or whatever wouldn't be dismissed as an odd little quirk but was instead something that could get you into a whole lot of trouble, up to and including getting burned at the stake.

She tried to tell herself this was a good development. If her cousin was already having nightmares and making her fiancé worry that she was getting cold feet, then maybe it wouldn't be too hard to convince her that there might be plenty of alternatives to getting married at the Angel's Dream chapel.

"Olivia," she said, trying to sound gently persuasive but not pushy, "maybe you should think about having the ceremony somewhere else."

Her cousin's voice sharpened. "Somewhere else?"

Here goes nothing. "Well, I've been doing some research on Vegas wedding venues—a client of mine was asking for some input, since she's also planning her wedding—and I've come across some absolutely beautiful places that might be even more perfect for you and Alec."

This was all an utter lie, but Delia spent so much time out and about in Las Vegas that she knew the chapels pretty well, even if she hadn't done any specific research on them in particular.

For the first time, Olivia sounded almost hopeful. "Really?"

"Really," Delia assured her. "In fact, if you want, I can scout out a few alternatives for you."

"Oh, that would be fabulous," Olivia replied at once, relief clear in her voice. "I've been wanting to do that, but Alec keeps saying we already paid in advance and they don't offer refunds. But if there's something better...."

Delia hadn't known that about the ceremony being nonrefundable, but she supposed it made sense. The last thing quickie wedding chapels wanted was people backing out at the last minute because they knew they wouldn't lose any money on the deal if they found something better.

Besides, this wouldn't be like pulling out of a country club wedding or something. At most, they would have sunk a couple of grand into the ceremony, and that was only if they'd bought the most expensive package.

She guessed most people would consider that an acceptable sacrifice if it meant avoiding getting sucked into a hellmouth.

"Oh, I'm sure there's something better out there," Delia said. "Just let me do some looking around, and then I'll get back to you."

"That would be awesome," her cousin responded, already sounding much more cheerful. "I really wanted to get married in Las Vegas so we could honeymoon in Alec's new house there, but I thought we were stuck with Angel's Dream."

"You're not stuck," Delia assured her. "It's going to be fine."

After delivering those reassurances and promising again that she'd call Olivia as soon as she had a list of four or five viable alternatives, she reached out to Caleb.

"My cousin is already having nightmares about

the chapel," she told him as soon as he answered her call. "And she wants me to scout some alternatives for her. The hardest part is going to be convincing her fiancé, but Olivia sounds ready to find something else."

"That's great news," Caleb replied, although something about his tone sounded almost distracted. "But there's been another development. Go to Channel 8's website."

That didn't sound very good. With her free hand, Delia opened her laptop and searched for the local ABC affiliate's website. Right at the top was an article about a series of "unexplained incidents" at wedding venues across the city—electrical fires, plumbing disasters, mysterious break-ins.

"It's escalating," she said.

"Fast," Caleb agreed. "We may have gotten Olivia on board, but—"

His words were cut off by a sharp ping, and Delia pulled the phone away from her ear so she could look down at the screen.

A text from Pru.

Emergency team meeting. Found something big. My place @ 6.

"I just got a text from Pru," she said.

"So did I. So much for getting together at my house."

Yes, it would have been nice to have a quiet

evening together. However, it didn't look as if "quiet" was going to be on the calendar for at least the next few days.

She released a breath. "I guess we're about to find out just how much worse this is going to get."

Chapter Five

——·‹‹‹‹ ✦ ›››·——

BECAUSE PRU'S CONDO WAS CLOSER TO Delia's office than either of their houses, Caleb had to drive straight there rather than swing by Delia's home to get her. He didn't much like having to go by himself, mainly because parking was tight in Pru's neighborhood, and this would have been a lot easier if they'd been able to carpool.

Well, that and he knew he'd been hoping that maybe he and Delia would have a chance to slip off together for dinner or something once this meeting was over.

The condo was located on the sixth floor of a twelve-story building, which meant he had to take the elevator. Just as the doors were closing, Ty appeared and slipped inside.

"You got the invite, too, huh?" Caleb said sourly.

Ty shrugged. "It sounds like Pru found something important."

The elevator climbed slowly, each floor seeming to take forever, and Caleb found himself drumming his fingers against the metal railing.

"You seem tense," Ty remarked.

"Just thinking about everything else I'd rather be doing right now."

Wasn't that the truth.

The elevator dinged, and the doors slid open on the sixth floor. Pru's place was halfway down the hall, and when Caleb knocked, she opened the door almost immediately. Her dark green hair was pulled back into a haphazard ponytail, and she wore skinny black jeans and a black tank top with a graffiti-style font that spelled out "Final Girl."

"About time," she said, even though they weren't remotely late, and stepped back to let them in. "Delia got here about five minutes ago."

Delia sat on Pru's big black sectional, a glass of water cradled in her hands. She glanced over when he and Ty entered, and despite his cranky mood, Caleb still experienced that familiar little jolt of warmth at seeing her.

"Hey," she said, although her smile didn't seem to have its usual brilliance. "How was your day of poking around?"

"Educational," he replied as he settled beside her, close enough that their thighs almost touched.

"I'll tell you about it in a minute." He looked over at Prudence. "So, what's this big discovery you made?"

Pru was already moving toward her laptop on the dining room table, which was covered in print-outs and hand-drawn charts. "Remember how I said I started tracking the power grid anomalies?" She turned the screen toward them, which showed a map of Las Vegas dotted with colored markers. "Every single location that's had infrastructure failures is on a ley line. Thirty-five locations so far. And they're all wedding venues."

Caleb sort of doubted that was a coincidence. "So...they're not just targeting the quickie chapels."

"They're targeting every place in the city where someone might hold a wedding," Delia said quietly.

Ty moved closer to examine the map, eyes narrowing. "Whoever's orchestrating this must have been planning it for months."

That observation matched what Caleb had found today—EMF readings spiking in too exact patterns, test runs like yesterday's water main break at the Venetian and this morning's transformer explosion at City Hall. It sure looked as if whoever was behind all this, it was someone with intimate knowledge of both ley line magic and modern infrastructure.

"There's more," Pru said as she clicked to

another tab. "The incidents aren't random. They're following a specific schedule." She pulled up a timeline showing the frequency spiking dramatically over the past week. "By Olivia's wedding, every major venue except Angel's Dream will be compromised."

"Forcing everyone into the chapel," Delia said. She looked calm enough, but her lips pressed together for a second, enough to tell Caleb that she was deeply worried. "Funneling as many people as possible into their convergence point."

His jaw tightened. "Were you able to find anything about who's behind it?"

A nod. "The permits for the electrical work causing these 'malfunctions'? They all trace back to shell companies owned by subsidiaries of—"

"The Styx Group," Ty finished for her.

Pru didn't seem overly annoyed by the way he'd cut in, although Caleb guessed if he'd done the same thing, she probably would have bitten his head off. "They've been systematically sabotaging their competition while positioning themselves as the only viable option."

"Right," Ty said. "They probably possessed some maintenance workers to cause the accidents. That kind of meddling would be very difficult to trace."

Caleb's phone let out a ping right then, and he

pulled it out of his jeans pocket. The number wasn't one he recognized.

Having fun playing detective? You have no idea what you're dealing with, boy. Stop now, or we'll make sure tonight's emergencies become tomorrow's tragedies.

"What is it?" Delia said. "You look like someone just walked over your grave."

As much as he would have liked to pretend all this wasn't happening, he knew that wasn't an option. So he read the message aloud.

Ty's expression immediately darkened. "They're monitoring our communications."

"Which means they know exactly what we're doing," Pru said. However, her chin lifted, and it seemed clear she wasn't about to let herself get bullied out of what needed to be done.

Caleb moved to the huge window that over-looked the city. In daylight, Vegas was much more subdued, the sun washing out the bright neon lights, but he knew the streets were choked with tourists nonetheless. And somewhere out there, demonic forces were weaving a web to trap all those unsuspecting people.

"We can't stop," he said at last. "Whatever they're planning, it's bigger than just one wedding."

"But if we keep pushing and they escalate...."

Delia's words trailed off, and she made a frustrated gesture with one hand.

More than ever, Caleb wished he could go and take her in his arms. Instead, he turned back, feeling the unwelcome weight of leadership settling on his shoulders. He'd only wanted to make a new life here in the desert, far from his dark past, but it looked as if the universe wasn't on board with him having a quiet existence.

"Then we'll move fast and smart," he said. "Pru, can you map out the most critical locations?"

She nodded and turned back to her laptop.

"Ty, what's your range for detecting demonic activity?"

"Depends on the source strength," the half angel replied. "For something this organized, probably within a few hundred yards."

"Delia, I know this isn't what you signed up for, but—"

"You know I'm in," she said, voice firm as she rose to face him. "This is my family they're threatening. Besides, someone has to keep you guys from doing anything too stupid."

Despite everything, he smiled. "All right, then. Let's go hit 'em where it hurts."

An hour later, Caleb was crouched behind a delivery truck in the parking lot of the Silver Bell Wedding Chapel, trying to get a read on the supernatural energy emanating from the building. The place looked normal enough from the outside—white stucco walls, a small bell tower, tasteful landscaping with lilies of the Nile and white marguerite daisies—but his demon senses screamed that something was very wrong.

The energy patterns were all off, twisted into configurations that made his skin crawl. Whatever was happening inside that building, it wasn't natural.

His earpiece crackled as Ty came online. "I'm getting massive distortions from the north side of the chapel. Definitely demonic, but it's not like anything I've encountered before."

Pru had taken up a position across the street, hiding in some convenient shadows cast by an unoccupied bus stop. "Same here," she said. "The electromagnetic readings are crazy. It's like they're using the building's electrical system as some kind of amplifier."

Caleb activated his throat mic. "Delia, what's your status?"

"I'm in position by the main entrance," came her whispered response. "And I've got company. Three figures in dark cloaks just went inside. Not exactly your standard attire for late May in Las Vegas."

No, it wasn't. Caleb pulled in a breath and said, "Okay, we're going in. Ty, can you create a distraction on the north side? Something to draw their attention away from the main entrance?"

"Already on it."

A few seconds later, the sound of shattering glass came from the opposite side of the building, followed by what Caleb thought was a small explosion. Emergency lighting flickered on inside, and he spied shadowy figures moving past the windows.

"Now," he said into his mic, then moved toward the main entrance where Delia was waiting.

She fell into step beside him as they approached the front door. While they were prepping for this raid, she'd borrowed some of Pru's clothes so she could get out of the work outfit she'd been wearing. Her face was a pale oval above the all-black ensemble. "Any idea what we're walking into?"

"Nothing good," he replied as he tested the door handle. Locked, but that had never been much of an obstacle for him. A small touch of demon-generated heat to the metal mechanism, and the lock clicked open.

They slipped inside and found themselves in a small foyer decorated with artificial flowers and inspirational quotes about love. The space felt normal enough—if a bit cheesy for his taste—but

Caleb could already sense the wrongness emanating from deeper in the building.

"This way," he whispered, following the pull of dark energy down a narrow hallway lined with framed wedding photos. The images looked innocent enough, but something about them made him feel vaguely sick to his stomach. Were the faces in the photos shifting when he wasn't looking directly at them?

He couldn't allow himself to get distracted, though, so he kept his gaze fixed forward on their destination.

They reached a set of double doors that presumably opened onto the main chapel. Caleb pressed his ear against the wood, trying to make out what was happening on the other side. He could hear voices—multiple voices—chanting in a language that made his very bones ache.

That same language had echoed in the halls of Hell, and he'd hoped he'd never have to hear it again.

"Demons," he mouthed to Delia, who gave a grim nod.

His earpiece crackled again. "Whatever you're going to do, do it fast." Ty sounded less than thrilled with life right then, and Caleb couldn't really blame him. He didn't know what the half angel generally did during his downtime, but it probably didn't involve acting as bait for some of

Hell's minions. "I've got at least six demons converging on my position, and they don't look very happy."

Well, that was just fabulous.

"Pru, is there any way you can cut the power to the building?" Caleb asked, keeping his voice pitched low so he couldn't be overheard.

He hoped.

"As if I'm able to do something like that," Pru replied, clearly annoyed. "I'm just a private investigator, remember? You want a hacker, go find one on the dark web."

Like they had time to do something like that... even if Caleb had possessed the foggiest idea how to accomplish such a thing. He knew he'd been lucky enough just to find the people who'd supplied his fake birth certificate and credit report, and they'd been a couple of petty criminals and not much more.

Okay, his little team would just have to deal with these demons the hard way.

Caleb looked at Delia and saw his own determination reflected in her clear, blue-gray eyes. "Ready?"

A brief nod. "Ready."

He placed his hands on the double doors and took a deep breath, calling up the fire that lived in his demon blood. The heat flowed down his arms, gathering in his palms until the metal door handles began to glow.

"On three," he whispered. "One...two...."

The doors exploded inward in a shower of flame and splinters.

The chapel beyond was clearly a far cry from the saccharine space it used to be. Now it was a nightmare of twisted geometry and impossible shadows, the sort of place any sane person would want to avoid. The pews had been arranged in a complex pattern that seemed to twist the laws of physics, and in the center of it all, three figures in hooded robes stood around what looked like a portable altar covered in symbols that appeared to writhe and shift in the firelight.

But it was the thing hovering above the altar that made Caleb's heart pound in fear.

It wasn't quite a portal—not yet—but it was close, a tear in reality that leaked darkness and whispered with voices that belonged to no earthly creature. Through it, he caught a glimpse of red skies the color of old blood and landscapes of bone and ash.

A place he'd never wanted to see again.

One of the robed figures turned toward them, and beneath its shadowy hood, yellow eyes glared with unholy light. "The half-breed," it said. "How delightfully convenient."

"Caleb." Delia's murmur practically vibrated with fear. "Tell me you have a plan."

He flexed his fingers, feeling fire dance between them. "Working on it."

The demon smiled, revealing rows of needle-sharp teeth. "You're too late, boy. The network is nearly complete. Soon, every chapel in this city will be a gateway, and your precious mortals will walk willingly into our embrace."

"Like hell," Caleb said, and hurled fire at the nearest robed figure.

It ducked, but the fireball still caught the edge of its hooded robe. Judging by the way it quickly and efficiently extinguished the blaze, he guessed these weren't the low-level demons he'd tangled with before—these were scouts, advance units of something much larger and more organized. They seemed to work together, almost as if they understood one another's thoughts, and he could see they were using the twisted geometry of the chapel to their advantage as they melted away from the altar.

But Caleb knew he had advantages of his own. His demon blood blazed in his veins as he rolled left, avoiding a lance of shadow that speared through the air where his head had been. The twisted geometry worked both ways—he used the angled pew as a springboard, vaulting over it as flames wreathed his fists like living things.

The second robed figure raised its hands, and the air around Caleb suddenly thickened, pressing against him, reminding him of spring days back in Indiana when the snow melted and left viscous mud in its wake. He gritted his teeth and pushed harder, his supernatural strength allowing him to burn through that resistance and turn it to so much ash. Behind him, he heard Delia's sharp intake of breath.

"The symbols," she called out, her voice cutting past the demonic whispers that leaked through the tear in the universe above them. "I think they're feeding power to the ritual!"

As she spoke, the demons' heads all swiveled toward her, sensing fresh prey.

Shit.

Something about the chapel's acoustics was all wrong—sounds echoed in directions that shouldn't exist, and Caleb hoped he could use that disorientation against his enemies. His boots scraped against stone as he feinted right, then pivoted left, drawing the demons' attention away from Delia.

The first demon he'd hit was already regenerating, its burned robe mending itself with threads of darkness. It hissed something in syllables that made Caleb's hair want to stand on end, and in the next moment, all three figures moved in perfect synchronization, as if they shared a single malevolent consciousness.

Definitely not good.

Caleb dropped into a crouch, wishing he'd been more of a brawler when he was back in school so he'd have a better idea of just what the hell he should be doing. But the demon blood within him was a whisper telling him to stop thinking and allow instinct to take over.

Time seemed to slow as his enhanced reflexes kicked in. The leftmost demon's claws whistled over his head while he spun, sweeping the legs of the one coming from his right. As it stumbled, he drove an uppercut wreathed in hellfire into its solar plexus, feeling oversized ribs crack under the impact.

But the third demon was already on him, its needle teeth snapping at his throat. Caleb jerked backward, feeling the wind from those jaws brush his skin. His back hit one of the impossibly angled pews, and for a split second, he was trapped.

Out of nowhere, Delia swooped in low and fast, a heavy brass candlestick brandished in both hands like a club. The demon, focused entirely on Caleb, never saw her coming. The candlestick connected with a wet crunch that echoed horribly in the warped space, sending the creature sprawling across the altar.

The portable altar rocked, and several of the writhing symbols flickered and dimmed.

"The altar!" Caleb shouted, realization flooding through him. "It's the focal point!"

He rolled away from the pew as shadow-fire erupted from the spot where he'd been standing. The stone floor cracked and hissed, releasing sulfurous steam. His demon blood responded to the hellish energy, making him faster, stronger...but also harder to remain himself. He could feel his human side struggling to maintain focus as primal fury tried to take over.

The demon Delia had struck was already rising, yellow eyes blazing with rage. It backhanded her almost casually, sending her flying into a cluster of pews with a sickening crash.

Something cold and furious exploded in Caleb's chest. His fire flared white-hot, surrounding him with the angry energy of a supernova. He closed the distance to the demon in two bounds, grabbed it by the throat, and drove his knee into its midsection with enough force to crater the floor beneath them.

The creature doubled over, gasping with something that might have been surprise. But Caleb couldn't give it time to recover. He spun it around and hurled it straight at the altar, putting every ounce of his supernatural strength behind the throw.

The demon hit the altar dead center. The impact sent symbols scattering, some of them winking out entirely as they separated from the ritual circle. The tear above them shuddered, its edges becoming less stable, and the whispers from beyond grew more frantic.

But the other two demons were adapting, learning from his tactics. They split apart, forcing him to divide his attention. One began making complex movements in the air, rebuilding the ritual pattern that had been damaged a moment earlier. The other circled toward the scattered pews where Delia was struggling to get back on her feet, her breath coming in short gasps.

Caleb's mind raced, measuring angles and distances with a cold calculation that felt utterly unlike him. The chapel's twisted geometry created blind spots and unexpected sight lines. If he could use that, maybe —

The circling demon lunged at Delia.

All calculation fled. Caleb simply moved, crossing the space between them faster than should have been possible. He caught the demon mid-leap, his fists pounding into its chest as they both crashed into the wall.

Stone cracked. The demon's yellow eyes went wide with something that might have been fear.

"Bad choice," Caleb growled, his voice rougher than it should have been. He could feel his human control slipping, his demon blood rising to make sure the creature would never have a chance to hurt the woman he loved.

And for the first time since the fight began, he didn't try to hold it back.

Fists pounded again and again, and he could feel the thing beginning to dissolve beneath the pummeling. No, he couldn't kill it, but he could make sure it never wanted to return to this plane again.

Oily black blood spattered everywhere. Agonized yellow eyes met his...and then the thing winked out of existence.

Behind him, Caleb heard an unearthly howl and whirled. A white-faced Delia stood there, an empty vial of holy water clutched in either hand, while the demon she'd just splattered was doing a pretty good imitation of the Wicked Witch from *The Wizard of Oz,* melting into the stone floor in a puddle of gooey black liquid.

As it dissolved, the portal above the altar began to collapse in on itself. The wrongness in the air faded, replaced by the normal atmosphere of an ordinary—if horribly saccharine-sweet—wedding chapel.

Delia shot him a lopsided smile as she patted the purse slung across her body. "You know I never leave home without it."

And thank God for that. Caleb had also had a

few bottles stuffed into the pockets of his jeans, but his demon rage had opted for a more primitive solution to their problem.

He'd have to watch that in the future. While he didn't regret using violence to dispel their foes, he also didn't want to Hulk out to the point where he didn't even know what he was doing.

Ty's voice came through his earpiece, sounding slightly winded. "Is everyone all right?"

"We're good here," Caleb replied, surveying the destruction inside the chapel. It would take weeks to fix the damage, which meant there was no way it could be back online in time for whatever the demonic masterminds behind the Styx Group were plotting. "How about you?"

"Six demons down," Ty replied, "and I found something you're going to want to see. There's a control room hidden behind the north wall. It looks like they've been coordinating the entire operation from here."

A chill moved down Caleb's spine, and he looked over to see Delia's arms wrapped around herself, as if she, too, suffered from a cold that had nothing to do with the temperature inside the chapel.

If this was just one control room, how many others were there?

"Pru," he said into his mic, "we could really use that map of critical locations."

"Working on it," she replied. "But based on what I've found so far, I think this was just the beginning. The real target isn't the individual chapels."

He frowned. "What do you mean?"

A pause that seemed to stretch forever. Then she said, "I'm not an expert or anything, but I think they're building a citywide summoning circle. Every location and every ley line is all part of one massive ritual."

Caleb looked at Delia, seeing his own realization reflected in her face. This wasn't about stopping one wedding or protecting one chapel from turning into a hellmouth.

No, this was about preventing a full-scale invasion.

"Well, hell," he said.

Chapter Six

———·‹‹‹·⟡·›››·——

THE SILENCE IN CALEB'S MERCEDES seemed almost oppressive as they drove away from the Silver Bell Wedding Chapel. Delia kept stealing glances at him, noting the tight set of his jaw and the way his knuckles had gone white where he gripped the steering wheel. The adrenaline from their confrontation with the demons was still coursing through her system, making her jittery and hyperaware of every sound, every shadow that passed by the car windows.

And if she was feeling like that, she could only imagine what Caleb must be experiencing. Although she'd seen him use his demonic abilities before, something had seemed different about this last battle, as though his demon blood had ramped up a few levels.

She wasn't sure what to think about that.

"Your place or mine?" Caleb asked, his voice almost harsh, deeper and rougher than usual.

Some kind of lingering effects from the almost berserker fury he'd exhibited a few minutes ago?

That possibility scared the hell out of her. What if he allowed his demon blood to take over so much that he couldn't find his way back to the man she loved?

That's not going to happen, she told herself. *He knows what he's doing.*

At least, she hoped he did.

"My place," she said, and prayed that was the right answer. Maybe Caleb would have preferred to be at his house, but her home was a little closer to Pru's, and right now, Delia thought the familiar comforts of her own space were exactly what she needed. "I've got some of that wine left over from dinner last night, and I think we both could use a drink."

He nodded, and they drove the rest of the way in an uncomfortable silence. Every so often, Delia found herself touching the small cuts on her arms where she'd been scraped by debris during the fight, doing her best to reassure herself that the injuries were minor and the important thing was that they'd both made it out in one piece.

She definitely couldn't say the same for the demons.

When they pulled into her driveway, she

noticed her porch light was still flickering in that odd pattern from the night before. She looked over at Caleb and wondered if she should say anything, but then decided that right now, a twitchy light-bulb seemed like the least of their concerns.

Inside, she headed straight for the kitchen while Caleb sat down on the couch, something about his ongoing silence and the stiff set of his shoulders telling her that he was probably dealing with his own doubts after that ferocious battle. She got out a couple of stemless wine glasses and poured Montepulciano into each of them. Once that was done, she put the now-empty bottle in the trash and headed into the living room.

Even a month earlier, she might have taken one of the chairs that faced the couch. Now, though, she sat down next to him, so close that her knee almost brushed against his.

Whatever else, she needed to let him know that seeing him in action like that hadn't changed anything about the way she felt about him.

"So," she said, then took a sip of wine and did her best to relax into the sensation of its rich, fruity warmth sliding down her throat. "That was educational."

Caleb chuckled, but there wasn't much humor in the sound. "I suppose that's one word for it." He picked up his wine glass but didn't drink from it, instead staring down into the dark liquid as if it held answers he desperately needed. "I keep thinking about what could have happened if you'd been hurt in there."

The quiet intensity in his voice made her reach over and lay a gentle hand on his knee. She'd seen him worried before, but this felt different.

Was it simply because he thought the stakes were a lot higher now that they'd both made their feelings for one another clear?

"But I wasn't hurt," she said, her tone low but firm. "We both made it out, and we stopped those demons from completing whatever they were doing with that portal."

"This time." He finally looked over at her, and what she saw in his dark eyes made her breath catch. Bone-deep fear, the kind that had nothing to do with demons or ley lines and everything to do with her. "But what about next time? What about when we're up against something even worse?"

She set her wine glass down on a coaster and turned to face him. "Caleb—"

"I can't lose you, Delia." The words came out in a rush, as if he'd been holding them back for too long. "I know we haven't talked a lot about what's been going on between us, what we're doing, but I need you to know that you're the most important thing in my life. The only thing that matters."

The vulnerability in his voice, the way he was looking at her as if she might disappear at any moment, made her heart ache. All the reasons she'd been holding back from letting their relationship progress any further, all the careful distance she'd been maintaining, suddenly seemed meaningless and downright foolish compared to the raw pain on the face of the man sitting next to her.

"You're not going to lose me," she said softly as she reached over to take his hand. His fingers were warm and shook slightly when she touched him, but that didn't prevent her from clasping his hand. "We're in this together, remember? You said so yourself."

"I know, but—" He stopped there and gave a frustrated shake of his head. "I've spent most of my life keeping people at arm's length. I knew it was safer that way. But with you...." His fingers tightened on hers. "With you, I can't seem to maintain any distance at all."

She leaned closer, close enough that she could see the amber shimmers in his warm brown eyes, could smell the faint scent of smoke that lingered on his hair and clothes from the battle at the chapel. "Maybe that's not such a bad thing."

For a moment, they just looked at each other. Then Caleb lifted his free hand to cup her cheek, his thumb brushing across her skin with heartbreaking gentleness.

"I love you," he said simply, and those words made a shudder go through her. Not because she hadn't heard them from him before, but because this time seemed even more heartfelt, more intense.

And she wouldn't hold back, not when she knew this was a simple truth she understood to the very depths of her soul.

"I love you, too," she whispered, "more than anything."

His expression shifted from fear to wonder to something so tender, it made her eyes sting with unexpected tears.

Had he been worried that she wouldn't be able to say those words anymore, that something in her feelings might have changed over the course of the past hour?

When he kissed her, their embrace seemed different from all the others they'd shared...deeper and more desperate, somehow a claiming and a promise all at the same time. She could taste the wine on his lips, could feel the barely leashed power that ran through his veins, and yet, none of it frightened her.

Maybe it should have. Maybe all this was utter insanity. But she knew him, had come to see him as the man who made her laugh and who somehow managed to light the fire in her heart and who also allowed her to be utterly comfortable at the same time, and she knew she could never walk away from that.

No matter what happened.

When they finally ended the kiss, it was only so she could move even closer and rest her head against his shoulder. "We should probably talk about what comes next," she said, even though part of her wanted to forget about talking altogether.

Caleb brushed a gentle hand across her hair. "Tomorrow," he told her. "We can figure out tomorrow later. Right now, I just want to hold you."

So he did, as they sat curled together on her couch with the wine forgotten on the coffee table, and for a little while, demons and portals and city-wide conspiracies faded into background noise nearly drowned out by the steady rhythm of his heartbeat beneath her cheek.

The next morning, Delia woke up alone on the couch, covered with the throw blanket from the back of the sofa. She honestly didn't even remember falling asleep, but she supposed Caleb had decided it was better to leave her there than move her into the bedroom and risk waking her up.

It seemed he'd taken their wine glasses into the kitchen, since the only thing on the coffee table now was a note from him explaining that he'd had to leave early to meet with contractors at the flip house but that he'd call her later.

She smiled a little as she read the note, remembering the way he'd looked at her the night before when he'd told her he loved her. The memory sent warmth spreading through her entire body, even as her practical side reminded her that they still had a supernatural crisis to deal with, not to mention the usual round of life, like meetings with clients and contractors and a trip to the dry cleaners' that she couldn't put off any longer.

After toast and coffee and a quick shower, she sat down at her kitchen table with her phone, steeling herself for the conversation she'd been dreading. But after what Pru had discovered about the systematic targeting of wedding venues across the city, Delia knew she couldn't put it off any longer.

She touched Olivia's entry in her contacts and waited, hoping her cousin would be in a receptive mood that morning.

"Delia!" Olivia's voice sounded cheerful enough, but it also seemed a little tense around the edges. "I was just thinking about you. Did you have a chance to look at those alternative venues you mentioned?"

"I did," Delia said, glad her cousin had given her such an easy opening. "And I found some really beautiful places. But how are you feeling? Any more bad dreams?"

A long pause, followed by a shaky sigh.

"They're getting worse," Olivia replied. "Last night I dreamed that the chapel caught on fire during the ceremony just as Alec and I were about to exchange rings. All the guests were trapped inside, and...oh, God, Delia, I could see them burning, could practically feel all their pain, like I was burning along with them." She paused there before finishing simply, "I woke up in a cold sweat."

That sounded absolutely horrible. Whatever psychic sensitivity her cousin might or might not possess, something was clearly trying to warn her away from danger. "Did you talk to Alec about changing the venue?"

"I brought it up at dinner last night, but he just laughed it off again. He said I'm having pre-wedding jitters, and I need to calm down. And of course he had to tell me all over again that we've already paid for Angel's Dream and it would be crazy to throw that money away over a couple of bad dreams." Another pause. "The problem is, they don't feel like normal dreams, or even normal nightmares. They feel like warnings. That's totally stupid, though...right?"

Not stupid at all. Unfortunately, Delia knew she couldn't tell her cousin the whole truth, or even the smallest part of it.

"I don't think it's stupid," she said gently. "And if your gut is telling you something, then I think you should listen to it. I've done some research, and there are several other chapels that could fit you in. The Little Chapel of Hearts, the Chapel of Love, Graceland Wedding Chapel—all of them have availability for your date."

"Really?" For the first time, Olivia sounded hopeful. "And you're sure they could fit us in on such short notice?"

"I've made some calls," Delia replied.

Okay, that was a total lie, but right now she just wanted to make sure she got her cousin firmly on board with changing the venue. Maybe this was all an exercise in futility, and what she should really be doing was trying to get her cousin to move her wedding out of Las Vegas altogether, but she knew that was never going to happen, not when she knew Olivia and Alec wanted to spend their honeymoon in his new vacation house in Henderson. No, the best she could do was make sure the ceremony took place in a chapel that wasn't owned by one of the Styx Group's shell companies.

Anyway, she'd have to make those calls after she was done talking to Olivia, but Delia was confident she could make something work.

She continued, "The key is being flexible about timing. You might have to move the ceremony to earlier or later in the day, but at least you'll be able to have it on the same date."

"That would be amazing," Olivia said, relief practically pulsing across the miles that separated them. "I just couldn't stop worrying about the whole thing...but I also didn't want to sound like I'd totally lost my mind."

"There's nothing crazy about trusting your instincts," Delia assured her. "If something feels wrong, then it probably is. The most important thing is that you and Alec have a beautiful wedding day without any stress or worry."

"You're absolutely right." Olivia's voice sounded stronger now, more determined. "I'm going to talk to Alec again tonight. If he refuses to listen, then I'll just have to make the decision myself. It's my wedding, too, even if he's paying for most of it."

Thank God that it sounded like her cousin had started to grow a spine. Things often got tricky when money was involved, but wasn't the bride supposed to make the final decision about anything like this?

"Good for you," Delia said. "And if you need someone to help you coordinate the change, just let me know. Sometimes it's easier when you can do this kind of stuff in person."

"Well, maybe we can do it together, then." Olivia paused, and when she spoke again, she sounded almost guilty. "I probably should have brought it up before this, but Alec and I are going to be in Las Vegas late tomorrow. My parents are flying in at the same time, and Alec's family is coming a few days early, too. His parents thought it would be nice to have a family dinner before the wedding. Not exactly a rehearsal dinner, since the ceremony won't be that elaborate, but a little kind of get-together."

Well, hell. More family members meant more people potentially in danger if Olivia couldn't convince Alec to change venues. It also meant more voices weighing in on wedding decisions, which could make it harder for her cousin to follow through with her plan to switch to a different chapel.

"That sounds like fun," Delia managed, even though the words wanted to strangle in her throat. "How many people are we talking about?"

"Well, my parents, obviously. Alec's parents and his sister and her husband. His grandmother, who's flying in from Phoenix. And I think a couple of his cousins." Olivia chuckled, but the laugh sounded a bit strained. "It's going to be a full house. That's part of why we're worried about changing venues—what if the new place can't accommodate everyone?"

"Don't worry about that," Delia said quickly. "Most of the chapels I mentioned can handle groups of fifty or more. The guest list won't be a problem."

"Okay, that's a relief," Olivia replied. "I just want everything to be perfect, you know? And with all the family arriving early, there's going to be so much pressure to have everything locked down."

The pressure was exactly what worried Delia. Family dynamics could be complicated under the best of circumstances, and adding wedding stress to the mix often made people dig in their heels about decisions they'd already made.

"Just remember that it's *your* wedding," she said. "Whatever you and Alec decide, that's what matters. The family will understand."

"I hope so." Olivia released a breath. "I'm beginning to think we should have just eloped."

"It's not too late for that, either," Delia said lightly, although inwardly, she was dead serious. If she couldn't get Olivia and Alec to change venues, maybe she could convince her cousin that changing the entire plan wasn't a bad idea, and it would be better if they just ran off to Cabo or Cozumel or something.

Olivia laughed, and this time, she sounded much more genuine. "Don't tempt me. But I suppose after all the money we've spent on flights and hotels for everyone, that ship has sailed."

They chatted for a few more minutes about logistics and timing, and by the end of the call, Delia felt cautiously optimistic. Olivia seemed motivated to make a change, and her growing unease about Angel's Dream could only work in their favor.

But the mention of arriving family members had introduced a new complication. The more people involved in the decision-making process, the harder it would be to steer things in the right direction without raising any suspicions about her motives.

As soon as she ended her call with Olivia, Delia started reaching out to the wedding chapels she'd mentioned. She needed to have concrete alternatives ready to present, complete with availability and pricing, if she was going to help her cousin make the switch, and although doing all this might make her a little late for work, she wanted as much of this handled as possible before she went into the office.

The first chapel she called was able to offer a Saturday evening slot that would work perfectly. The second had a late afternoon opening that might be even better, since it would give the wedding party more time for photos before dinner. By the time she'd made five calls, she had three solid options with availability and hoped that would be enough.

Now the only thing left was to wait and see if Olivia could convince Alec—and the rest of the family—that a last-minute venue change was worth the hassle.

Her phone pinged, and she looked down to see she'd gotten a text from Caleb.

How'd the call with your cousin go?

Better than expected. She wants to change venues, but she has a bunch of family arriving tomorrow, and that might complicate things.

We'll figure it out. Meet for lunch later? I want to hear everything.

Sure. Just let me know where.

After last night's revelations, the prospect of seeing him again sent a happy rush of warmth through her. Whatever challenges lay ahead with the demons' plot or the family's dynamics, at least she wouldn't be facing them alone.

Her phone rang again, and this time it was her mother.

"Hi, Mom," she answered, wondering if Linda had somehow sensed the drama brewing around Olivia's wedding...or was maybe wondering why Delia hadn't come in to work yet. The hour was inching dangerously close to ten, and usually she would have been in the office at least half an hour earlier than that.

But it turned out her tardiness wasn't what was on her mother's mind.

"Morning, Delia," Linda said. "I just sent your father off to find a new suit for Olivia's wedding. Things have been so busy that I just realized you and I hadn't really talked about whether you're even planning to attend."

"Yes, I'm going," Delia replied. "Olivia asked

me to be involved with some of the local arrangements, actually. I'm helping her scout some venues."

"'Venues'?" Her mother repeated, voice sharpening a little. "I thought everything was already set with Angel's Dream. That's what was on the invitation, anyway. Is there a problem with the chapel?"

Okay, time to come up with a plausible explanation for such a last-minute change. While Linda wasn't exactly an expert on the wedding industry, she still knew enough, mostly because selling real estate in a city where destination weddings were big business lent itself to picking up a few things. Anyway, her mother would definitely notice if something seemed off about a last-minute venue change.

"Not a problem, exactly," Delia said, doing her best to sound casual. "Olivia's just been having some second thoughts about the chapel. You know how brides can be—she wants to make sure everything is perfect and that she made the right choice."

"Hmm." Her mother didn't sound entirely convinced by this explanation. "The Angel's Dream chapel is fairly new, isn't it? I seem to remember it changing hands recently."

Trust her mother to remember a detail like that. "Yes, I think it was sold a few months ago. Maybe that's part of what's making Olivia nervous

—it sounds as if the staff is the same, but I can see why she's worried that the new management might make some last-minute changes."

Linda seemed to think that was a reasonable concern, since she only said, "Well, if she needs help with alternatives, you know I'd be happy to lend a hand."

"I appreciate that, Mom," Delia replied, "but I think I have it taken care of. Besides, you and Dad will probably have enough to do, what with all those out-of-town family members showing up in the next day or so."

"True enough. Your Aunt Vicky is flying in tomorrow, and she's always been a bit high-maintenance when it comes to travel." Linda paused there before adding, "Just let us know if you need anything, okay? Family weddings can be stressful enough without venue drama."

Delia assured her mother that everything was under control, and then said she'd be at the office in the next half hour or so. Technically, theirs was a partnership, and Linda didn't have any say in the hours her daughter worked, but she knew her mother wouldn't be too thrilled if she decided to start showing up after ten o'clock every day.

After they ended the call, Delia realized the situation had just gotten even more complicated. If nothing else, her mother's sharp business instincts meant she'd be watching for any inconsistencies in Delia's explanations about the venue change.

Oh, and let's not forget that somewhere in the background, a citywide demonic conspiracy was building toward whatever climax they had planned for May thirtieth.

She thought about Caleb's words from the night before, his fear about losing her, and couldn't hold back a corresponding chill of her own. They were walking into something much bigger and more dangerous than anything they'd faced before, and the people she loved most were going to be right in the middle of it.

But there was no backing down now. Too many lives were at stake, including her cousin's and her parents'. Whatever it took, she was going to find a way to keep them safe.

Even if it meant lying to everyone she cared about in the process.

Her phone pinged to let her know she had another text, this one from Olivia.

Talked to Alec. He's still resistant, but I think I can wear him down. Can we meet tomorrow afternoon to look at those other chapels? Our flight is getting in at one, and I want to have all the facts in hand before our families arrive.

Good thing Delia didn't have any house showings scheduled for tomorrow. She'd planned to use the slow day to get some paperwork taken care of and swing by to check on the contractors at the flip house, but none of that was totally urgent. *Absolutely. I'll pick you up & we'll make an afternoon of it.*

At least Olivia was taking the initiative. That was something. Now Delia just had to hope that between the two of them, they could present a compelling enough case to overcome Alec's reluctance and the inevitable family pressure that would come with all the early arrivals.

She glanced at the clock and realized she needed to get going, especially if she wanted to get any significant work done before she had to meet Caleb for lunch. Once she got to the office, she could do more research on the alternative chapels and maybe come up with a strategy for handling all the complicated family dynamics that wouldn't result in a total meltdown.

Because one way or another, she was going to make sure her cousin didn't walk down the aisle at Angel's Dream on May thirtieth.

Even if she had to kidnap the bride to make it happen.

Chapter Seven

—·‹‹‹·◎·›››·—

THE ALARM ON CALEB'S PHONE WENT OFF at seven-thirty the next morning, the same time he'd had it set for the past few months. Unlike his old life in Greencastle, where his mother had insisted that the household follow her schedule—well, at least until he made his escape at twenty, when he'd bought his loft apartment in Greencastle's historic downtown and was able to assert some measure of independence—here in Las Vegas, he'd found himself settling into his own rhythm. Morning workouts in the home gym he'd set up in one of the spare bedrooms, followed by whatever needed attention at the flip house he was working on at the moment, with the rest of the day open for any crises that might emerge.

And lately, there had been plenty of those.

He rolled over and picked up his phone from

the spot where it rested on the nightstand, then squinted at the screen. Three missed calls from Pru, all within the last twenty minutes. That wasn't good.

Maybe he should rethink putting the thing on "do not disturb" overnight.

Before he could even sit up properly, the screen showed another call coming in. This time, it was Ty.

"We've got a problem," the half angel said as soon as Caleb answered. Obviously, he didn't want to waste time on "good mornings." "Multiple incidents across the city. The activity started a little before six this morning."

Of course it did. Right then, Caleb found himself wishing for the good ol' days back in January when all he'd had to deal with was a bunch of demons trying to chase him out of town because he was hurting their bottom line by winning all that money at the gaming tables. Simple greed had been a lot easier to deal with than this current clusterfuck.

"What sort of incidents?" he asked as he moved toward his dresser to grab some clothes. It sure looked like he was going to have to skip the workout this morning.

"Coordinated attacks on wedding venues," Ty replied. "But not just the chapels we've been watching—it looks like they've expanded to every major event space in the city...hotels, restaurants, convention centers. Anywhere people might gather for celebrations, just like we were afraid might happen."

This unwelcome news made every muscle in Caleb's neck and shoulders tense. Deep down, he supposed he'd been hoping that after he and Delia had vanquished the demons at the Silver Bell, things might quiet down, if only for a little while.

No such luck.

"How many locations?" he asked, scrubbing a hand through his hair, inwardly glad that it was never what you could exactly call controlled.

"At least twenty that we've confirmed so far," Ty said. "Pru's been monitoring her police scanner, and the reports are still coming in. Electrical fires, structural collapses, unexplained equipment failures. The city's emergency services are starting to get overwhelmed."

Caleb pulled on jeans and a T-shirt, trying to figure out what this kind of widescale activity meant. If the demons were making such bold moves in broad daylight, then they were either desperate or supremely confident.

Neither option was particularly comforting.

He also hated the idea of innocent bystanders getting caught up in a mess that was none of their making. "Any injuries?"

"So far, no. That's what's strange about all this.

Every incident seems to have happened when the venues were empty—overnight cleaning staff had already left, morning setup crews hadn't arrived yet. It's like the demons timed everything perfectly to cause maximum disruption with minimal casualties."

Which suggested they wanted chaos, not a body count. At least, that was the impression Caleb was getting from Ty's report. Right now, it seemed as if the havoc the demons were causing in the city probably wasn't quite enough for anyone to start connecting the otherworldly dots.

"Where do you want to meet?" he asked, already knowing he'd need to see some of these sites firsthand to get a sense of what the gang was dealing with.

"Pru's place. It's closest to the center of town, and Delia's already on her way over. We need to coordinate our response before they escalate further."

Caleb hated the idea of her getting caught up in this mess any more than she already had. After what they'd shared last night—the openness he'd seen in her eyes when she'd told him she loved him, the way she'd fit so perfectly against him as they sat on the couch—the idea of her walking into danger made something fierce and possessive rise within him.

But she was part of this, whether he liked it or

not. Hell, she might be better equipped than any of them to handle supernatural threats, given her growing psychic abilities.

"I'll be there in fifteen minutes," he said.

"Make it ten if you can. I've got a feeling we're running out of time."

Of course they were.

Despite the half angel's urgency, Caleb stood in his bedroom for a moment after he ended the call, doing what he could to allow his enhanced senses to stretch out across the city. Even here, far from most of the affected locations, he could sense a kind of wrongness in the air—a spiritual disturbance that set his teeth on edge and made the demon blood in his veins respond with restless energy.

Whatever was happening, it was bigger than anything his little group of friends had faced so far.

He grabbed his keys and wallet, and on his way to the garage, he paused by the coat closet in the foyer. Then he reached inside and pulled out a small gym bag he'd been keeping there for emergencies. In the bag were bottles of holy water, a few basic first aid supplies, and a knife that had been blessed by three different priests. He'd put the gear together after returning from Laughlin, figuring he needed to have a kit for the supernatural interruptions that seemed to be occurring in his life with more and more frequency.

But he really hadn't thought he'd need to use it this soon.

The drive to Pru's condo building should have taken fifteen minutes, but Caleb made it in seven. He'd pushed his Mercedes harder than he probably should have, using his enhanced reflexes to navigate morning traffic with a kind of reckless skill that would have looked impressive to any observers—but not so impressive as to attract any unwanted attention from the local authorities.

He guessed that morning, they were probably busy elsewhere.

After leaving the car in one of the condo building's guest parking spaces, he took the elevator up, noting that he could sense increasingly strong energetic disturbances the higher he went. By the time he reached the sixth floor, the feeling was strong enough to make him slightly nauseated. Whatever Pru had been monitoring from her condo, it was definitely affecting the local energy patterns.

When he knocked at the door to Pru's condo, a tense-looking Delia opened it and stepped out of the way so he could come inside. He gave her a brief squeeze of the hand—he kind of doubted Ty or Pru would appreciate any obvious displays of affection—and followed her into the dining room. There, he saw the two others standing in what looked like a war room setup—multiple laptops, printed maps taped to the walls, and EMF meters and other gadgets scattered across the table, among them a police scanner, its antenna tacked to the ceiling so Pru could get the best reception.

Clearly, she'd been busy over the past few hours. Where had she even gotten all this stuff?

Maybe former boyfriends, he thought with an inner grin. After all, if she'd once dated a pick-pocket, as she'd revealed during their time in Laughlin, who knew what other useful SOs might be lurking in her past?

"About time," she remarked as he approached. Today, her green hair hung loose, as if she couldn't be bothered with even a ponytail, and, judging by her jittery air, she'd probably been subsisting on coffee and not much else. "You need to see this."

She gestured toward the largest laptop screen, which displayed a real-time map of Las Vegas with dozens of red dots scattered across it. As Caleb watched, three more dots appeared.

"Each dot represents a supernatural incident," Ty explained, shifting slightly so Caleb and Delia could move closer. "The pattern is becoming clearer as we hear more reports."

He studied the map, trying to see what the others had already figured out. The dots appeared random at first, but as he let his gaze unfocus slightly, a pattern began to emerge. It sure seemed as if all those dots formed a rough geometric shape that encompassed most of the Las Vegas valley.

"We'd already guessed they were trying to create some kind of ritual circle," Delia said quietly. She stood close enough to him that Caleb could sense her body's warmth, and despite the chaos unfolding in the city around them, he wished he could wrap an arm around her waist and pull her even closer. "But now we can tell it's not just any circle. Look at the spacing."

She was right. Now that he could see it, the pattern was unmistakable. Each incident site corresponded to a specific point in what appeared to be an elaborate summoning diagram—one that used the entire city as its foundation.

"How big is it?" Caleb asked, even though he suspected he already knew the answer.

"Big enough to summon something we really don't want to deal with," Ty replied, his tone grim. "Best guess is that they're attempting to create a portal large enough for a major demon lord to cross over. It has to be someone from the upper echelons of Hell's hierarchy."

That was what Caleb had been afraid of. He'd spent two years in that place, and while most of his time had been devoted to survival rather than demon politics, he'd learned enough about the power structures there to know that the really dangerous entities rarely bothered with the mortal plane unless they had something specific in mind.

Something like revenge.

"Any idea which lord they're trying to summon?" he asked, already guessing that the answer was going to make his day significantly worse.

Pru clicked through several screens on her laptop, bringing up what looked like occult diagrams and arcane symbols. Maybe she'd started out investigating cheating spouses and people lying about their workmen's comp cases, but it seemed as if she'd slid into the whole supernatural milieu pretty easily. Then again, research skills were research skills.

"Based on the geometric patterns and the timing of the incidents, there are three possibilities," she said. "Malphas, Marchosias, or—"

"Vinea," Caleb broke in, his voice flat.

"Who's that?" Delia asked.

Right. Most people didn't know anything about the hierarchy of Hell, beyond the obvious suspects like Beelzebub or Asmodeus or even Belial, the demon lord who'd had the most effect on Caleb's life.

But, thank God and all the choirs of angels, Belial was now dead, not just banished.

However, that didn't mean they didn't have plenty of remaining evil entities to deal with.

"Vinea is an earl of Hell who can build towers, demolish walls, and make waters rough," Ty replied. "He often appears as a lion riding a black horse while holding a viper...although I assume he'll probably try to maintain a lower profile while here on the mortal plane."

"And he's no one to mess with," Caleb added. "He gets his jollies destroying the works of man, so it's not too much of a stretch to guess he's behind the destruction in the city this morning."

"Do you think he's trying to get back at you specifically?" Delia said. She inched even closer, and he got the impression she also wished he could take her in his arms and provide some much-needed reassurance, however spurious it might be.

"Maybe." He pushed a hand through his already disheveled hair as he tried to work his way through the possibilities. Even though he was part demon, the motivations of the higher-level demons were often pretty murky to him. "Or maybe he's just tired of being stuck in Hell and sees Las Vegas as a convenient entry point."

"Either way," Ty said, apparently deciding they'd wasted enough time on ancient history, "we need to disrupt the ritual before they can complete it. The question is how."

Pru pulled up another screen, this one showing a timeline of the morning's incidents. "If the pattern holds, they'll need to hit at least twelve more locations before the circle is complete. Based on the current rate of attacks, that gives us maybe six hours."

Six hours to prevent a demon lord from potentially taking over Las Vegas. Well, that should be simple enough.

Not.

"We'll have to split up," he said, then moved closer to the table where Pru's laptop rested so he could study the map in detail. "If we can disrupt even a few of the remaining ritual sites, it should be enough to throw off the entire summoning."

"Agreed," Ty replied. "But we need to be strategic about which sites we target. Some locations will be more critical to the overall pattern than others."

Delia had been studying the map as well, her expression tight with concentration...and worry. "It looks like Angel's Dream is right in the center of all this. If they're building a city-wide summoning circle, that chapel is probably going to be the focal point."

Oh, crap. In all the chaos of the morning's revelations, he'd temporarily forgotten about Delia's cousin and the wedding that was now only two days away. If Angel's Dream was indeed the center of the ritual....

"We need to get your family out of the city," he said at once. "All of them. Today."

But Delia was already shaking her head. "You know they won't go. Not without a really good reason, and obviously, we can't tell them the truth.

Olivia's parents, Alec's family—they're all flying in for the pre-wedding events, and Olivia and Alec's flight is supposed to get here a little after one o'clock."

"Then we have to make sure the ritual never gets completed," Caleb said, knowing he sounded a lot more confident than he felt. "Whatever it takes."

Pru glanced away from her laptop. "I've been trying to track the attack patterns, and I think I can predict which sites they'll hit next."

"You 'think'?" Caleb asked dubiously.

Ty, on the other hand, didn't seem too worried about the lack of a ringing endorsement. "Show me," he said, shifting his position so he could more easily look over Pru's shoulder.

As the two of them began coordinating tactical details, Caleb pulled Delia aside. Now that they were away from the others, he could see the strain in her face more clearly. The dark circles under her clear, blue-gray eyes suggested she'd gotten even less sleep than he had, and there was a tension in her shoulders that spoke of deeper worries than just the supernatural crisis they were facing.

"How are you holding up?" he asked quietly.

She managed a small smile. "I've been better. I keep thinking about what will happen if we don't stop this, and...." The words trailed off there, and then she seemed to gather herself. "My parents are going to be at that wedding, Caleb, along with a lot of other family members. If something happens to any of them—"

"Nothing's going to happen to them," he said firmly as he reached out to squeeze her hand. "We're going to stop these bastards before it gets that far."

"You can't promise that," she replied, but she didn't pull her hand away. "We're not even sure what we're really up against yet. For all we know, this could be the opening move in something much bigger."

She wasn't wrong. The level of coordination they'd seen so far suggested resources and planning that went well beyond what a few rogue demons plotting their usual mischief could accomplish. Someone with serious power and influence was orchestrating all this—maybe the demon lord Vinea, maybe someone even worse—and Caleb had a sinking feeling that they'd only scratched the surface of what was really going on.

"Then we'll learn more," he said. "But we'll do it together, and we won't give up. No matter what."

Before Delia could respond, Pru called out from across the room. "Guys, get over here. I just heard something important."

They hurried back to the computer setup, where Pru had a set of earphones half on and half off so she could listen to them and monitor the police scanner at the same time.

"Multiple units are responding to a disturbance at the Little Chapel of Hearts," she went on. "That's one of the venues Delia suggested as an alternative for her cousin's wedding."

A chill ran down Caleb's spine. "What kind of disturbance?"

"Witnesses reported seeing figures in dark clothing entering the building around dawn. When the first responders arrived, they found the front doors standing open and signs of some kind of ritual activity inside. No perpetrators on scene, but...." Prudence paused there so she could turn back to her laptop and open up a new tab. "Then they found this."

The screen switched to a photo that had apparently been taken by one of the responding officers. It showed the inside of the chapel, with chairs overturned and what looked like arcane symbols burned into the carpet. But it was the message scrawled across the wall in what appeared to be ash that made Caleb's blood run cold.

THE HALF-BREED KNOWS OUR WORK. LET HIM COME TO US.

Ty folded his arms. "It sure looks like they're actively trying to draw us out."

"Or specifically trying to draw me out," Caleb replied. The reference to a "half-breed" was clearly meant for him, even if technically he wasn't a half-breed at all, but a quarter-breed.

Delia moved closer to the screen, her expression even more troubled. "If they're targeting the alternative venues, too, that means even if we convince Olivia to change locations, she—and the rest of my family—still won't be safe."

"Unless we stop this entire operation," Caleb told her. "So we need to take the offensive instead of just reacting to their moves."

Pru was already typing rapidly on another, smaller laptop, a little MacBook Air instead of the Pro she seemed to favor. "I can track their movements in real time now that I know the demons are using the city's emergency frequencies to monitor response times. If they stick to their pattern, the next attack should be...."

She paused, appearing to cross-reference several screens of data. "The Venetian's wedding pavilion. They'll probably hit it within the next hour."

Ty nodded. "That gives us enough time to get into position. We can set up surveillance and try to intercept them when they arrive."

"Or we could turn the tables completely," Caleb said as an idea began to form in his mind. "Instead of trying to stop them from completing individual attacks, what if we gave them a target they couldn't resist?"

They all stared at him, and he could see Delia's

expression morph into one of even deeper worry as she began to guess where his thoughts were heading.

"You want to use yourself as bait," she said flatly.

"Not just me. All of us." Caleb moved closer to the map displayed on Pru's MacBook Pro, then pointed to the center of the ritual circle. "They need Angel's Dream for the final stage of whatever they're planning. If we can draw their attention there, force them to make their move before they're ready, we might be able to disrupt the entire operation."

"That would be unbelievably dangerous," Ty said at once. His frown had only deepened, and it was obvious that he thought Caleb had lost his ever-loving mind. "If we're wrong about the timing, or if they have more resources than we realize, we could end up walking into a situation we wouldn't be able to escape."

"So...what, then?" Caleb returned. "We just stand back and let them complete a ritual that could open a permanent gateway to Hell in the middle of Las Vegas?" Before anyone could respond, he went on, "Sometimes the risky play is the only one that makes any sense."

Pru pushed her chair away from the dining room table a few inches so she could get a better look at all of them. "Actually, that might work.

There's a way to get into the city's response system so I can create enough false emergency signals to confuse their monitoring systems. That would make it look like we're hitting multiple sites simultaneously, when in reality, we're really only concentrating our efforts on Angel's Dream."

Delia put her hands on her hips, and Caleb could tell she was dubious at best. "You can really do that?"

"Well, on my own, no," Pru responded with a grin. "Let's just say I know a few people who owe me favors. You don't need to be a hacker if you've already got people on the inside."

And what Prudence Nelson had on those "people," Caleb wasn't sure he wanted to know. A private investigator probably had all kinds of dirt that could be used for persuasion. Or maybe they were just grateful former clients, like the assistant city manager with the cheating wife. Either way, it sure looked as if they had an in.

Delia still looked somewhat disapproving, but it seemed she'd decided the stakes were too high to worry too much about how they were accomplishing their goals. "Okay," she said. "I think I could probably create some barriers around the chapel to contain whatever supernatural energy they're trying to summon."

"You're sure about that?" Ty inquired, expression openly skeptical, and she shrugged.

"I'm not 'sure' about anything," she said. "But I know my abilities were getting stronger anyway, and after being exposed to that portal in Laughlin...." The sentence died away, and her shoulders lifted again. "It just feels like I might have gotten an additional boost. So that means I might be able to hold a containment field long enough for you two to disrupt the ritual directly."

Ty nodded, but he still appeared less than enthusiastic. "I suppose it could work. But we'll have to coordinate perfectly. One mistake, and we could end up making the demons' job easier instead of harder."

"Then we won't make any mistakes," Caleb said.

By mid-morning, they thought they were ready to move. The attacks had continued across the city, each one adding another point to the growing ritual circle. According to Pru's calculations, they had maybe three hours before the demons would be ready to attempt the final summoning at Angel's Dream.

"Remember," Caleb said as they prepared to leave Pru's condo, "the goal is disruption, not confrontation. We go in fast, hit the key points, and get out before they can coordinate a response."

"And if they've set up more defenses than we're expecting?" Delia asked.

"Then we improvise," he replied. Not a very good answer, he supposed, but the only one he was able to give. They had to be flexible, since they were walking into a situation with way too many unknown variables. They didn't know how many demons they were actually facing and what kind of backup plans their enemies might have. And they had absolutely zero idea whether their own abilities would be sufficient to counter whatever supernatural forces were currently surging in the city.

But they also didn't have the luxury of waiting for more information, not when the circuit was due to close sometime right at high noon. Sometimes the only thing you could do was act...and hope for the best.

"Do what you can to stay in contact," Ty told everyone once they were inside the elevator and headed down to the ground floor. "If any of us runs into more than we can handle, then we'll abort and regroup."

They split up, with Delia and Caleb and Ty going toward the guest parking lot to retrieve their vehicles and Pru heading toward her car in the parking garage under the building. After that, they all scattered to their assigned positions around the city.

Caleb pointed his E-Class toward Angel's

Dream, taking a circuitous route that would allow him to scout the surrounding area for signs of supernatural activity. As he got closer to the chapel, the uncomfortable buzzing sensation in his demon blood grew stronger until it felt like every nerve ending was zinging with unwanted energy.

Whatever was happening here, it was big.

He parked three blocks away and approached on foot, doing what he could to scan for any demonic presences nearby. The chapel itself looked the same from the outside as it had when he and Delia had visited here for the first time—a white-painted clapboard structure meant to mimic a charming church that might have been plucked from somewhere in America's heartland. But the spiritual atmosphere around the building was thick and oppressive, like the air before a thunderstorm.

A text came through from Delia.

I'm in position. Energy readings are off the charts here.

Immediately afterward, he received similar messages from Ty and Pru. Whatever the demons were planning, they weren't being subtle about it anymore.

Which was fine. That just made them easier to find.

Caleb found a good vantage point in the shadow of a nearby office building and settled in to wait.

The plan called for him to hang back and simply observe until the others were ready to begin their coordinated disruption, but as the minutes ticked by, he began to sense something was very wrong here.

The energy patterns around Angel's Dream weren't just strong...they were oddly familiar as well. Although he probably wouldn't have been able to articulate such a thing before now, the specific resonance of the supernatural disturbance tugged at memories from his time in Hell, reminding him of the aura that had surrounded certain high-ranking demons he'd encountered there. Luckily, they hadn't paid him much mind, thinking a quarter demon like himself beneath their notice, but they still had a particular smell, so to speak.

And this stink definitely reminded him of Vinea.

His phone buzzed—he'd put it on vibrate for obvious reasons—and he answered immediately. "Ty?"

"We've got a problem." The half angel didn't sound too happy about his life choices right then, and Caleb couldn't blame him. "I'm picking up movement at multiple sites around the city. It looks like they're accelerating their timeline."

Well, that was just peachy. "How accelerated?" Caleb asked, doing his best to sound as if this latest development hadn't sent adrenaline shrilling along every nerve ending.

"Like, right now," Ty responded. "I can see figures moving around the Desert Rose Wedding Chapel, and they're definitely not human. Whatever they were waiting for, they've decided not to wait anymore."

Before Caleb could respond, a new voice cut through the phone connection—one that made the blood freeze in his veins, deep and harsh.

"Hello, nephew."

The line went dead.

Caleb stared at his phone for a moment, trying to process what he'd just heard. Then the implications of those two simple words hit him like a pair of punches to his gut.

Nephew.

There were only a very few beings in existence who would refer to him that way. While the demons and devils who occupied the highest levels of Hell's hierarchy weren't technically related to one another, they still referred to the others of their kind as "brother" from time to time.

Often ironically, but still.

And his demon grandfather had been among them.

Somehow, Vinea was already here. The demon lord must have found a way to cross over without completing the city-wide summoning circle. His early arrival implied he had some kind of assistance, someone powerful who'd used their own ritual to bring him here.

And that meant everything the little group of defenders thought they knew about the situation was wrong.

Delia and Pru and Ty needed to regroup, get back to Pru's apartment, where they would have at least a modicum of safety.

Abort, he typed, replying to Ty since he was the last person in their team he'd communicated with. *Go back to home base. Now.*

Ty's response came back almost immediately.

Are you coming?

Soon. Just do it.

All right. I'll message Delia and Pru.

The convo ended there, but it was enough. Caleb knew Ty would do as he asked, mainly because the half angel also understood that this was not the occasion to waste any precious time on arguments.

Caleb's phone vibrated again...a text from an unknown number.

The chapel. Come alone, or watch your city burn.

Chapter Eight

---·‹‹‹•☾•›››·---

The silence in Pru's living room after they'd all regrouped there was the most terrifying sound Delia had ever heard. She sat on the edge of the black sectional, her phone still stubbornly pressed to her ear even though repeated calls to Caleb's number just went over to voicemail.

Fifteen minutes earlier, Ty had received Caleb's urgent message telling them all to abort and return to home base, and he'd passed it along to the other two. Despite her own misgivings, Delia had dropped everything—to be honest, she'd been only too glad to get back someplace she hoped was relatively safe—and driven at top speed to Pru's condo, expecting to find Caleb waiting for the group with an explanation for the sudden change in plans.

Instead, they'd found an empty condo and a

phone number that no longer seemed to connect to anything.

The last thing any of them had heard from him was that voice—deep, harsh, utterly inhuman—calling Caleb "nephew" before his line went dead.

"Try his number again," Pru said from her position at the dining room table, fingers flying over her laptop keyboard with desperate speed. Her tourmaline-green hair swung forward, halfway hiding her eyes, and her jaw was tight as she worked.

Delia knew that feeling all too well, the knot of worry deep in her gut, the desperate belief that if she did something...*anything*...she might be able to change the situation. She touched the screen to call Caleb's number again, knowing it was pointless but still unable to stop herself.

Same result. Straight to voicemail, the cheerful recorded message a jarring contrast to the supernatural nightmare unfolding around them.

Hey, you've reached Caleb Lowe. I'm probably at my latest flip getting my hands dirty, so leave a message, and I'll get back to you.

The normality of those casual words—*latest flip, get back to you*—felt like relics from another lifetime. Had it really been only a few days ago that their biggest worry was choosing the right flooring for Caleb's latest acquisition?

Ty stood by the window, his usual calm

cracking enough to show the strain beneath. "That voice," he said, not turning around. "I'm not saying I've heard it before, but it didn't sound like your regular garden-variety demon. Too cultured for that."

"Who was it?" Delia asked, even though some part of her already knew the answer.

"We've already guessed that Vinea is involved in all this. The way he called Caleb 'nephew'...." Rather than bothering to complete the sentence, Ty finally turned to face the two watching women, his expression very sober. "Now I'm almost sure he's the one involved, because high-level demons often think of each other as brethren. That explains the 'nephew' reference, although I suppose 'great-nephew' is probably more accurate. Anyway, Vinea has been trapped in the underworld ever since the Fall, so you know he wants to get out."

"But that's impossible," Pru said, brows pulled together in frustration. "If he's trapped in Hell, how is he here, somehow breaking into Caleb's phone calls? How is he communicating with us?"

"I don't know," Ty replied. "Demons...especially demon lords...can be very difficult to predict."

There was an understatement. Resolutely, Delia set her cell phone down on the coffee table. Maybe if she wasn't holding it, she wouldn't be consumed by the need to keep trying to call Caleb.

"Do you know anything about who Caleb's grandfather is?" she asked. "How do you know it's not Vinea? I mean, he's a high-ranking demon lord, right?"

A certain stillness settled over Ty's model-handsome features. Did that mean he knew the answer but didn't want to reveal it, or simply that he didn't like having to confess how he didn't hold all the answers at his fingertips?

Apparently the latter, because he said, "We don't know. Although Caleb's forebear would have occupied a high position in Hell, he was still only one of Belial's servants. There are many who were in service to Belial, so even though I suppose it might be possible to narrow it down to a list of suspects, we can't really say for sure."

"But it wouldn't be Vinea," Pru said, when it seemed clear Delia wasn't sure how to respond.

"No. Vinea is an Earl of Hell. Still a lord, but a higher rank than the servants Belial brought with him to Greencastle."

Delia supposed that was something, although she realized the important thing here wasn't which demon might or might not be Caleb's grandfather. No, what they really needed to focus on was how to track Caleb down. He'd been observing outside the Angel's Dream chapel, but if he'd really been intercepted by demons, he could now be anywhere in the city.

Or at least, anyplace where the ley lines ran, giving the demon cohort the additional power they needed to make sure their terrible plans came to fruition.

Before Ty could answer, Delia's phone vibrated on the coffee table. Heart pounding, she reached out to pick it up, praying that it was Caleb texting to let her know he'd had phone issues but was fine and on his way over to Pru's condo even now.

But the message she read on the home screen made her entire body stiffen in terror.

The chapel. Come alone, or watch your lover burn.

"They have him," she said, then rose from the sectional so she could show the screen to Pru and Ty. Her hand shook, but their horrified trembling didn't seem to prevent her friends from seeing the words displayed there.

Ty's expression darkened further. "They're using him as bait."

"Of course they are." The words came out bitter, laced with a helpless fury that made Delia want to throw her phone against the wall, even though the logical side of her mind knew she would never do anything so pointlessly destructive. Instead, she set the iPhone back down on the coffee table as she said, "It's what I would do if I were an ancient demonic entity trying to lure someone into a trap."

But even as she spoke, Delia thought she felt something else stirring within her—a response to the ley line energy that had been building across Las Vegas all morning. Her psychic abilities, which had been growing stronger in fits and starts since her capture and imprisonment in Laughlin, spiked with an intensity that made her gasp and stumble backward.

Pru's voice came to her, sounding very far away. "Delia? Are you okay?"

It was like someone had suddenly turned up the volume on a radio that had been playing at barely audible levels. The supernatural energy of the city crashed over her in waves, each pulse bringing with it new information, new awareness of the vast network of power that crisscrossed Las Vegas like a spiderweb.

The room around her seemed to shimmer, the normal world overlaid with patterns of light and shadow that revealed the true nature of the city beneath its neon façade. Every ley line, every inter-section point, every place where supernatural power gathered—it was all visible to her now, a vast network pulsing with malevolent purpose.

And at the center of it all, Angel's Dream Wedding Chapel blazed like a beacon of concentrated darkness, a black hole at the center of the world.

"Delia?" Pru's voice was more urgent now, and she realized her friend had gotten up from her seat at the dining room table and paused a few feet away. "You're...you're glowing."

She looked down at her hands and realized that Pru wasn't exaggerating. A faint luminescence surrounded her fingers, a cool blue-white light that reminded her of LED bulbs. But this was different, because it was coming from her. The light pulsed in rhythm with her heartbeat, and she could feel it spreading up her arms with a warmth that was both comforting and terrifying.

"I can see it," she said, and her own voice sounded strange to her ears, as if it had somehow emanated from somewhere outside her body rather than her vocal cords. "The whole network. They've obviously been building this for months. Every property the Styx Group bought, every chapel they acquired—they're all connected."

She tried to focus on Pru's and Ty's faces, on the worry and wonder she could detect there, but the energy patterns kept intruding, overlaying her normal vision with geometric designs that made her want to squint. She could see the flow of power moving through the building's electrical systems, could sense the way the ley lines intersected three blocks south of here, could feel the pulse of supernatural activity radiating out from dozens of points across the valley.

It was overwhelming and beautiful.

And it was absolutely terrifying.

She wasn't supposed to be able to do any of this.

Pru's laptop screen flickered, displaying the map she'd put together of Las Vegas with dozens of red dots scattered across it. But now Delia could see what the map couldn't show—the lines of energy connecting each point, creating a massive ritual circle that encompassed the entire valley. Not just a circle, she realized with growing horror, but a complex geometric pattern that would focus and amplify whatever energy was channeled through it.

"And Caleb's right in the middle," she said, the words coming out flat, weighed down with an unwelcome certainty. She could sense him now, a familiar warmth surrounded by darkness...a candle flame flickering in a hurricane.

They had to do something, or that flame might be snuffed out forever.

Ty moved closer. It seemed the strange glow that surrounded her hadn't put him off too much, or she guessed he would have kept his distance the way Pru was doing right now, her expression that of a woman who still wasn't quite sure what she was seeing and definitely didn't know what to do about it.

"Delia," he said, "you need to listen to me carefully. I can sense at least six high-level demons converging on Angel's Dream. Vinea's brought backup. *Serious* backup."

The energy surge within her pulsed again, and suddenly, Delia could sense what Ty was talking about. Dark presences moved through the city like sharks circling their prey, all of them heading toward the same destination. She could feel their hunger, their anticipation, their absolute certainty that they were about to achieve something they'd been planning for a very long time.

They were heading toward Caleb.

"We have to help him," she said, the words fierce, not allowing any argument. "We can't just leave him there."

"No," Ty replied sharply, and she could hear the strain in his voice, as if he was saying what he knew he had to say, even if he didn't like it very much. "That's exactly what they want. You and Caleb together, in the same place, with all that ley line energy at their disposal. Your combined abilities are part of whatever ritual they're planning."

Delia crossed her arms, and the white glow surrounding her sparked for a moment before blinking out altogether. Had she closed a circuit, or had the energy simply done what it needed to do?

She had way too many questions, and she had a

feeling none of them would be answered anytime soon.

"So, what?" she demanded, voice hard. "We just leave Caleb there? We let the demons do whatever they want to him?"

A muscle in Ty's cheek twitched, but he sounded calm enough as he replied, "We'll regroup. We'll find another way."

But even as Ty spoke, another part of Delia's mind was reaching out, trying to sense Caleb across the supernatural network that connected Las Vegas. For a moment, she thought she felt something—a familiar warmth, tinged with anger and fear and a stubborn determination that was so quintessentially Caleb Lockwood that it made her heart ache. But then it was gone, blocked by something much darker and stronger, and she wanted to cry.

No time for that, though, not when trouble was assailing them from all sides.

"I have to call my family," she said abruptly. She'd been so caught up in what was happening with Caleb that she'd almost forgotten about the members of her extended family converging on Las Vegas in the very near future. "Olivia's flight lands in a couple of hours, and her parents are arriving a short time after that. My parents are supposed to pick them up at the airport. If this escalates any further...."

She didn't finish the sentence because she didn't need to. Everyone in that room knew what could happen if a supernatural battle erupted in the middle of Las Vegas while her family members were scattered across the city. Her parents, her aunt and uncle, Olivia and Alec, his family, the rest of the wedding guests—all of them flying blindly into a war zone with no idea of the danger that waited for them.

The thought of her mother trying to navigate McCarran Airport while demons stalked the city made Delia's hands clench in frustration and terror. Linda Dunne was supremely competent and more than capable in her own world of real estate deals and client meetings, but obviously, she didn't have any defenses against the kind of supernatural predators that had decided to take up residence in Las Vegas.

"Do whatever you can to keep them away from here," Ty said at once. "Try to get them to delay their arrival, or better yet, cancel entirely."

The laptop screen flickered, and Pru cursed under her breath, even as she hurried back over to take a seat in front of it and look at what was going on. She picked up her headphones and stuck them back on. "Shit," she said, even as she reached over to adjust one of the dials on the scanner. "Something's jamming the signals. Maybe someone figured out that I've been listening in."

This just kept getting better and better. Pru might have built her career on being unflappable, on being dedicated to finding the truth no matter how deeply it was buried, but everyone knew she was working way above her pay grade here. That she'd been able to discover as much as she had already was something of a miracle.

Maybe someone was looking out for them after all, even though it didn't feel much like it at the moment.

"Can you get around the jamming?" Delia asked, although she suspected she already knew the answer.

"I'm trying." Pru's voice was still even enough, but Delia caught the underlying note of frustration anyway. "I can't tell if they're blocking everything, or just me. I have to guess it's the latter, because first responders would know something was up if all their radios suddenly went dead."

Were demons usually that technologically sophisticated? The infernal entities Delia had encountered so far preferred more direct methods of creating chaos, and they also tended to be much more physical beings, not much interested in technology. The mere fact that these ones could be using these kinds of electronic warfare tactics disturbed her more than she wanted to admit.

What else might they be capable of?

With that unnerving thought floating through

her mind, Delia went to her contacts and found Olivia's number, her thumb hovering over the call button as she tried to figure out what she could possibly say. Her cousin would definitely be in the air by now, probably somewhere over the Great Plains, but the plane should have wifi. Maybe Delia could reach Olivia, convince her to get off the plane during her layover in Denver or wherever it might be, convince her that some vague "vendor problems" were serious enough to warrant canceling the wedding and sending her straight back to Chicago...or maybe to that possible elopement in Cancun.

It was a long shot...but it was the only shot they had.

The phone rang twice before Olivia answered, her voice crackling with static and sounding harried. "Delia? I can barely hear you. We've been hitting a bunch of turbulence."

A silent thank-you to the universe that she'd been able to get through at all, and then Delia said, "Olivia, listen to me. I really need you to think about postponing your arrival by a day or so."

"Are you crazy? Why? The wedding is in two days, and we have a ton to do."

Those everyday concerns—wedding preparations, vendor meetings, a family dinner—seemed absolutely surreal when contrasted with a demonic invasion. How could she possibly explain to her cousin that Las Vegas was currently being used as the focal point for a ritual that could tear holes in reality itself?

"There's been an, um, situation with some of the vendors," Delia said, hating herself for the lie but knowing she couldn't tell her cousin the truth. Not yet. Not over a crackling phone connection while Olivia was trapped thirty thousand feet in the air. "Some kind of issue with permits. It might be better to wait until things settle down."

"That doesn't make any sense," Olivia said, her voice crackling and distorting. Silence fell for a second or two, and Delia wondered if the connection had been cut off. But then her cousin went on, "The people at the chapel said they would take care of all that stuff. It's part of the package we bought."

Maybe it was. Delia would be the first to admit that she didn't know all the ins and outs of wedding planning in Las Vegas, or what a specific venue might offer its clients.

"It's something to do with the new management at Angel's Dream," Delia said desperately, even as she reflected that those words weren't a complete lie. "They've really dropped the ball. I just don't want you to get here and realize your wedding isn't going to happen because they screwed up."

Static crackled across the connection, and again Delia thought they'd lost the call entirely. Then

Olivia's voice came back, even more strained than before.

"Delia, what aren't you telling me? You sound scared."

Because I am *scared,* she thought. *I'm scared shitless because demons are trying to turn your wedding into the opening ceremony for Hell on Earth, and the man I love is being held hostage by an evil being who just happens to be a lord of Hell.*

"I just think it would be safer for everyone," she said instead.

Another burst of static, and then Olivia repeated, "'Safer'? What kind of vendor problems have anything to do with safety considerations? Delia, you're freaking me out."

The energy within her surged again, a white glow rippling out from the hand that held the cell phone, and suddenly, Delia could sense every supernatural presence in the city. Vinea at Angel's Dream, ancient and powerful and utterly without compassion. The six other demons Ty had mentioned, circling like vultures. And somewhere beneath it all, something else—a presence that felt familiar in the worst possible way.

Something that felt like Caleb, but wrong. Twisted. As if his demon blood was being forced to the surface against his will.

"Delia?" Olivia's voice sounded very far away. "Are you still there?"

She forced herself to focus on the immediate problem. "Yes, I'm here. Look, can you please trust me on this? Just deplane during your layover and go back to Chicago."

A huff of breath came through the phone's speaker. "Delia, it's a nonstop flight. Besides, my parents' flight lands half an hour after ours. Alec's family is already in the air, too. Even if I wanted to stop all this—which I don't—it's too late."

Of course it was. Delia closed her eyes, the weight of responsibility settling on her shoulders, heavy as a lead blanket. In less than two hours, Olivia's and Alec's families would be in Las Vegas, walking into a supernatural nightmare they couldn't even begin to imagine.

Time for Plan B.

"Okay," Delia said, then opened her eyes and looked over at Pru and Ty, both of whom were watching her with obvious concern. "When you land, I'm picking you and taking you straight to Alec's house in Henderson. We're not going anywhere near Angel's Dream Wedding Chapel."

"Why would we?" Olivia asked, sounding puzzled. "I thought we already agreed to sit down and talk about alternate places to have the ceremony after Alec and I got to Vegas."

Of course. So much had happened so fast, Delia couldn't seem to keep anything straight. "You're right. I'll see you at the airport."

"Delia—"

"I have to go," she said, hating herself for cutting off her cousin but knowing she couldn't maintain this conversation much longer without breaking down entirely. "I'll see you in a little while."

She hung up before Olivia could protest further, then immediately tried Caleb's number again. It went straight to voicemail.

Of course it did.

"Any luck with the emergency frequencies?" she asked Pru, who gave a grim shake of her head.

"Nothing. It's like they've created a dead zone around the affected areas." Pru slid off her headphones, expression now almost defeated. "This is all way above my pay grade."

Delia could relate. Her psychic powers might have taken a quantum jump this past month, but that didn't mean she knew what she was doing.

"You're doing better than you think," Ty said, and she raised an eyebrow.

Had he meant that, or had he just decided to play angelic cheerleader?

She didn't have much time to ponder the question, not when another energy spike suddenly smashed through her, this one strong enough to make her stagger. The apartment around them seemed to flicker, and for a moment, Delia could see through the walls, through the entire building, out across the city to a place where supernatural forces were gathering like storm clouds.

"This is getting worse," she said as she gripped the arm of the sectional to steady herself. "The ley line energy is building toward something big."

"How big?"

Before Delia could answer, the clocks on the appliances in the kitchen flickered for a second before going out. Emergency sirens began wailing in the distance, and both of Pru's laptop screens went completely black.

Light still came through the big picture window overlooking the city, although she could see the sky outside was darkening as well, becoming heavy with unseasonable monsoon clouds.

Another text from an unknown number lit up her phone's screen.

One hour. Come alone. Last warning.

"They're escalating," she said after she read the message aloud.

"And we still don't have a plan," Pru replied, her voice tight with frustration.

No, they didn't. Delia's powers might have been coruscating with energy like a flare-up of the aurora borealis, but she couldn't control them, had no idea when they might be at their strongest...or whether they might abandon her when she needed them the most.

That meant she couldn't go to Caleb's rescue,

not with any real hope of success. It killed her to be occupied with what seemed on the surface to be utterly mundane matters, but she knew there was nothing else she could do.

Right now, she just had to trust that he could take care of himself. If he'd managed to claw his way out of Hell, then he should be able to hang on for a few more hours.

"Keep monitoring the situation," she told Pru, whose eyebrows lifted slightly.

"Going somewhere?" she asked.

"Yes," Delia said as she slung her purse over her shoulder.

"I'm going to the airport to pick up my family."

Chapter Nine

—·«·‹‹·◎·››·»·—

The interior of Angel's Dream Wedding Chapel looked nothing like it had during his previous visits with Delia. Gone were the tasteful white roses and elegant simplicity that had fooled them into thinking this was just another Vegas wedding venue, one that Delia's cousin had chosen exactly because it wasn't your typical neon-lit temple of kitsch, including Elvis standing in as the minister.

No, now the space had been transformed into something that belonged in the deepest circles of Hell.

Caleb stood in what had once been the main aisle, his hands zip-tied behind his back with what felt like steel cable rather than plastic. The pews had been rearranged into a complex geometric pattern that reminded him of the one he and Delia had broken up at the Silver Bell chapel, and the air itself seemed to shimmer with malevolent energy. Symbols that definitely hadn't been there before were carved into every surface—the walls, the floor, even the ceiling overhead—all of them pulsing with a sickly red light that made his demon blood respond with uncomfortable heat.

But it was the figure standing at what had once been the altar that commanded his attention.

Vinea.

The Earl of Hell looked nothing like the classical depictions Caleb might have expected. No horns, no tail, no scaly black skin and red eyes. Instead, he appeared to be a man in his late forties, impeccably dressed in an expensive charcoal gray suit that looked as if he'd had it custom-tailored on Savile Row. His blond hair was silver at the temples, and his dark eyes might have been borrowed from a shark, since they contained roughly the same amount of humanity.

For all that, though, he still could have been a CEO, or a senator, or the president of an Ivy League university.

Which, Caleb supposed, made him infinitely more dangerous than any horned beast breathing fire.

"Welcome, nephew," Vinea said, his voice cool

and clear. He had a very faint accent, something that might have been British but felt much older, as if English was a language the demon lord had learned long after his native tongue had been forgotten by any mortal civilization. "I trust my servants weren't too rough with you?"

Caleb flexed his fingers, testing the bonds that held his wrists. The cable didn't budge, and he suspected it had been treated with something specifically designed to neutralize his abilities. When the demons had grabbed him outside the chapel, he'd tried to teleport away and found himself...stuck. Not completely powerless, but bound in a way that blocked his usual escape routes.

"Can't say I was impressed with their manners," he replied, doing his best to keep his tone light. No point in letting Vinea see how rattled he was, even though the demon lord probably knew that already. "Your people need to work on their customer relations."

Vinea chuckled, a sound that somehow managed to be genuinely amused and utterly chilling at the same time. "Ah, yes. I can see why Daniel was so fond of you. That particular brand of defiance in the face of overwhelming odds—it's quite the family trait."

His father's name was the last thing Caleb

wanted to hear, but he somehow managed to sound casual as he responded, "I wouldn't know. We weren't what you could call close."

"No, I suppose you weren't." Vinea began to move, not toward Caleb but in a slow circuit around the perimeter of the chapel, his footsteps echoing strangely in the transformed space. "Daniel always was rather focused on the bigger picture. I can see how that dedication might have come at the expense of those closest to him."

One way of looking at it, Caleb supposed. Mostly, it seemed as if his father had worked very hard to exert his influence on the cambions and quarter demons in their circle, making sure that no one did or said anything that might attract attention. His iron control had ensured that no one thought they were anything except the high school principals and doctors and lawyers they were pretending to be, their sons nothing more than the good students and athletes they were on the surface.

More than once, Caleb had wondered how Daniel Lockwood had been able to exert so much control over the others. Was it merely a "first among equals" sort of thing, or had Daniel's father been a slightly higher level of demon than the others?

It was the sort of question he'd never had the guts to ask.

His gaze flicked back to Vinea. The energy patterns in the room shifted and flowed around him like living things, as if reality itself somehow bent in his presence.

"But enough family reminiscences," the demon lord continued. "I'm sure you're wondering why you're here."

"The thought had crossed my mind," Caleb said dryly. "Along with wondering how the hell you managed to get to this plane in the first place. Last I checked, your kind was pretty firmly locked up downstairs."

Another chuckle, this one with a sharper edge. "Oh, my dear boy. You really don't understand how any of this works, do you? The boundaries between planes are much more porous than most people realize. Especially when one has the right kind of help."

Meaning, Caleb supposed, that someone must have summoned him here. Someone very powerful.

"What kind of help?" he asked, still trying to sound neutral and not terribly concerned about the whole situation. If he could get Vinea to spill the beans on who'd brought him here, then maybe Pru and Ty and Delia would have an actual target in the mortal realm they could hunt down.

Because Caleb wanted to do whatever he could to keep the woman he loved away from the demon lord and anyone else he might have brought here with him.

Instead of answering directly, Vinea paused in his circuit of the chamber and fixed Caleb with that unsettling black stare, such an unnatural contrast to his pale hair. "Oh, what would be the fun in my telling you that?"

Typical. Caleb didn't know about "fun," but if he had a bead on who had summoned the demon lord to this plane in the first place, at least he'd have some kind of target to track down once he got out of here.

If he got out of here.

"No fun at all, I suppose," he said.

An unpleasant smile tugging at his thin lips, Vinea resumed his slow pacing around the chapel, and Caleb could swear the symbols carved into the walls pulsed brighter in response to the demon lord's amusement. "I see we understand each other."

Before Caleb could even begin to formulate a reply to that comment, Vinea raised one hand and gestured toward the far end of the chapel. The air there began to shimmer, and in a flash, Caleb could see through the walls, out across Las Vegas, to dozens of points of light scattered throughout the city.

"Behold," Vinea said, his voice taking on a deeper, almost ceremonial intonation that made the carved symbols flare even brighter. "The fruits of months of careful preparation. Every wedding chapel, every event venue, every place where mortals gather to celebrate their pathetic little rituals of love and commitment. All of them connected, all of them feeding power into this central nexus."

The vision expanded, and Caleb could see the ley lines that crisscrossed the city, every one of them leading back to Angel's Dream like spokes on a wheel. But more than that, he could sense the supernatural energy building at each point, power being gathered and focused with the kind of accuracy that implied careful planning and intimate knowledge of both the mystical and mundane aspects of the city.

"This isn't about random demon-summoning or even a one-time portal, is it?" he said. Understanding had come to him in a flash...along with an additional resolve that the demon lord and his ilk should never succeed in their plans. "You're building permanent gateways."

"Very good." Vinea lowered his hand, and the vision faded, leaving them once again in the transformed chapel. "Although I prefer to think of it as 'infrastructure development.' The mortal plane has so much to offer, but the current transportation system between worlds is terribly inefficient."

"'Transportation system,'" Caleb repeated, his tone flat. "Funny way to talk about an invasion."

"No, I'm talking about emigration," the demon lord corrected him, his tone patient as if he were explaining something obvious to a particularly slow child. "There are so many of us trapped below, nephew. Entities of power and intelligence who could contribute so much to this world...if only they had a reliable way to reach it."

The casual way he uttered those words made Caleb's skin crawl. "Call it what it is. You're trying to give every demon in Hell a highway to Earth."

"Among others." Vinea's black eyes glittered with anticipation. "There are cambions and their sons currently languishing in the underworld, beings with just as much right to walk this plane as you do. All of them people you know."

Caleb wouldn't allow himself to flinch, but he knew the words had hit their target. He thought of his friends from Greencastle, the other quarter demons who'd been banished along with their fathers when the Project Demon Hunters gang had turned the cambions' Belial-summoning ritual on its head and sent them to Hell instead. He'd escaped eventually, but they hadn't.

And although he couldn't be too guilty about leaving his father and the other half demons behind, Caleb knew his friends Sean and Kevin and the rest of them were largely blameless. They'd only been trying to live their lives, and although of course they'd been roped into participating in the ritual to bring Belial back to this world, he kind of doubted any of them had been too thrilled about it.

"Of course," Vinea continued, "the ritual requires a very specific type of energy to stabilize the gateways, the kind that can only be provided by someone with both human and demon blood, someone who can serve as a bridge between the two planes."

Now they were getting to it. "Someone like me," Caleb said, figuring there wasn't much point in dancing around the issue.

"Someone exactly like you." Vinea shot him a triumphant smile. "Your blood, willingly given, will anchor the network and ensure that the portals remain stable indefinitely. Think of it, nephew— you could be responsible for reuniting so many families. You could give your trapped friends a second chance at life."

The offer was horribly tempting. The idea of seeing his friends again, of undoing the terrible fate that had befallen them, tugged at something deep inside, a desire to be around those who knew who he was and from whom he had no reason to hide.

You have that in Delia and Pru and Ty, he told himself. A smaller circle of friends, sure, but one he thought was just as loyal.

Besides, he also knew there was no way Vinea was telling him the whole truth.

"And all the innocent people who get trampled when your 'emigrants' arrive and take up residence here?" he asked. "What happens to them?"

Vinea's cool expression didn't change, but something flickered in his eyes, a reddish flame Caleb recognized all too well, since he'd seen it in his father's eyes as well.

Usually when he wasn't doing quite as good a job at reining in the demonic side of his nature as he should have been.

"Regrettable, perhaps, but ultimately necessary," Vinea replied. "You can't make an omelet without breaking a few eggs."

"'Eggs,'" Caleb repeated, eyes narrowing as he glared at the demon lord. "You're talking about millions of people."

"I'm talking about evolution," Vinea snapped, those irritated words the first crack in his urbane exterior. "This plane has been stagnant for far too long, dominated by cattle who squander their potential and waste the gifts they've been given. A little supernatural guidance could help them reach their true capabilities."

Caleb quirked an eyebrow. "Under demonic rule."

"Under proper management." The demon lord's tone was calm again, but Caleb could see the predatory gleam in his night-dark eyes. "Really, nephew, you're being quite dramatic about this. It's not as if we're planning genocide. Most humans would hardly notice the change, once they adjusted to the new reality."

The casual dismissal of human autonomy made the anger rise again, snarling like a rabid animal, and he stomped it down as best he could. Losing his temper wouldn't help anything.

"And if I tell you where to shove your interdimensional portal?"

"Well, that would be unfortunate." Vinea gestured with one pale hand, and the air around Caleb shimmered. At once, he could see Delia, Ty, and Pru—Delia behind the wheel of her little white Hyundai SUV, knuckles tight on the steering wheel, Pru and Ty with their heads bent together as they appeared to discuss something in urgent whispers. The image was so real he could almost reach out and touch Delia's beautiful, worried face. "You see," the demon lord went on, "the ritual can be powered by demon blood, regardless of whether it's given willingly or not. Voluntary participation simply makes the process more efficient."

"And my friends—"

"Will meet with tragic accidents," Vinea responded smoothly, not missing a beat. "Starting with the lovely Ms. Dunne. I understand you've grown quite attached to her."

The threat sent anger flaring through Caleb all over again, his demon blood roaring inside, wanting to reach out and snap the neck of this creature that threatened the woman he loved, but he knew he needed to think rather than react. Vinea was powerful, no question about that, but he was also talking. Gloating. Playing the Bond villain.

Which meant he either wanted something from Caleb beyond simple compliance...or he was buying time for something else.

"There's something you're not telling me," Caleb said then. "If you can take my blood by force, why all the theater? Why try to convince me to cooperate?"

For the first time since he'd entered the chapel, Vinea looked genuinely pleased. "Excellent question. You really are Daniel's son, aren't you? Always thinking three moves ahead."

The demon lord moved closer, close enough that Caleb could see his own reflection in those dark eyes, like the black mirrors mortals sometimes used for scrying. Up close, Vinea's human guise was less convincing—his skin had a waxy, bloodless quality to it, and there was no warmth in his breath despite the words that emerged from his thin lips.

"The truth is, nephew, that while I could certainly bleed you dry and use your essence to power the ritual, doing so would create instabilities in the gateway network. Your willing participation would ensure the portals remain stable for centuries. Your unwilling sacrifice would give us perhaps a decade...if even that much...before the whole thing collapsed."

Caleb's lip curled. "A decade's not enough time?"

"Not for what we have planned." Vinea's smile turned predatory again. "You see, this isn't just about creating escape routes for the entities currently trapped below. It's about establishing a permanent foothold in this reality, one that will allow us to reshape it according to our vision."

The reality Vinea had just described made Caleb's stomach churn. No simple invasion, but a complete transformation of reality itself.

And he would be the key to making it all possible.

"The choice is yours," Vinea continued. "If you're a willing participant, your friends will live to see the new world we'll create. If you refuse, they'll die knowing they failed to save the very plane they sought to protect."

Caleb tested his bonds again, but the mystical cables still held firm. Whatever they were made of, they were specifically designed to contain someone with his particular abilities. He could feel his demon blood responding to the supernatural energy in the room, but every time he tried to channel it, the cables seemed to absorb the power and turn it back on him.

"I need time to think," he said at length, since he knew he had to give the demon lord some sort of reply.

"Time is the one thing we don't have," Vinea replied. "The celestial alignment will reach its peak in less than forty-eight hours. After that, we'll have to wait another three hundred years for conditions to be optimal again."

"Then I guess you'll have to wait," Caleb said, meeting the demon lord's black stare without flinching. "I'm not agreeing to anything until I know exactly what you're planning."

Vinea studied him for a long moment, and Caleb had the uncomfortable feeling that he was seeing far more than just his physical form. At last, the demon lord nodded.

"Very well. I suppose a few hours won't make much difference." He gestured again, and two figures materialized from the shadows at the edges of the chapel—lesser demons, from the look of them, but still powerful enough. "Take our guest to the holding area. Make sure he's comfortable, but don't let him out of your sight."

As the demons moved to flank him, Caleb caught another glimpse of that predatory smile.

"Oh, and nephew?" Vinea called out as the pair of demons began to escort Caleb toward a door that definitely hadn't existed during his previous visits. "Don't even think about attempting to escape."

Like he would do anything so stupid when he knew the demon lord would retaliate the second he tried anything funny.

The holding area turned out to be a small room that had probably once been used for storage, now furnished with a single chair and nothing else. The demons shoved him down onto the chair and took up positions on either side of the door, their red eyes fixed on him with predatory patience.

Caleb leaned back and tried to look relaxed, even as his mind raced, considering first one possibility, then another. Vinea was powerful, no question about that, but he was also arrogant. And arrogant people made mistakes.

They also tended to underestimate their opponents.

The demon lord thought he had Caleb trapped, and physically, that was probably true. But he'd made one crucial error—he'd assumed that Caleb's only connection to the outside world was through conventional means.

Vinea didn't know anything about the psychic bond that Caleb and Delia shared. It was far from reliable, true, but he still hoped it was strong enough that if he concentrated hard, he would be able to sense her emotions across the city. And if he could sense how she felt....

Caleb closed his eyes and reached out with his mind, feeling for the familiar warmth that was uniquely Delia's. At first, there was nothing but the oppressive supernatural energy of the chapel, pressing on him like a physical weight. But then, faint as a whisper, he felt her.

She was afraid, but also angry, filled with a sort of furious resolve. And she was moving through the city, although he got the sense her destination was elsewhere, someplace south of where he was being held.

Delia, he thought, putting all his concentration behind the mental call. *Can you hear me?*

For a moment, nothing. Then, so faint he almost missed it, came her response.

Caleb? Where are you?

Angel's Dream. But it's a trap. Don't come here directly.

I'm not. A hesitation, and then she added, *But mostly because I knew there wasn't anything I could do. Are you hurt?*

Not yet. But Vinea's planning something big. Citywide portal network. He needs my blood to stabilize it.

A pause, and when her mental voice came back, it was laced with steel.

We'll figure out a way to stop him.

Be careful.

Before Delia could respond, one of the demons guarding him stirred, its red eyes narrowing as if it sensed something was off. Caleb quickly severed the mental connection and opened his eyes, doing his best to look like he'd simply been dozing.

The demon stared at him for another moment, then settled back into its watchful pose.

Caleb allowed himself a small smile. Vinea might think he had all the advantages, but the demon lord had just made his first major mistake. He'd underestimated the bond between Caleb and Delia, and that oversight might be exactly what they needed to turn the tables.

Now he just had to figure out how to stay alive long enough for his team to mount a rescue—and more importantly, learn how to sabotage Vinea's ritual without getting everyone he cared about killed in the process.

The door to the holding room opened, and Vinea himself stepped inside, no longer wearing his human guise. The thing that stood before Caleb was still roughly man-shaped, but much taller, with skin that looked like polished obsidian and eyes that burned with actual flame. When he smiled, his teeth were sharp as razors.

"I've been thinking about our conversation, nephew," the demon lord said, his voice different now, harsher as it emerged from an inhuman throat. "And I've decided to sweeten the deal."

Caleb kept his expression neutral, even though every instinct was screaming at him to run...not that he was able to go anywhere, not tied up and with three demons close by on the off chance he did somehow manage to free himself. "I'm listening."

"Your friends from Greencastle," Vinea continued. "The ones trapped below. You know I can bring them back. All of them. Give them new lives, a new chance for them to prosper and be happy."

The same offer the demon lord had hinted at before, only now he was being much more direct about the situation, as if he'd felt the need to reinforce with Caleb what it would be like to have his full circle of friends again.

"And all I have to do is help you turn Earth into Hell's summer vacation spot?"

"You make it sound so crude." Vinea's burning eyes flickered with what might have been amusement. "Think of it as expanding the definition of family. Your friends, reunited with you. Their fathers, finally able to claim their birthright. Even some of the more...civilized...full demons, ones who could contribute to human society rather than simply consuming it."

"Like you?" Caleb inquired, not bothering to hide the scorn in his voice.

"Like me." Vinea inclined his head graciously, the elegant movement horribly at odds with his reptilian appearance. "I have so much to offer this world, nephew. Centuries of knowledge, power that could solve so many of humanity's problems, wisdom gained through ages of existence. All I need is a reliable way to maintain my presence here."

It was a seductive vision, Caleb had to admit. But he knew enough about demons to understand that their ideas of "helping" humanity rarely aligned with what humans actually wanted or needed.

"And if I say no?"

"Then your friends will remain trapped...and you'll get to watch as I drain every drop of demon blood from your body to power a ritual that will last perhaps a tenth as long as it could have." The demon lord's smile turned cold. "Oh, and everyone you care about dies screaming. Did I mention that part?"

Caleb forced himself to meet those burning eyes without flinching. "Give me until tomorrow morning. I want to think it over."

"You have until dawn," Vinea intoned. "After that, willing or not, we will begin."

The demon lord turned and walked out, leaving Caleb alone with his demonic guards and the weight of an impossible choice.

Save his friends and damn the world, or protect humanity and live with the knowledge that he'd condemned the people who'd once been his best friends to an eternity of suffering.

Unless, of course, he could find a third option.

Caleb settled back in his chair and closed his eyes, reaching out once more for that connection to Delia. He didn't know what she and Pru and Ty were planning...but he hoped like hell it was going to work.

Chapter Ten

—‹‹‹•☽•›››—

THE HARRY REID INTERNATIONAL Airport pickup area was a special kind of chaos on any given day, but today it seemed like every stress Delia had ever experienced in her life had melded into one perfect storm of family logistics and demonic dread.

She sat in her Hyundai Kona at the curb, engine idling, and watched the stream of travelers emerging from the sliding glass doors while her psychic abilities sparked and flickered, making it feel as if her brain was some AM band radio, hiccupping from one station to another. Every few seconds, another wave of ley line energy would smash into her, making her grip the steering wheel until her knuckles went white.

Get it together, she told herself. She pulled in a deep breath and did her best to center her thoughts on something other than the terrifying fact that Caleb was being held captive by a demon lord who happened to be his great-uncle.

Or something like it. She still wasn't entirely certain how relationships worked among demon-kind.

Now, though, she needed to focus on a much more down-to-earth kind of relationship.

Your family needs you to be normal right now.

Normal. Right. As if anything about her life had been normal since she'd first started talking to ghosts. Then again, communing with spirits and helping them move on to the afterlife felt like a walk in the park compared to what she'd been through over the past few months.

Her phone vibrated from inside her purse. A text from Olivia, and Delia's heart skipped a beat before she realized the message was just a standard arrival update and not anything sinister at all.

Flight's on time. Should be at baggage claim in about twenty minutes. Thanks again for picking us up!

Twenty minutes to get her head together and figure out how to explain why it was so important that her cousin had to choose an alternative to Angel's Dream Wedding Chapel without revealing that the venue was currently serving as headquarters for an interdimensional invasion attempt.

Piece of cake.

As she sat in the car and tried very hard not to think about Caleb trapped in the chapel...and her utter inability to mount any kind of successful rescue...Delia watched a family of four struggle with an overloaded luggage cart, the father looking harried while two small children ran circles around their mother. Such normal problems. Such beautifully, blessedly, normal problems.

Someday she hoped to have problems like those of her own. Now, though, she had to focus on the very real threat facing her and her friends...and the man who'd stolen her heart.

Another family emerged from the terminal, this group of three consisting of two parents and a daughter who might have been in her early teens, looking much more organized as they made their way toward the ride-share pickup area. Delia envied their brisk efficiency, their obvious confidence that they knew exactly where they were going and what they were doing.

Her phone vibrated again, this time with a text from her mother.

Just left the house to head to the airport. Your dad's grumbling about traffic, but excited to see everyone. Any word on when you'll be free to join us for dinner tonight?

Dinner. Right. Because in addition to managing a supernatural crisis and coordinating a wedding venue change, she also needed to be a dutiful daughter and participate in the extended family reunion.

Working on it, she texted back. *Might need to juggle a few things with the venue situation.*

The response came back almost immediately.

Everything okay?

Just wedding logistics. You know how it is.

Well, don't let Olivia's drama stress you out too much. This is supposed to be fun, remember?

If only it were that simple.

Another wave of energy coursed through her, stronger this time, and for a moment, the airport around her seemed to shimmer and shift. She could see the ley lines running beneath the concrete and asphalt, could sense the way they connected this location to the network that spiderwebbed across the entire Las Vegas valley.

And at the center of it all, Angel's Dream Wedding Chapel blazed, a dark star embedded in neon and plate glass.

The connection to Caleb was still there, thank God, the thin, unbreakable thread of psychic energy that he'd used to contact her as she was on her way to the airport. But she could also sense something else through their bond—his anger, his frustration, and underneath it all, a growing determination that made her worried he was planning something dangerously heroic.

Don't do anything stupid, she thought,

directing the mental message toward the corrupted chapel. *Just stay alive until we can figure out how to get you out of there.*

Whether he received the message or not, she couldn't tell. The psychic static from the ley line network was making it harder and harder to maintain clear contact.

A familiar laugh caught her attention, and she looked up to see Olivia and Alec emerging from the terminal. Her cousin looked pretty much the same as she had during the last family visit to Chicago, if a few years older—tall and willowy, with the kind of effortless elegance that made Delia feel slightly underdressed even when she was wearing her best outfit. Her dark hair was pulled back in a sleek ponytail, and she wore slim, expensive-looking jeans and a pair of strappy sandals that were more than a little impractical for hauling luggage through an airport terminal.

Alec complemented her well—broad shoulders, perfect hair, and the kind of confident smile that probably served him well when dealing with his hedge fund clients. Or at least, Delia assumed his work must involve something like that. Her mother had only vaguely said that he worked in finance, which could have meant almost anything. However, she kind of doubted that a bank manager had the cash on hand to buy a million-dollar house outright.

They made a beautiful couple, Delia had to admit. They definitely were the kind of people who belonged in wedding magazines and luxury travel brochures.

The kind of people who definitely didn't belong anywhere near a demon-infested wedding chapel.

She got out of her car and waved, pasting on her best "everything is perfectly normal" smile as they spotted her and headed in her direction.

"Delia!" Olivia's smile was genuine, if a little strained around the edges. Up close, Delia could see a hint of shadows under her cousin's eyes that hadn't been entirely erased by concealer, a subtle tension in her shoulders that spoke of too many restless nights. "Thank you so much for doing this. I can't tell you how much it means to have someone local helping us coordinate everything."

"Of course," Delia replied, giving her cousin a quick hug. "That's what family's for."

Alec stepped forward and shook her hand, his grip confident but not so strong that she had to worry about him crushing her knuckles. "Nice to meet you, Delia. I can't thank you enough for stepping in to help with all the last-minute arrangements. Olivia's been so worried about the venue situation."

If only you knew how much more worried she should be, Delia thought. Making sure her pasted-on smile didn't waver, she said, "It's really no problem. I'm just glad I was able to find some alternatives for you to consider."

"About that," Olivia said, and something in her tone made alarm bells start going off in Delia's mind.

Like it wasn't already busy enough in there.

"I've been thinking about what you said, about the management issues at Angel's Dream, and I'm wondering if maybe we're being a little hasty. I mean, we've already paid in advance, and the ceremony is only the day after tomorrow. Maybe we should just stick with what we've got and hope for the best."

No. Absolutely not. Over her dead body.

"I really think you should at least look at the alternatives," Delia replied, doing her best to keep her tone light and casual. "Some of the places I found are actually quite a bit nicer than Angel's Dream. More elegant, better settings for your wedding photos, that kind of thing."

"But we've already paid them," Alec interjected, frowning. "We're talking about losing a decent chunk of change here. It's not just a simple deposit. And frankly, I'm not sure I understand why we need to make a change at all. The chapel looked fine when we did the virtual tour."

Another spike of ley line energy coursed through Delia's system, and this time it was accompanied by something else—a vision, brief but terri-fyingly clear, of Angel's Dream Wedding Chapel filled with writhing shadows and the sound of otherworldly screaming.

"Trust me," she said, realizing even as she spoke that she sounded much too intense. "You do *not* want to get married at Angel's Dream."

Olivia and Alec exchanged a look, and Delia realized she'd probably come on way too strong. Normal people didn't usually speak with such vehemence about wedding venues, not unless there was a really good reason.

"Is there something specific you're not telling us?" Olivia asked, voice almost too neutral. "Because if there's a serious problem with the chapel, then we need to know about it."

There it was. Now Delia had to decide just how much truth she was willing to share with her family members. Not the whole truth—she couldn't tell them about demons and ley lines and interdimensional portals. But maybe she could give them enough information to under-stand that this wasn't just about wedding aesthetics.

"There have been some incidents," she said after a pause she knew must have been horribly conspicuous. "At Angel's Dream and some of the other recently acquired venues. Electrical problems, safety violations, that sort of thing. Nothing that's made the news yet, but the city's been investigating."

It wasn't entirely a lie. There had been electrical incidents across Las Vegas, and people in the city government were undoubtedly investigating them, even if they had no idea what they were really dealing with.

Alec's frown deepened. "What kind of safety concerns?"

"Mostly infrastructure issues," Delia replied, improvising as she went. "Wiring problems, electrical surges, that sort of thing. They could definitely cause problems during a ceremony if they're not addressed."

"How do you even know about all this?" Olivia asked, and there was something sharp in her cousin's voice now, a note of suspicion that made Delia's pulse quicken.

"I have lots of contacts in the real estate industry and with the city," Delia said, which at least was perfectly true. "Word gets around when there are problems with commercial properties."

Another exchange of glances between the couple, and then Alec's expression shifted from suspicion to concern. "Are we talking about serious safety hazards? Like, could people actually get hurt?"

More than you can begin to imagine, Delia thought. "It's possible," she said. "Which is why I really think you should consider one of the alternatives. Just to be safe."

Olivia was quiet for a long moment, staring at something over Delia's shoulder. When she finally spoke, her voice was soft and uncertain, barely audible above the bustle of people coming and going from the terminal. "And there are my dreams," she said. "About the wedding. Terrible dreams where something goes wrong and people get hurt."

"You've had more of them?" Delia asked gently.

"Yes," Olivia said, voice flat, as if she didn't want to allow any betraying emotion to creep in. "I always see fire and people screaming, people dying. And there's also this horrible feeling like something dark and awful was coming right through the walls." She shook her head. "I know it sounds crazy, but they feel so real, almost like they're warnings or something."

"They very well may be," Delia said, and meant it. "Sometimes our subconscious picks up on things that our logical mind dismisses. If your instincts are telling you something's wrong, then I think you should listen to them."

Alec wrapped his arm around Olivia's shoulders, and now Delia could see the protective concern in his expression. Whatever else she might think about the man—she instinctively distrusted people who looked so glossy and perfect—it was clear that he cared about her cousin's well-being.

"Okay," he said after a pause. "After we get to the house, you can show us the alternatives. If there are safety concerns with Angel's Dream, then we need to take that seriously."

The relief that flooded through Delia was so intense, it made her knees a little weak. "Sounds good," she said. "I know you won't regret making the change."

"I hope not," Olivia replied, but she was smiling now, and some of the tension had left her shoulders. "Because my parents' flight lands in a little over an hour, and I'm really hoping we can have some good news to share with them."

Right. Uncle Doug and Aunt Vicky. Along with Alec's family, who were also already in the air. More people flying into the heart of darkness, more family members who would need to be protected while having absolutely no idea what they were being protected from.

As they walked toward the baggage claim area, Delia got another text. This one was from Ty.

Multiple new incidents reported across the city. Pattern suggests acceleration. How's the family situation?

Working on it, she texted back quickly while Olivia and Alec were distracted by locating their luggage carousel. *Convinced them to switch venues. Parents arriving soon.*

Good. Keep them away from Angel's Dream at all costs. Situation deteriorating.

Of course it was.

She acknowledged the text with a terse, *Okay,* and the text conversation ended there, leaving Delia with the uncomfortable knowledge that while she was managing family logistics, Caleb was still trapped in that horrible chapel with no immediate prospect of rescue.

"Delia?" Olivia's voice pulled her back to the immediate situation. "You okay? You look a little pale."

"Just tired," Delia replied, forcing another smile. "It's been a busy week."

The luggage carousel hummed to life, and they joined the crowd of passengers waiting for their bags to appear. Around them, the normal bustle of airport life continued—reunions and farewells, business travelers checking their phones, families corralling tired children.

They had to be kept safe. No matter what.

"So, what are these alternative venues like?" Alec asked as he and Olivia waited for their luggage to come around. "Are we talking about the same level as Angel's Dream, or are we looking at some pretty major compromises?"

"Actually, I think you're going to be pleasantly

surprised," Delia said, grateful to be back on solid ground with a topic she could discuss without revealing any supernatural secrets. "The Little Chapel of Hearts is probably the nicest of the options. It's got that Vegas vibe without being too kitschy. Good photo opportunities, very professional staff."

"And availability?" Olivia asked. "We're cutting this really close."

"Like I told you before, they can accommodate your original date and time slot," Delia assured her. "It's not going to be a problem."

What she didn't mention was that the Little Chapel of Hearts had suddenly found itself with much more availability than usual, thanks to the systematic sabotage of competing venues across the city and many people deciding they didn't want a Vegas wedding after all, opting instead for Lake Tahoe or Reno or something out of the state altogether. The supernatural chaos that was threatening to destroy Las Vegas was at least making it easier to book last-minute wedding venues.

Silver linings and all that.

"There," Alec said, pointing toward the carousel as their luggage began to make its way toward them. "The black Samsonite set."

As the couple retrieved their bags and made their way over to the spot where Delia's Kona still waited at the curb, another wave of ley line energy rolled over her. This one was strong enough to make her stumble slightly, and she had to catch herself against a support pillar.

"You sure you're okay?" Olivia asked, genuine concern in her voice now. "Maybe you should see a doctor. No offense, but you look kind of rundown."

"I'm fine," Delia said quickly. "I just need some coffee, or maybe an iced tea."

But she wasn't fine, and she knew it. The psychic overload from the citywide ley line activation was getting worse, and she wasn't sure how much longer she could function normally while supernatural energy coursed through her system like lightning in her veins.

She needed to get Olivia and Alec safely settled at his house—both sets of parents were staying nearby at the M Resort and Casino—and then she needed to figure out how to help Ty and Pru rescue Caleb before Vinea completed whatever horrific ritual he was planning.

And she had to do all of it while pretending that everything was perfectly normal.

No pressure at all.

As she closed the Kona's rear hatch and Olivia and Alec moved forward to get in their seats, Delia's phone rang. Her mother's number showed on the home screen.

"Hi, Mom," she said as she lifted the phone to

her ear, doing her best to sound cheerful and unstressed.

"Delia, where are you? We're almost at the airport."

"I just picked up Olivia and Alec," she said. "We're heading to Alec's house now so they can get settled. What time were you thinking of for dinner?"

"Six o'clock," her mother replied. "We figured it would be better to eat a little early, since all our visitors will still be on Chicago time."

Delia wished she could beg off from the whole thing, but she knew her mother would ask too many probing questions if she bailed on the get-together. No, she'd just have to endure a few hours of pretending everything was normal while Caleb remained captive and the supernatural threat level continued to escalate.

"Sure," Delia said. "That sounds great."

"Wonderful. And how's it going with the venue?"

"Just fine. I have a good alternative, so the three of us are going to sit down and talk about it when we get to Alec's house in Henderson. I'm pretty sure we'll have it all sorted out by the time we meet for dinner."

"Thank you so much for doing all this," Linda said, sounding grateful that she wasn't the one having to deal with all the last-minute changes. "We'll see you at dinner."

The call ended there, and Delia dropped her phone in her purse and got in behind the wheel. As she fastened her seatbelt, Olivia leaned forward from her place in the back seat.

"I can't tell you how much I appreciate everything you're doing," she said. "I know this is a lot to ask, especially on such short notice."

"It's really not a problem," Delia replied, and realized that despite everything else that was going on, she meant it. Family was family, and she would do whatever it took to keep them safe.

Her phone, which was resting in the cupholder, lit up. Another text, this one from an unknown number.

Family reunions can be so dangerous in a city like this. Be a shame if something happened to them.

Delia's grip tightened on the steering wheel, but she made herself keep driving as if she'd only gotten a text from a client or someone else equally innocuous. Inside, though, her resolve hardened to steel.

Vinea wanted to play games with her family?

Okay, Vinea, she thought.

I'll play.

Chapter Eleven

———— ·‹‹‹·◯·›››·————

THE HOLDING ROOM HAD NO WINDOWS, NO clock, and no way to tell how much time had passed since Vinea had left him alone with his demonic guards. Caleb had tried counting heartbeats and estimating minutes, but the supernatural energy saturating the chapel seemed to play havoc with his internal clock. Minutes felt like hours... and hours felt like eternity.

Which meant he had plenty of time to think.

And what he'd been thinking about was how he needed to play this. Vinea expected him to cooperate eventually—that much was clear from the demon lord's casual confidence. The real trick would be figuring out how to appear compliant while actually working to sabotage whatever massive ritual the bastard was planning.

Caleb had spent two years in Hell, and if there

was one thing he'd learned during his unwilling residency in that place of eternal torment, it was that demons respected strength but expected cunning. They didn't trust easily, but they also didn't expect their enemies to be completely honest with them. A little deception was pretty much a given.

After all, no one wanted to be accused of acting like a goody-two-shoes angel or something.

The trick in dealing with Vinea would be finding the right balance between seeming defeated and maintaining just enough defiance to be believable.

When the door to the holding room opened again, Caleb looked up with what he hoped was the perfect combination of resignation and simmering anger as Vinea entered, still wearing his human guise but somehow managing to make a simple charcoal suit look like the formal attire of a crocodile who'd decided to hit the Strip for some drinks and maybe a show.

"Have you had sufficient time to consider my offer, nephew?" the demon lord asked, his tone conversational, as if they were discussing stock options rather than the potential destruction of human civilization.

Caleb really wished the guy would stop calling him "nephew." It was a way of trying to put him off balance, to remind him at regular intervals that he wasn't entirely human and never would be.

But since he'd recognized the strategy for what it was, he wouldn't let it affect him.

Not much, anyway.

He allowed a few seconds to pass before he answered the demon lord's question, doing his best to project the image of a man who'd been wrestling with an impossible choice and had finally reached a decision he didn't like at all.

"I want to know more about the specifics," he said at length. "If I'm going to help you, I need to understand exactly what we're talking about here."

Something flickered in Vinea's coal-black eyes... satisfaction, maybe, or perhaps nothing more than greedy anticipation. "A reasonable request. Very well. Follow me."

The two demon guards flanked Caleb as Vinea led them out of the holding room and down that brain-twistingly long corridor. As they walked, Caleb tried to map the layout of the building in his mind, noting doorways and intersections, searching for anything that might serve as an escape route if things went sideways.

Which they almost certainly would at some point.

"Tell me, nephew," Vinea said as they walked, his footsteps making odd echoes in the narrow space, "what do you know about the current state of affairs in the underworld?"

An odd question, and one Caleb wasn't sure he knew how to answer. During his time in Hell, he'd been focused mainly on survival rather than supernatural politics. Keeping his head down and avoiding as many demonic entanglements as possible had been his main strategy.

"I know it's not a vacation destination," he remarked.

That comment earned him a dry chuckle. "Indeed. But more specifically, are you aware of the...well, let's call them overcrowding issues?"

Caleb frowned. He hadn't really thought about Hell having capacity problems, but then again, he supposed the prospect made a certain amount of sense. If demons and the souls of the condemned had been accumulating there for millennia, eventually the place would start to get pretty packed.

However, he'd wandered its cold, deserted spaces far more than he would have liked, and so he knew that trying to refer to the underworld as "overcrowded" was a bit of a stretch. For whatever reason, those condemned to Hell—whether human or fallen angel—liked to congregate in certain population centers, cities of steel and stone that possessed an utter lack of anything that could be called creature comforts.

So, once again, Caleb knew Vinea wasn't telling him anything close to the truth.

"Not really," he allowed, and decided to leave it there so he could see where the demon lord was going with this.

"The underworld was never designed to be a permanent prison," his unwelcome guide continued as they reached what appeared to be a large set of double doors. "It was meant to be a place of punishment, yes, but also a waystation. Souls were supposed to move on after serving their sentences. Demons were supposed to have the opportunity to earn redemption. But the celestial bureaucracy has become...shall we say, less than efficient...in recent centuries."

The demon lord paused with his hand on the door handle, and when he looked back at Caleb, something that looked almost like genuine anger flashed in his dark eyes. "Do you have any idea what it's like to be trapped for uncounted millennia in a place where hope itself has been systematically crushed?"

Caleb recalled his two years down there—the constant danger, the grinding despair, the way every day had seemed like an eternity. Then he multiplied those terrible conditions by a thousand...by ten thousand...and tried to imagine what that would do to someone's sanity.

When you put it that way, you could see why

some demons were willing to take extreme measures to escape.

That didn't mean he was going to help them turn Earth into their new permanent residence, but at least he could understand their motivations.

"I have an inkling," he said.

Vinea gave a satisfied nod and pushed open the double doors in front of them, revealing a vast chamber that definitely hadn't existed when the building was just a simple wedding chapel. The space stretched out before them like a cathedral, but instead of containing stained glass windows and religious iconography, the walls were covered with what looked like massive television screens, each one displaying a different location around Las Vegas.

In the center of the room, a three-dimensional map of the entire Las Vegas valley hung suspended in the air, complete with tiny points of light that pulsed and flickered in complex patterns. Ley lines were visible as streams of energy connecting various locations across the city, all of them flowing toward a central nexus point that Caleb realized, with a sinking sensation, was directly beneath their feet.

"Welcome to the command center," Vinea said as he gestured toward the floating map with obvious pride. "From here, we can monitor every aspect of the ritual network. Each light represents a portal site, each energy stream a connection between this plane and the next."

Caleb moved closer to the map and tried to count the number of active sites. There were dozens—maybe hundreds—scattered across the valley. They had to be far more than the wedding chapels and event venues his little group of demon slayers had been tracking.

"This is bigger than we thought," he said, and knew the awe in his voice was genuine.

How in the world were he and Delia and Pru and Ty supposed to combat something like this?

"Oh, yes, much bigger," Vinea agreed. "The wedding venues were simply the most emotionally charged locations. But we've also been working on restaurants, hotels, casinos, shopping malls...even some residential developments. Anyplace where humans gather in large numbers and experience strong emotions."

The scope of what the demon lord was describing only increased the nauseated sensation in Caleb's gut. From what he could tell, Vinea planned to turn the entire city into a supernatural transit hub.

"How long have you been planning this?" he asked.

"Planning? About five years. Active preparation? A bit less than that." Vinea's smile turned predatory. "We had to wait for the right celestial alignment, of course. The conjunction of Mercury retrograde with a full moon while Mars is in opposition to Jupiter—it only happens once every few hundred years."

Well, at least he wouldn't have to worry about this becoming a weekly occurrence.

Caleb filed that information away for later consideration and turned his attention back to the floating map. "So, what do you need from me?"

"Now we're getting to the heart of the matter." The demon lord moved to stand beside the map, his hands clasped behind his back like a general surveying a battlefield. "The portal network requires a very specific type of energy to remain stable. Not just demon blood, but blood that contains both infernal and mortal essences. The combination creates a sort of bridge between the two planes."

Caleb nodded, having suspected something like this. "And you need that bridge to be permanent."

"Exactly. A temporary portal—the sort that is typically used in summonings—is useful for individual crossings, but what we want to build here is infrastructure. We need gateways that will remain open indefinitely, allowing for the systematic relocation of entities who've been trapped below for far too long."

The casual way Vinea described such a mass

exodus of demons made Caleb's skin crawl. "And once they're here?"

A shrug. "They'll integrate into human society, of course. Many of them have skills and knowledge that could benefit this plane enormously. Architecture, engineering, medicine—demons have had millennia to perfect various disciplines."

"'Demons,'" Caleb repeated. "What about the souls who were condemned to Hell for the sins they committed while alive? Are they going to have free rein to come back here and commit those crimes all over again?"

Vinea waved a negligent hand. "Oh, we have no intention of setting them free. As you said, they are souls only. They have no corporeal forms like we demons do. Even if they managed to cross over, they would be nothing more than empty spirits, unable to do much at all."

Caleb wasn't so sure about that. He remembered how the spirit of that dead serial killer had almost pushed Delia into an empty pool when the two of them had gone to inspect his current house before he bought it. Somehow, Caleb doubted a soul like that would be content to merely float around and observe what humans and demons were up to.

However, he had a feeling the demon lord wouldn't care to hear such arguments, so he thought he had better try a different tack. "What about the humans who are already here? Something tells me they might not be too enthusiastic about this 'integration process.'"

Vinea's smile might as well have been the rictus of a corpse. "Change is always difficult, nephew. But humans are remarkably adaptable. Those who embrace the new reality will find their lives greatly improved. Those who resist...." He gave an elegant lift of his shoulders, the sort of negligent shrug Caleb might have expected of a member of the French nobility back in the days before the Revolution. "Natural selection has always been a harsh mistress."

Such a casual dismissal of human concerns only served to remind Caleb exactly of who...or, more to the point, what...he was dealing with. Whatever sympathetic motivations Vinea and his demonic cohort might have for wanting to escape Hell, his final solution involved the subjugation— or downright elimination—of anyone who got in his way.

"How many are we talking about?" Caleb asked. He was trying his damnedest to sound disinterested, as if such concerns didn't matter much to someone like him and that he was inquiring only to satisfy his intellectual curiosity.

Inwardly, he knew he wanted nothing more than to reach out and wrap his fingers around Vinea's thin neck and squeeze as hard as he could.

If that made him a murderer, fine. He thought he was okay with sacrificing one demon lord to save all of humanity.

Too bad that he knew he would never get away with such a gambit. Vinea would swat him like a fly the second he made even the slightest hostile move.

"How many what?" the demon lord asked, his tone utterly indifferent.

"How many humans are you planning to kill or displace?"

Vinea considered the question for a moment, his head tilted and mouth slightly pursed, as if he was doing nothing more consequential than trying to determine how many board-feet of flooring he needed to order for a remodel. "Initially? Perhaps a few million, while the transition period works itself out. Long term? It's difficult to say. Much will depend on how quickly the remaining humans learn to accept their new place in the hierarchy."

A few million. Was that all?

Caleb forced himself to nod, as if the numbers were regrettable but acceptable. Inside, though, his stomach roiled, and he had to pray that none of his nausea was reflected in his expression. "And my friends from Greencastle? The other quarter demons who got trapped with the cambions?"

"They'll be among the first to cross over," Vinea assured him. "Think of it, nephew—you'll be reunited with people who truly understand what you are. No more hiding, no more pretending to be something you're not. You could all live openly, using your abilities without fear of discovery."

The same temptation that the demon lord had dangled before him during their previous conversation. Sure, Caleb couldn't deny that seeing Sean and Keith and the others again, being part of a community where he didn't have to hide his demon heritage, tugged at emotions he'd tried to suppress and downright ignore for most of his life.

The need to belong. Anyone looking in from the outside—anyone who didn't know what he truly was—would have thought he'd had the perfect life in Greencastle, with his wealthy family and his role as the hometown hero star quarterback at his school.

It had all been a lie, though. Sure, the other quarter demons had known what he was, but everyone else only saw a shell, a façade.

But then he thought of Delia, of how she'd been startled to learn the truth about his identity but had accepted him into her life anyway. Of how she'd made him believe Las Vegas could become the home he'd always wanted.

Of the expression on her face when she told him she loved him. No artifice there, just a simple, honest acknowledgment of feelings she knew she couldn't ignore any longer.

And then there were Pru and Ty, who also knew what he was and didn't seem to treat him any differently than they would anyone else. True, Ty wasn't exactly your regular guy off the street, either, but it had to mean something that the half angel was willing to work with someone who should have been his bitter enemy.

There were all the others as well—Delia's parents and her cousin and her fiancé, and all the innocent people in Las Vegas who were going about their daily lives with no idea that their world was about to be turned upside down.

He was the only one standing between them and the fall of night.

A swallow, and then Caleb asked, "When do we start?" About all he could do was hope that his voice conveyed reluctant acceptance rather than his growing determination to sabotage every damn thing Vinea was planning.

"Tomorrow evening," Vinea replied. "The celestial alignment reaches its peak at 11:47 p.m. on May thirtieth. We'll need to begin the final ritual phase several hours before that to ensure everything is properly synchronized."

Tomorrow night. May thirtieth. The same day as Olivia's wedding.

Of course it was.

"All right," Caleb replied. He was somewhat proud of himself for sounding as if none of this was a terribly big deal. "What's my role in the ritual?"

Vinea gestured toward one of the wall screens, which immediately shifted to show what looked like a detailed schematic of some kind of arcane circle. "You'll be positioned at the central nexus point, here beneath the chapel. Your blood will be drawn slowly over the course of several hours, ensuring that the energy release is gradual and controlled."

That sounded like tons of fun. Maybe he should ask the demon lord to throw in a root canal while he was at it.

"Drawn how slowly?"

"The process should take approximately three to four hours to complete," Vinea said, his matter-of-fact tone somehow far more chilling than any demonic hiss. "And don't worry—we'll make sure you remain conscious throughout the procedure. Your willing participation is essential for the stability of the network."

Of course it was. So...three to four hours of having his blood slowly drained while remaining awake and aware the entire time, feeling himself getting weaker and weaker. Even a part demon could withstand a lot more physical abuse than a regular human, but Caleb still didn't want to think too hard about how that would feel.

No, better to focus on the tactical possibilities

the setup might allow. If the ritual ended up taking that long, all those hours would provide his team with multiple opportunities to intervene and get him out of there.

Assuming, of course, that they could actually infiltrate the building and at the same time come up with a way to disrupt a citywide supernatural working that was being overseen by an earl of Hell.

No pressure at all.

"I understand," he said aloud, hoping he hadn't paused long enough to rouse the demon lord's suspicions. "Anything else I need to know?"

"Just one." Vinea moved closer, close enough that Caleb could see his own reflection in the creature's black eyes. His tone turned silky as he went on, "I hope you understand that any attempt to sabotage this operation will result in the immediate and extremely painful deaths of everyone you care about. Ms. Dunne, in particular, would suffer exquisitely for your betrayal."

The not-so-casual threat sent a flare of rage through Caleb, and his demon blood roared, wanting to strike out. For just a moment, the air around him shimmered with heat, and small flames licked up and down his arms before they disappeared again.

Impossible for Vinea not to notice, of course. His smile widened, revealing those too-sharp teeth.

"Excellent," the demon lord said, sounding

amused. "I was beginning to wonder if you'd lost your edge during your time playing house with the mortals. But I can see the fire is still there."

Caleb forced himself to take a deep breath, wrestling his demon blood into some semblance of control. Getting angry wouldn't help anyone, least of all Delia.

He needed to be smart about this.

"I'm not going anywhere," he said, his voice steady despite the fury that still coursed through his veins. "I'll do what you need me to do."

"I'm sure you will," Vinea replied. "After all, you wouldn't want anything unfortunate to happen to your precious mortal while you're helping to usher in a new age for our kind." The demon lord turned away then, the very movement utterly dismissive. "Take him back to the holding room," he told the guards. "Make sure he gets some rest. Tomorrow will be a long day."

No point in resisting as the demons escorted him back down the corridor. Instead, Caleb tried to work through his options, which he had to admit weren't as numerous as he would have liked. He had maybe eighteen hours before the ritual began—eighteen hours to figure out how to sabotage a citywide supernatural rite without getting himself or his team killed in the process.

The psychic bond he shared with Delia was still there, the delicate thread of connection that let him know she was alive and relatively safe. But he could also sense the supernatural static building across the city, the ley line energy that was making it harder and harder to maintain clear contact.

Soon, he might be completely cut off from any outside help.

Which meant he needed to start preparing for the possibility that he'd have to handle this on his own.

Back in the holding room with the two demons once again taking up guard stances on either side of the door, Caleb settled into the uncomfortable chair and closed his eyes, reaching out with his enhanced senses to map the supernatural energy flows around him. The chapel sat at the center of a massive web of power, ley lines converging from across the valley to focus their combined energy on this single point.

But every web had its weaknesses. He just had to find them.

The guards' red eyes were fixed on him, unblinking. They probably expected him to sleep, or at least rest quietly until it was time for the ritual.

Instead, Caleb began to explore the limits of his captivity.

The mystical bonds that held his powers in check were sophisticated, but they weren't perfect. He could feel them responding to his demon blood, siphoning away energy whenever he tried to access his abilities directly. But they seemed to be designed to counter brute-force applications of power, not subtle manipulations.

Maybe there was a way to work around them.

Carefully, slowly, Caleb began to test the boundaries of what the wards would allow him to do. Not break free or teleport away—anything that obvious would definitely be noticed—but simply feeling around the edges of his supernatural prison.

After what felt like hours of patient exploration but might have been only minutes, he found it. A tiny flaw in the binding, a place where the mystical cables didn't quite mesh perfectly with his particular energy. It wasn't much—barely enough to let him access a fraction of his normal abilities—but it might be enough.

Enough to send a message...enough to plant a few surprises for Vinea's ritual.

And, with any luck, enough to give his team the information they'd need to mount a rescue.

As the hours ticked by and the supernatural energy around the chapel continued to build, Caleb began to lay the groundwork for his rebellion. Small things, subtle manipulations that would hopefully go unnoticed until it was too late for Vinea to stop them.

He thought about Delia, about the way she'd looked at him the night before when she'd told him she loved him. And then he thought about Ty and Pru, about the unlikely team they'd formed and the trust they'd placed in each other.

Whatever happened tomorrow night, he wasn't going to let them down.

And if Vinea thought he could use Caleb's blood to open permanent gateways to Hell, the demon lord was about to discover just how wrong he could be.

The door to the holding room opened, and one of the guards entered carrying a tray of food. Human food, Caleb noticed with some surprise. Apparently, even demon lords understood the importance of keeping their sacrificial victims properly nourished.

"Compliments of Lord Vinea," the guard said, its voice a harsh rasp that sounded like grinding stone. "He wants to make sure you maintain your strength for tomorrow."

Caleb accepted the tray without comment, noting that the food actually looked quite good— some kind of grilled chicken with roasted vegetables and rice pilaf, along with a couple of rolls that seemed fresh from a bakery. Either Vinea had excellent taste in catering, or he was trying to demonstrate that cooperation would be rewarded with civilized treatment.

As he ate, Caleb continued his careful exploration of the mystical bonds that kept him trapped there. The guards watching him wouldn't have noticed anything different, but in the background, the part of his mind that wasn't quite human pushed here and tested there, doing whatever it could to find weaknesses he could exploit.

By the time he'd finished the meal, he'd managed to create several small gaps in the binding network. Not enough to escape, but enough to plant seeds of sabotage throughout Vinea's carefully constructed ritual framework.

When the guards came to collect the empty tray, they found their prisoner apparently asleep in his chair, looking—he hoped—defeated and resigned to his fate.

They had no way of knowing that behind his closed eyelids, Caleb's mind continued to work furiously, laying the groundwork for what he hoped would be the demon lord's spectacular failure.

Now just twelve hours and counting.

He prayed it would be enough.

Chapter Twelve

—·‹‹‹·☾·›››·—

THE LITTLE CHAPEL OF HEARTS LOOKED
exactly like what it was supposed to be—an attractive, intimate venue for couples who wanted something a little more elegant than the Elvis-themed
establishments that made the Las Vegas wedding
scene famous but without the stuffiness of a traditional church ceremony. With its white clapboard
exterior, stained glass windows depicting doves and
roses, and a small garden area perfect for photos, it
really wasn't all that different from Angel's Dream.

Well, except for the part where Olivia's original
wedding site had been taken over by demons determined to use it as the nexus of their diabolical
plans.

Under normal circumstances, Delia would
have been thrilled to show the place off to her

cousin. The chapel seemed to be everything Olivia had said she wanted for her wedding—classy, romantic, and extremely photogenic.

Unfortunately, normal circumstances had flown right out the window the moment a demon lord decided to use Las Vegas as his personal summoning ground.

"This is beautiful," Olivia breathed as they approached the front entrance. She'd been quiet during most of the drive from Alec's house, but now her voice had the first note of genuine enthusiasm Delia had heard since she'd picked up her cousin and her fiancé at the airport. "It's even nicer than Angel's Dream."

"I knew you'd like it," Delia replied, doing her best to sound casual despite the energy spike that had just washed over her, the resulting disorientation enough to make her stumble slightly on the brick walkway. Luckily, both Alec and Olivia were so preoccupied with studying their surroundings that they didn't seem to notice anything wrong.

Still, the ley line activity across the city was building toward something big, and Delia's psychic abilities kept acting like the equivalent of a radio antenna in a lightning storm.

Every few minutes, another wave of supernatural energy would wash over her, and she'd get flashes of things she probably didn't want to see— shadowy figures moving through the city...red eyes watching from darkened windows...angular patterns of power that connected every supernatural site in Las Vegas, all of them pulsing with an ominous rhythm that made her head ache.

But then Alec looked over at her, and his dark brows drew together. "Are you all right?" he asked, stepping closer as if he wanted to steady her. "You look a little pale."

"Just tired," she said quickly. "It's been a busy week."

That was putting it mildly. At the moment, she felt like she was running on nothing but adrenaline and caffeine.

The chapel's manager, a woman in her fifties with perfectly styled, highlighted hair and the kind of professional warmth you'd expect from someone with years of experience dealing with nervous brides, met them at the door with a welcoming smile.

"You must be the Gunderson party," she said as she extended her hand to Olivia. "I'm Jeannette Hatch."

"Yes, that's us," Olivia replied. "Thank you so much for accommodating such a last-minute change."

"Of course. Why don't we go inside, and I can show you around?"

As they followed Jeannette through the entrance, another energy spike erupted, this one strong enough to make Delia gasp and reach out to steady herself against the wall. For just a moment, the chapel's everyday interior flickered and became overlaid with those same geometric patterns of light that revealed the supernatural network hidden beneath Las Vegas.

Once again, she saw it all—every ley line, every intersection point, every place where supernatural power gathered. And at the center of it all, Angel's Dream might as well have been a black hole, pulling energy from across the entire valley.

"Delia?" Olivia's voice seemed to come from very far away. "Are you sure you're all right?"

Delia blinked hard, forcing herself to focus on her cousin's worried face. The supernatural overlay faded, returning her to the tastefully decorated chapel with its arrangements of white roses and carefully soft lighting.

"I'm fine," she replied. "Just got a little dizzy for a second. I think they really amped up the caffeine in that grande iced tea I drank before we left the house."

Jeannette's brows pulled together in concern. "Would you like some water? Or maybe you should sit down for a moment?"

"No, I'm okay," Delia said at once, even though she knew that wasn't entirely true. The energy building across the city seemed to be affecting her more strongly with each passing hour.

What if she overloaded completely? What if the supernatural static building across Las Vegas fried her brain like a computer in a power surge?

Not helpful, she told herself firmly. *Focus on what you can control.*

"Let's see the chapel," she said aloud, putting on a brisk smile.

The main ceremony space was everything the website had promised—elegant without being ostentatious, with good sight lines and sunlight streaming through stained glass windows, casting jewel-toned patterns across the white carpet.

"This is perfect," Olivia said, sounding happy and sure of herself for the first time since she'd landed in Las Vegas. "It's exactly what I was hoping for."

Another wave of energy hit Delia, and this time, the surge came with horribly vivid images. She saw Caleb in what looked like a holding room, his hands bound behind his back while shadowy, red-eyed figures stood guard. She saw Vinea in his human guise, moving through what had once been Angel's Dream but was now transformed into something that belonged in the deepest circles of Hell, shadowed and dark and smoky, with arcane symbols blazing on the walls. And she saw dozens of other demons converging on Las Vegas, drawn by the growing network of power that crisscrossed the city.

The visions were so vivid, so immediate, that for a moment she forgot where she was. She took a step forward, reaching out as if she could somehow touch Caleb through the psychic connection they shared.

"Delia?" Alec's voice was sharp with concern. "What's wrong?"

She blinked, and realized she was standing in the middle of the chapel's center aisle, one hand extended toward empty air, while Jeannette and Alec and Olivia stared at her with expressions ranging from mildly concerned to deeply alarmed.

"Sorry," she said quickly, and dropped her hand. "I thought I saw something move, but now I realize it was probably just a reflection from the stained glass."

Jeannette's frown deepened, and Delia had the uncomfortable feeling that the chapel manager was beginning to suspect there was something seriously wrong with one of her potential clients.

"Why don't we step outside for a moment?" Olivia suggested. "Maybe we should get some fresh air before we finalize anything."

Delia gave a grateful nod, then followed her cousin and Alec back toward the entrance. As they walked, she tried to create some kind of mental barrier around her psychic abilities. She visualized a high wall surrounding a garden, a wall of stone covered with climbing roses. And within that wall,

all was serene and beautiful, a place darkness could never touch.

The pulsing energy that had been pushing on her all day seemed to retreat a little.

Was it actually working?

Outside the chapel, the late afternoon sun had begun to sink toward the mountains that ringed the Las Vegas valley, painting the heavy clouds overhead in shades of orange and red and purple. The scene should have been beautiful but somehow seemed ominous instead. The air itself seemed to hum with tension, as if the entire city was holding its breath.

"Okay," Olivia said once they were out of Jeannette's earshot, "what's really going on? And don't tell me you're just tired, because I know it's more than that."

Delia looked at her cousin and reminded herself that Olivia had been having prophetic dreams about her wedding for weeks. That had to mean she must also possess some level of psychic perception.

Maybe it was time to trust her with at least part of the truth.

"Something is happening in the city," Delia said. "Something that's affecting sensitive people more than others. I think you might be experiencing it, too—that's why you've been having all those nightmares about the wedding."

Alec frowned. "What kind of 'something'?"

How could she possibly explain that Las Vegas was currently being used as the focal point for a massive supernatural ritual without sounding like she'd lost her mind?

"There have been some unusual incidents over the past week or so," she replied, choosing her words with care. "Electrical disturbances, structural problems, that sort of thing. And weird vibes. Some people seem to be more aware of these disturbances than others."

It wasn't technically a lie.

Olivia was quiet for a moment, her eyes searching Delia's face. "Is that the real reason why you wanted me to change venues? Not because of permit issues, but because you sensed something wrong with Angel's Dream specifically?"

The insight revealed in that question caught Delia off guard. "Yes," she admitted. "I've always been sensitive to the atmosphere in particular locations. And something about that chapel felt very wrong to me."

"Like my dreams," Olivia said quietly.

"Exactly like your dreams."

Alec looked back and forth between the two women, his expression skeptical but not completely dismissive. "So...we're talking about what, exactly? Some kind of psychic phenomenon?"

The infernal energy spiked again, but this time, it seemed oddly muted, as though most of its power had been absorbed by the protective wall she'd built around her consciousness. When it passed, Delia could tell she felt more centered, more in control.

"I know it sounds crazy," she said, relieved to hear that her voice sounded steady. "But some people are just more sensitive to certain kinds of environmental changes."

Olivia gave a slow, considering nod. "And you think whatever's happening, it's going to peak around the time of the wedding?"

"I think it's possible," Delia replied. "Which is why I wanted to make sure you were somewhere safe."

"And this place is safe?" Alec asked, inclining his head toward the chapel.

Delia allowed her psychic senses to extend beyond the wall she'd built, testing the energy patterns around the building. The chapel sat on a minor ley line, but not one of the major intersection points the demons were targeting. More importantly, she couldn't sense any of the twisted supernatural signatures that marked the places where Vinea's people had been working.

"Yes," she said with more confidence than she'd felt all day. "This place should be fine."

"Then let's book it," Olivia said.

Inside, Jeannette was waiting, wearing a professional smile although she had obvious questions in her eyes.

"We'd like to book the chapel for tomorrow," Olivia said. "Seven-thirty in the evening, if possible."

"Wonderful." Jeannette's smile looked genuinely warm now. "With so little lead time, I'm afraid I'll need the entire amount up front."

"That's fine," Alec said, pulling out his wallet.

While they handled the paperwork, Delia's phone vibrated. A text from Ty appeared on the screen.

Multiple new incidents reported across the city. Pattern suggests major escalation within the next twenty-four hours. How's the family situation?

The venue's taken care of. Everyone's in town now. Any word on Caleb?

Still working on it. Keep family away from downtown area if possible.

The text conversation ended there, leaving Delia with the uncomfortable realization that whatever Vinea was planning, it was accelerating faster than any of them had anticipated.

"Is everything all right?" Olivia asked, brow puckering in a small frown.

Lord knows what she must have looked like as

she was texting with Ty. "Just coordinating all the other arrangements," Delia said, which was true enough. "Making sure your vendors are on the same page about the venue change."

Jeannette handed Alec a folder with copies of all the contracts. "I think you two are going to have a beautiful ceremony."

As the three of them left the chapel and walked toward Delia's little SUV, Olivia looked over at her cousin with an expression that was part gratitude and part concern.

"Thank you for all of this," she said. "I know there's more going on than you're telling me, but I trust you."

"You're family," Delia replied simply. "I'll always do whatever it takes to make sure you're happy."

And safe, she added mentally.

Even as she got out her key fob to unlock the Kona, another wave of energy rolled over her, and this time it came with a vision so clear and immediate, she had to grip the door handle to keep herself from falling.

Once again, she saw Angel's Dream transformed into something that belonged in a nightmare, with symbols carved into every surface and dark energy swirling through the air like smoke. This time, she also saw Vinea in his true form—not the urbane businessman but something ancient and terrible and utterly without mercy, a thousand times worse than the other demons they'd battled so far.

But she also saw something else—a network of light that connected her to Caleb, to Ty, to Pru, and even to the city itself. Power flowed through the ley lines, true, but it also ran through the bonds of love and friendship and determination that held them all together.

"Delia?" Alec's voice came to her from somewhere, tinny and faint. "Are you having another one of those...episodes?"

He sounded uncertain, and she couldn't blame him.

Delia opened her eyes—when had she even closed them?—and found her cousin and Alec standing beside the car, concern obvious in every line of their faces.

"I'm okay," she said, and realized that for the first time all day, she actually meant it. The energy still surged through her system, but now it felt less like a foreign invasion and more like a natural part of who she was becoming.

"Let's go get that coffee," she said, managing a genuine smile. "And then we need to pick up your parents at the hotel."

As they drove away from the chapel, Delia found herself focusing on all the changes she could sense in the supernatural landscape around them...

more and more active sites, accompanied by stronger energy flows. Thrown into the mix was the unmistakable presence of entities that had no business being on this plane of existence.

But she could also sense something else—a growing network of resistance. People like herself, scattered throughout the city, whose natural psychic abilities were being awakened by the chaos. There weren't enough of them to mount a direct challenge to Vinea's operation, but maybe there were enough to provide the kind of support her team would need when the time came.

Her phone vibrated again. This time, the message was from Pru.

Emergency meeting tonight after family dinner. Ty found something big.

Good or bad big?

Let's go with 'complicated' big. Can you get away around eight?

Under normal circumstances, Delia would never have contemplated bailing on a family commitment. Everyone was meeting at Santorini's at six, which should have given her plenty of time. But any get-together associated with a wedding tended to run long.

These weren't normal circumstances, though. And if Pru and Ty had discovered something that could help them rescue Caleb and stop Vinea's operation, then she had to be there.

I'll make it work.

Yet another energy spike smashed into her just as she was shutting off the engine. But this time, instead of fighting it or trying to shield herself from it, Delia simply let it flow through her, accepting the power as part of who she was becoming.

Whatever happened tonight, whatever they learned at Pru's emergency meeting, she would be ready.

By the time Delia managed to extract herself from the family dinner at Santorini's, it was nearly eight-thirty. The evening had stretched on longer than expected, through multiple courses, several rounds of toasts, and the kind of cheerful chatter that always seemed to happen when relatives who rarely saw each other tried to catch up on years' worth of news in a single evening.

Under normal circumstances, she would have enjoyed every minute of it. Olivia's relief at having the venue situation resolved was infectious, and both sets of parents seemed genuinely pleased with how smoothly everything was falling into place. Even Alec, who'd been skeptical about the last-minute change, admitted that Little Chapel of Hearts seemed to be a better place for the ceremony than Angel's Dream.

But with every passing hour, Delia found it harder to ignore the supernatural energy building across the city, pressing against the mental walls she'd constructed. By the time she'd finally made her excuses and headed for Pru's condo, her nerves were stretched, so frayed that they might as well have been made of old string.

The building's elevator seemed to take forever, and when she finally reached Pru's door, she thought she could hear voices from inside before she even knocked.

"About time," Pru said as she opened the door, then stepped aside to let Delia enter. Her dark green hair fell around her face, and the faint circles under her eyes told Delia that she must have been working nonstop for hours.

Ty stood by the window that overlooked the city, his fingers tapping on the glass in a nervous rhythm that seemed very unlike him. When he turned away so he could face the two women, the strain in his handsome features was obvious even from all the way across the room.

"How bad is it?" she asked, figuring there wasn't any point in wasting time on greetings.

"Even worse than we thought," Ty replied as he moved away from the window to join them in the living room. "The timeline's accelerated. Vinea's not waiting until midnight tomorrow to get started."

Delia sank onto Pru's sectional, all of her muscles suddenly sore, as if the day's accumulated stress had finally caught up with her. "How much time do we have?"

"The ritual begins at eight tomorrow evening," Pru said. She also settled on the sectional, but perched at the far end of the L, as if she thought she might need to get up and go over to her laptop at any second. "Peak power will be at 11:47, but by then it'll be too late to stop anything."

"How do you know all this?" Delia asked, looking from her friend over to Ty. It was good that they'd been able to unearth this information, but it wasn't the sort of thing they could have picked up from a simple Google search.

The half angel's expression darkened. "Because I've been monitoring my people's communications all day, and the higher-ups are in full crisis mode. This isn't just about Las Vegas anymore. If Vinea succeeds in opening those permanent gateways, it'll destabilize the barriers between planes across the entire continent."

All this unwelcome news made Delia want to throw up her hands in despair, but she knew that wasn't an option. No, they'd have to soldier through this, no matter what happened. "And they're not sending help?"

"They can't intervene directly without risking an all-out supernatural war," Ty said. With an impatient hand, he reached up to pull away the rubber band that held his heavy dark hair away from his face, then neatly bound it up again, as if it had been bothering him. "There are rules about these kinds of things. I'm allowed to work with you because I'm half mortal and have a stake on this plane, the same as you do, but any actual angelic intervention is completely off the table.'"

That was a nugget of information she hadn't possessed previously, but, interesting as it might have been, it certainly didn't change anything about their current situation.

"Great," Delia said. She'd had a glass and a half of wine with dinner, but any "good feelings" buzzes were long gone by that point. "So it's still just us."

"Oh, but it gets worse," Pru said. "Ty helped me get into the communication network the demons have been using to coordinate the operation. Vinea knows about your family. He knows about the wedding, the venue change, where everyone's staying. *Everything.*"

The excellent osso bucco Delia had eaten for dinner turned over in her stomach. "I assume that's not good."

"That's an understatement," Ty replied. "Vinea is planning to use them as leverage if necessary. From what we've been able to find, the demons are just fine with turning this into a hostage situation. If we try to interfere, innocent people will die."

Delia thought about her parents, her Aunt Vicky and Uncle Doug, Olivia and Alec and all of his family members who'd flown in for the wedding. They would be the worst kind of sitting ducks.

"We have to get them out of Las Vegas," she said.

"And tell them what?" Pru asked, clearly frustrated. "That demons are planning to turn their family celebration into the opening ceremony for Hell on Earth? They'll think we've lost our minds."

Delia knew her friend was right, of course. There was no way to explain the situation to anyone outside the loop without sounding completely insane. And even if she and Pru and Ty could, by some miracle, convince everyone to leave, wouldn't Vinea just find other hostages? Other innocent people to threaten?

"There's something else," Ty said, his tone even grimmer than before...if that was possible. "The ley line activation is awakening every psychically sensitive person in the city. People with even a spark of latent ability."

"To do what, exactly?" Delia asked. She'd already sensed this happening, even if she wasn't sure what it meant. "Or is this just a byproduct of all the wild energy that's getting flung around?

Pru and Ty exchanged a weighted glance. "To create a network of human batteries, we think," Pru said.

Well, that didn't sound good.

Ty crossed his arms. "From what I've been able to tell, the network's growing exponentially. By tomorrow night, there could be hundreds...maybe thousands...of people involuntarily connected to Vinea's ritual."

The sinking feeling had returned. "Including me," Delia murmured.

"Including you," Ty replied. "Your abilities have been expanding over the past couple of months anyway, but now you're being pulled into the network. If we can't stop the ritual, you'll become part of it...whether you want to or not."

The thought of being psychically enslaved, of having her newly acquired powers used to fuel the demons' invasion, made her skin crawl. At the same time, though, she knew she couldn't let herself be lost to worry and despair.

No, they had to do something to make sure none of that ever happened.

"Then we have to stop it," she said simply.

"How?" Pru asked. Her voice shook a little, although Delia wasn't sure that was because she was afraid or just so very damn tired. "How are the three of us supposed to go up against a lord of Hell and however many demons he's brought with him? The math doesn't exactly work in our favor."

Delia was quiet for a moment. Although she still wasn't entirely comfortable with using these strange new gifts of hers, she also realized this wasn't the time to be squeamish. So she pulled in a breath, then reached out with her enhanced senses to test the supernatural energy flowing through the city. The network was vast and incredibly powerful. But it also felt incomplete. She could locate gaps in the pattern, places where the connections weren't quite stable.

"What if we don't try to fight the network directly?" she said, the words coming out slowly as she tried to work her way through to a solution. "What if we turn it against itself?"

Ty's eyebrows lifted, but Delia thought she saw a light of interest flicker in his sky-colored eyes. "Explain."

Easier said than done. But she knew she had to articulate what she'd sensed, put it out there so both Ty and Pru would understand what she was driving at.

"The ley line energy is building toward critical mass, right?" she said. "All that power focused on a single point. But what if, instead of trying to block it, we redirect it? Use the network's own energy to overload the ritual?"

Ty rubbed his finger against his chin, expression thoughtful. "That could work. If we could coordinate the disruption across multiple nodes at the same time...."

"But that would require someone inside the network," Pru put in, sounding dubious. "Someone who could access the control points from inside the ritual framework itself."

"Someone like me," Delia said. She thought she sounded very calm, very brave.

Maybe that glass and a half of wine was doing something for her after all.

"Absolutely not," Ty replied at once, his voice flat. "If you're inside the network when it overloads, it could kill you...or worse."

"And if we don't try, a bunch of people in the city will die anyway," Delia pointed out. "At least this way, we have a chance."

Everyone went quiet. Delia could tell that both Ty and Pru were trying to come up with some other way of fighting the demons, but they were pretty much out of options at this point.

"One good thing," she went on when it became clear that neither of her friends had any other arguments to offer. "I can probably access the framework from anywhere in the city. It's not like I have to be right where the action is happening, so to speak."

"Sort of like hacking a mainframe from a remote terminal," Pru said.

"I thought you weren't a hacker," Delia replied, and her friend grinned.

"I'm not. But I watch a lot of movies."

Delia could only shake her head. At least now they had the faintest glimmer of a plan.

Even if she had no clear idea of how to execute it...or what might happen when she did.

Chapter Thirteen

—·‹‹‹‹·ⓘ·››››·—

Dawn slowly crept across the Las Vegas valley, as if it wasn't sure it wanted to be a witness to what the coming day might bring. Caleb watched the sunrise through the single narrow window in his holding room, noting how the light seemed to bend strangely around the chapel, as if the building somehow existed outside normal reality.

Which, he supposed, it probably did by now.

The demons guarding him had changed shifts twice during the night, but the routine remained the same—two red-eyed sentinels flanked the door while he sat in the uncomfortable chair, ostensibly resting before his starring role in Vinea's grand finale. What they didn't know was that he'd spent most of the night working on the subtle sabotage he'd been weaving into the ritual framework, tiny flaws and inconsistencies he hoped would cascade into something much larger when the time came, the way a tiny crack in a dam might turn into a flood when enough water tried to force its way through.

His phone had been taken away hours ago, but his psychic connection to Delia hung on despite everything. Every so often, he'd catch glimpses through their bond—flashes of her sitting down to a dinner with a large group of family members at a restaurant that thankfully was far from the center of the chaos, taking a late-night call from Olivia to walk her through some wedding details...working with Ty and Pru to piece together what Vinea was really planning.

She was safe for now. That was the one thing that really mattered.

The door to the holding room opened, and Vinea entered, once again wearing the human guise that made him look like a waxwork dummy in a bespoke suit. The demon lord carried a silver tray laden with what appeared to be an excellent breakfast—eggs Benedict, fresh fruit, toast, and a big mug of heavenly-smelling coffee.

"Good morning, Caleb," Vinea said as he set the tray down on a small table that appeared out of nowhere. "I trust you slept well?"

Actually, he hadn't slept at all, but he saw no reason to share that information. "Like a baby," he replied blithely, then gestured toward the food. "Room service in Hell has really improved since my last visit."

That comment earned him one of Vinea's razor-sharp smiles. "Oh, we're not in Hell, dear boy. We're very much on your beloved mortal plane, although I'll admit that the boundaries have become rather fluid in this particular location."

As if to emphasize his point, the walls of the holding room flickered for a moment, revealing glimpses of something vast and shadowy beyond them. Caleb caught sight of what looked like a cathedral made of black stone, with architecture that pained his eyes, all Escher-esque planes and angles, with some flourishes that could have come right out of a concept drawing for one of the *Alien* movies.

Then the illusion snapped back into place, returning them to the mundane, square room where he'd been held captive for almost a day.

"Eat," Vinea commanded, settling into a chair that materialized from thin air. It was large and almost throne-like, carved mahogany with blood-red upholstery, far grander than the hard, plain chair where his prisoner had been forced to sit. "You'll need your strength for tonight's festivities."

Tonight. The word sent a chill down Caleb's spine. Time continued to march on, although he really wished it wouldn't.

He picked up the fork and took a bite of the eggs Benedict, which were annoyingly delicious. If the food hadn't been so good, he wouldn't have wanted to eat all of it. As it was, he knew he'd probably clean the plate...which he guessed would please Vinea to no end.

"So...tonight," he said, figuring he might as well prepare himself for the worst. "Walk me through what happens."

"Eager to get started, are we?" The demon lord seemed pleased, as though he'd interpreted Caleb's request as a visible sign of cooperation. "Very well. The ritual will begin at sunset, which is approximately eight o'clock at this time of year. We'll need several hours to properly synchronize the portal network across the city."

Caleb popped a grape in his mouth, then asked, "And I'll be...?"

"Positioned at the primary nexus point, of course. Right here, in the heart of what was once Angel's Dream Wedding Chapel." Vinea gestured around them, and for the barest second, the walls became transparent again, revealing the vast supernatural architecture that existed beneath the mundane skin that most everyday observers would see. "Your blood will flow through channels carved into the foundation, connecting this location to every other node in the network."

The mental image of his blood literally flowing

through supernatural conduits made the eggs Benedict flip-flop in his stomach, but Caleb managed to keep his expression neutral. "And it'll take three to four hours?"

"Yes. The process must be gradual to ensure stability." Vinea's tone was matter-of-fact, as if they were discussing getting together to build a bookcase from Ikea rather than performing a ritual that would reshape reality. "The celestial alignment reaches its peak at 11:47 p.m., and that's when the final gateway will open."

The final gateway. Something about the phrasing suggested that it wasn't only the last portal in the sequence—it was the most important one.

"What makes that portal special?" Caleb asked.

For the first time since he entered the room, Vinea's mask of confidence slipped just the slightest bit. In that brief moment, Caleb caught a glimpse of something that might have been anticipation mixed with genuine uncertainty.

"That gateway will be large enough to accommodate entities that haven't walked this plane since before the human race learned to make fire," the demon lord said, his quiet tone somehow far more ominous than a loud declaration would have been. "Powers that make even someone like me look like a minor nuisance."

Entities that made a lord of Hell look puny.

Caleb didn't want to think about what that might mean, but his mind helpfully supplied images of a few unsettling things he'd glimpsed in the deepest parts of Hell during his unwilling residency there. Ancient beings that existed at the very foundations of reality, creatures so old and powerful that they reshaped the laws of physics through their mere presence.

If something like that crossed over to Earth....

"Having second thoughts, nephew?" Vinea asked, having apparently noticed his reaction. "I will remind you that the ritual will proceed with or without your cooperation. Your willing involvement simply makes everything simpler."

The threat was delivered with the demon lord's usual urbane courtesy, but Caleb could hear the steel beneath the silk. Vinea was confident that Caleb would ultimately cooperate...but he was also prepared to drain his blood by force if necessary.

Which meant the sabotage Caleb had been weaving into the ritual framework was his only real weapon.

"No second thoughts," Caleb said coolly. "I'm just trying to understand the full picture."

"Wise of you." Vinea rose from his chair, which dissolved back into nothingness as soon as he stood. "Knowledge is power, after all. And you'll need every advantage you can get if you hope to survive what's coming."

The casual admission that Caleb might not survive the ritual should have been terrifying. Instead, it was almost a relief. If Vinea hadn't been certain that his primary source of demon blood would live through the process, then the demon lord had probably built in redundancies and backup plans.

Which meant there were other targets, other sources of the mixed heritage that could power the portal network.

Other quarter demons.

But how was that possible when all the other quarter demons were safely locked away in Hell?

"Who else?" Caleb demanded, not caring how rough his voice sounded. "If something happens to me, who's your backup plan?"

Vinea's smile was all pointed teeth. "Why, your lovely Ms. Dunne, of course. Her abilities have been growing quite dramatically since her little adventure in Laughlin. I suspect her blood might be even more potent than yours."

The demon lord might as well have punched Caleb right in the gut, considering how breathless...how helpless...those words made him feel. Sure, he'd known Delia's psychic abilities had been expanding over the past few weeks, or he wouldn't have been able to maintain any kind of bond with her, tenuous as it seemed at the moment.

"Delia doesn't have any demon blood," he said.

Somehow, his voice stayed level, although he couldn't be sure that Vinea hadn't noticed some other physical reaction to that threatening comment— maybe just the slightest widening of his eyes, or a momentary increase in his body heat.

After all, demons' senses were far sharper than those of ordinary humans.

"Perhaps not," Vinea replied, "but she's something equally rare—a mortal whose psychic potential has been awakened by exposure to interdimensional energy. That sort of person doesn't come along very often, so in some ways, that makes her even more valuable than a quarter demon, since there are seven of you and only one of her." The demon lord began to walk around the small room, his footsteps silent, even though the leather soles of his expensive Italian lace-ups should have been clacking on the hard concrete floor.

His explanation made a horrible kind of sense. During the incident in Laughlin, Delia had been exposed to massive amounts of supernatural energy, first from the Colorado River guardian network, and then by the portal the demon masquerading as August Sellers had partly opened. If that exposure had changed her on some deep level that no one suspected....

"You're not touching her," Caleb said, and this time he didn't bother to hide the fury in his voice.

"Oh, I don't intend to," Vinea replied, looking

singularly unruffled. "As long as you fulfill your role in tonight's festivities, Ms. Dunne will be perfectly safe. It's only if something unfortunate were to happen to you that we'd need to explore... well, let's just call them alternative arrangements."

Another threat wrapped in silk, but this one sounded all too sincere. Vinea would use Delia's blood to power his ritual without a moment's hesitation if Caleb failed to cooperate.

Which meant the sabotage he'd been planning had to be subtle enough to avoid detection but still serious enough to bring down the entire operation. That was a balancing act even a high-wire artist might think about twice.

No pressure.

"I understand," Caleb said, and he meant it. He understood exactly what was at stake...and exactly what he had to do.

Vinea nodded, apparently satisfied that his message had been received. "Excellent. Now, if you'll excuse me, I have some final preparations to oversee. The catering alone for tonight's gathering is quite complex—we're expecting representatives from seven different circles of Hell once the portal has been opened, and their dietary requirements are somewhat specialized."

Caleb really didn't want to think about that. Technically, demons didn't need to eat, which was a good thing, since there was no food or water in

Hell. One simply existed without any sort of bodily functions at all. That had been yet another horrifying element of the whole ghastly experience, of knowing that he looked just like his old self but that certain parts of his biology had been put on hold. He'd lost weight during those two years, but at a much slower rate than would have been normal, considering his zero caloric intake.

A good thing, he supposed, or he wouldn't have been much more than a skeleton by the time he managed to claw his way back to the mortal plane.

The demon lord moved toward the door, then paused with his hand on the handle. "Oh, and nephew? Don't bother trying to reach out to your teammates through that charming psychic connection you share with Ms. Dunne. You'll find it blocked. We wouldn't want you coordinating any last-minute heroics, after all."

Son of a bitch....

The door closed behind the demon lord with a soft *click,* leaving Caleb alone with his guards and the growing certainty that he was running out of time.

He reached out to his bond with Delia, knowing he needed to find out whether Vinea's claim about blocking communications was true or whether he was merely waging more psychological warfare. The connection was still there—

Caleb could sense her presence, her emotional state—but when he tried to send a focused message, he might as well have been shouting into a hurricane. The supernatural static surrounding the chapel was too intense for clear communication.

Which meant his team would be operating blind when they finally came for him.

Caleb settled back in his chair and closed his eyes, then reached out with his enhanced senses to trace the supernatural energies building around the chapel. He soon learned that the portal network was much larger than he'd initially realized, encompassing not just Las Vegas itself but stretching out into the desert in all directions. Ley lines he'd never even known existed were being activated, their combined power funneling toward this single nexus point.

But energy networks, no matter how sophisticated, were still just systems. And every system had its vulnerabilities.

The sabotage he'd been weaving into the ritual framework over the past day was designed to exploit those vulnerabilities. Small inconsistencies in the flow patterns, tiny flaws in the geometric alignments, microscopic gaps in the binding matrices that held the portals stable.

Individually, none of them would be enough to bring down the network. But if they cascaded properly, if the timing was right, then the entire structure could collapse in on itself.

The real question was whether he'd have a chance to trigger the cascade before Vinea's ritual reached the point of no return.

The door opened again, only this time, it was one of the lesser demons who entered. It carried what looked like ceremonial robes made of some dark material that seemed to absorb light, blacker than black.

"Lord Vinea's compliments," the creature said in its gravelly voice. "He requests that you prepare yourself for the evening's activities."

Caleb looked at the robes, then at the demon, and then back at the robes. "You know," he remarked, "when I was growing up, nobody ever mentioned that saving the world would involve so many costume changes."

The demon stared at him with glowing red eyes that didn't blink. "Lord Vinea expects you to be ready within the hour."

"Wouldn't want to keep a lord of Hell waiting," Caleb replied as he took the robes from the creature.

Once it was relieved of its burden, the demon withdrew, leaving Caleb alone with his guards once more. He held up the ceremonial garments and examined them closely. The fabric felt wrong against his fingers, too smooth and too cold, and the symbols seemed to thrum with pure evil.

Definitely not something he'd find at Men's Wearhouse.

But as he held the robes, an idea began to take shape in his mind. The ceremonial garments were clearly designed to channel and focus supernatural energy during the ritual...which meant they must also be part of the network he'd been sabotaging.

If he could work a few more flaws into the system....

Caleb held back a smile. The demons watching him didn't seem to be paying any particular attention to what he was doing—he'd already gotten the impression that they weren't exactly the sharpest knives in the drawer—and as he pulled the heavy garments on over his black button-up and jeans, his fingers worked subtle modifications into the fabric, a pinch here and a loose thread there, places where he could insert a little of his own power, drawing it out in ways he wouldn't have even known existed a few short months ago. The changes he made were too small to be detected by casual inspection, but they would create interesting resonance patterns when the ritual energy really started flowing.

Outside his window, the sun flared out redly from behind its bank of obscuring clouds, and across Las Vegas, the shadows began to lengthen.

Soon.

Chapter Fourteen

—‹‹‹‹·☾·›››·—

THE ALARM ON DELIA'S PHONE WENT OFF way too early on Saturday morning, the lilting chime she'd chosen because it was supposed to be pleasant and not too jarring doing absolutely nothing to ease the sense of dread that had settled in her stomach like a lump of undigested oatmeal. May thirtieth. Olivia's wedding day.

She rolled over and silenced the phone, then lay there for a moment, staring at the ceiling while another wave of ley line energy washed over her. The protective walls she'd built around her consciousness the day before held firm—and because she was lying down, the rippling energy wouldn't have affected her as badly as it might have if she'd been standing up—but she could still feel power building across the Las Vegas landscape, pressing on her ears and her temples.

If she'd been flying in a plane and had experienced similar discomfort, she could have yawned to pop her ears and regain some equilibrium. Unfortunately, the solution to this particular sensation was a lot more complicated.

And they wouldn't arrive at that moment of relief until almost midnight.

She pushed herself out of bed and went down the hall to the kitchen, muscle memory guiding her through the familiar routine of starting coffee while her brain kept playing the day's impossible logistics over and over again. Wedding at seven-thirty and a late reception at the Anthem Country Club afterward with both families. Vinea's ritual scheduled to begin around eight, reaching its climax just before midnight.

And Caleb held somewhere in the supernatural maze that Angel's Dream had become.

Her phone, which Delia had brought with her into the kitchen, vibrated on the granite countertop as the coffeemaker gurgled to life.

A text from Ty.

I'm picking up multiple demonic signatures converging downtown, so I'm fairly sure Caleb is still at Angel's Dream. How's your family situation?

Well, that was one piece of semi-good news. Not that storming the chapel was going to be a walk in the park, but better that Caleb stayed put.

The last thing they needed was to have to go chasing all over town trying to find him.

Everyone's accounted for. All the visitors are staying at the M Resort, well away from downtown. The wedding is still on schedule.

Good. Whatever else you do, keep them there as much as possible. That area should be safer than anywhere downtown.

The conversation ended there, leaving Delia alone with her growing sense of unease. She poured coffee into her favorite mug, the one with the pretty reactive glaze in shades of sky blue and soft taupe that a client of hers, a potter, had given her as a thank-you after he closed on his house, and tried to reach out through her psychic bond with Caleb.

Still there, thank God. That thin thread of connection told her he was alive, but not much else was able to get through. She thought she could sense his determination, though, and maybe underneath it, a carefully controlled anger that made her think he was planning something.

Don't do anything stupid, she thought, directing the message toward Angel's Dream even though she had no idea whether he was able to hear her. *Just stay alive until we can get to you.*

Another energy surge hit her, stronger than any she'd experienced so far, and she grabbed the edge of the countertop to prevent herself from falling over. The coffee mug slipped from her hand, but luckily, it fell on the faux-Persian runner in muted shades of off-white and gray that filled in the gap between the main bank of cupboards and the island. Coffee spilled everywhere, but at least the mug seemed to have survived. She didn't know if she could say as much for the runner.

Not, she thought, that it mattered too much. Not in comparison with what she saw now.

Demons moved through the city like shadows, gathering at locations that pulsed with unnatural light. The demon lord Vinea stood in the center of what had once been Angel's Dream, now transformed into something that belonged in the deepest circles of Hell...or maybe one of H.R. Giger's worst nightmares. And beyond all that, she saw something else—a network of power that connected not only the supernatural sites Pru and Ty had already discovered, but every person in Las Vegas who possessed even a spark of psychic ability.

It was just like Ty had told her the night before. Only it felt far worse today, simply because now she understood what was going on.

Vinea would use the power of all those innocent people to make sure the portals opened on time...and stayed open.

Her phone rang, startling her. Good thing she'd already dropped her mug, or she probably would have spilled her coffee all over again.

Who the hell would be calling at this ungodly

hour? Had Pru and Ty unearthed yet another unsettling piece of information, something that would make the impossible task that lay ahead even more difficult?

But no, that was Olivia's ID on the screen. Delia muttered a curse, even though she supposed the one person who got a free pass on calls before 10 a.m. was a woman getting married that day.

"Hey," Delia said after she touched the screen to accept the call. She tried her best to sound cheerful and wedding-appropriate despite the utter lack of caffeine in her bloodstream. Well, she'd remedy that after she took care of this call. "How are you doing today?"

"A little nervous," her cousin replied, although she sounded more excited than anxious. "But good nervous, you know? I keep thinking about what you said, about trusting my instincts, and I'm so glad we changed venues. I slept better last night than I have in weeks."

At least one of them was getting some rest. "I'm glad to hear that," Delia said. "Any last-minute details you need help with?"

"Actually, yes. The florist is supposed to deliver the arrangements to the chapel at five, but I'm going to be getting my hair done then, and so are my mom and Alec's sister Abby. Could you meet them there and make sure everything looks all right? Alec's mom said she would do it, but just between you and me"—Olivia's voice lowered as though she was about to deliver a state secret— "Penny doesn't have the greatest taste in the world. She's awesome in every other way, but I just don't trust her to handle something like this."

Delia's first instinct was to say yes—she was family, after all, and wedding coordination was the sort of thing relatives were supposed to help with. But roping herself into yet another wedding-related task seemed like a stupid idea when she had no idea what else she might be called on to do today.

What if Ty and Pru managed to figure out a way to get to Caleb just as she was at the chapel, arranging lilies or whatever?

But then the words, "Of course," rolled out of her mouth, and Delia wanted to shake her head at herself. Maybe one of these days she'd learn to be a little less accommodating. "I'll be there."

A sigh of relief came through the phone's speaker. "You're the best. Thank you again for everything you've done. I know I keep saying it, but I really mean it. Having you here, knowing someone local is looking out for us—it's made all the difference."

The genuine gratitude in her cousin's voice made Delia feel a little better about agreeing to help with this additional task. Olivia had no idea what she was really being protected from, no idea that her destination wedding had almost become the focal point for Hell's exodus to Earth...and Delia was going to do everything in her power to make sure it stayed that way.

"That's what families are for," she replied, the false cheer in her voice almost fooling her.

Almost.

After they ended the call, she started another pot of coffee, then leaned against the kitchen island and allowed herself exactly sixty seconds to have an inner freak-out about the overwhelming odds she faced. She was responsible for keeping her extended family out of harm's way, and she also couldn't rid herself of the terrible inner certainty that her own psychic abilities might be the key to stopping Vinea's operation, even though she still had no clear idea how to use them effectively.

And above all else was her fear for Caleb's safety. If anything happened to him....

No, she wouldn't allow herself to contemplate that outcome. They'd find him, and the demon lord who thought he had everything in his pocket was going to find out the hard way that humans also knew how to play.

The coffee was ready. She poured herself a cup and held it in both hands, taking strength from its warmth.

Everything was going to be okay.

Most of the day seemed oddly calm. She met the family for lunch, located a seamstress who could do some last-minute alterations on the pretty blue dress Alec's sister would be wearing as Olivia's sole attendant, and then, along with her mother, ferried the group over to the Forum Shops at Caesar's Palace—mainly because Delia's Aunt Vicky was dying to see them, even though her main excuse for going there was that she'd decided she didn't like the shoes she'd chosen to go with her dress and wanted to find something different.

During all this busyness, Delia kept expecting to get assailed by another wave of rogue energy, but that didn't happen. Had the barriers she'd put in place somehow strengthened? Or was Vinea simply storing everything up for the ritual this evening?

She prayed it was the former...but she feared it was probably the latter.

By the time she pulled into the parking lot at Little Chapel of Hearts a little after five, the late-afternoon sun was casting long shadows across the desert landscape. Clouds had lingered all day, keeping temperatures to a more manageable level, but they did nothing to help the sensation of lingering dread that seemed to have permanently settled in Delia's stomach.

The florist's van was already there, and Delia could see two men moving the arrangements of white hydrangeas and peonies that Olivia had ordered, lush and old-fashioned, into the chapel.

She approached the front entrance, noting that the chapel's energy signature felt the same as it had yesterday—neutral and blessedly free of the twisted supernatural resonance that marked the places where Vinea's people had been working. At least she'd succeeded in getting the wedding moved to a safe location, even if everything else felt horribly unsettled.

"Ms. Dunne?" A woman around Delia's age emerged from the chapel, carrying a clipboard and looking harried. "I'm Taylor from Desert Rose. Everything's almost ready, but we wanted to check the placement of the altar arrangements with someone from the family."

Delia followed Taylor into the chapel, where the other members of the florist's team were putting finishing touches on displays that were, she had to admit, absolutely stunning. White peonies and sprays of miniature white orchids cascaded from tall arrangements flanking the altar, while smaller bouquets marked the ends of each pew. Everything looked elegant and romantic, exactly what Olivia had dreamed of.

"It's perfect," Delia said, glad that her words were no false praise. "My cousin is going to love this."

"Wonderful. We'll finish up here and be out of your way in about twenty minutes."

As the florists worked, Delia found herself drawn to a window near the back of the chapel where she could look toward downtown, about a mile away. It all seemed normal enough, neon lights flashing even though the sun wouldn't set for a few more hours. Those streets were probably filled with tourists and locals getting an early start on their Saturday evening activities, whether that was shopping or gambling or catching a show.

If she and her friends didn't do this right, all those people's Saturday nights were going to turn out to be horribly different from what they'd planned.

For the first time in hours, a surge of energy hit her, and she winced and grabbed hold of the pew nearest to where she stood. Behind closed eyes, she caught a brief glimpse of Caleb. He was being moved from the room where he'd been held, escorted through endless corridors that surely couldn't exist inside a structure built by human hands. More importantly, though, she sensed that his determination had crystallized into something specific—he was planning to sabotage Vinea's ritual from the inside.

Be careful, she thought, hoping the message would somehow reach him through the supernatural static that seemed to have filled the Las Vegas valley. *Don't sacrifice yourself to save everyone else. We need you alive.*

Luckily, no one from the florist seemed to have noticed anything off about her behavior. They finished their work and packed up their supplies, leaving Delia alone in the chapel with arrangements that seemed to glow in the late afternoon light filtering through the stained glass windows. She walked down the center aisle, letting her fingers trail along the smooth wood of the pews, trying to imprint this moment of peace before the chaos that was surely coming.

Her phone rang, and Delia pulled it out of her purse.

Linda Dunne.

"Hi, Mom."

"Delia, where are you? We're all gathering in the hotel lobby before heading to the chapel."

Right. The plan was for everyone to meet at the hotel where both sets of parents were staying and then caravan to the chapel together, a bit of last-minute pre-wedding bonding that Olivia had come up with during their shopping expedition earlier that afternoon.

"I'm actually at the chapel already," Delia said. "I just finished checking on the flowers. They're beautiful. After this, I'm going to head home and get changed. I'll meet you at the hotel after that."

Her mother must have detected some of the

tension in her daughter's voice, because she didn't urge her to hurry but only said, "Okay. Just come join us when you're ready."

"I'll be over as fast as I can."

They ended the call there, and Delia walked back to her car. The whole time, she kept tensing, thinking she was going to get hit by another blast of supernatural energy at any moment, but things seemed to have calmed down for now.

She couldn't take any real comfort from that, unfortunately. Not when she knew those waves of power could come at any time.

Her house was about fifteen minutes away from the chapel, and she drove faster than she should, wishing that Olivia hadn't insisted on everyone gathering at the hotel first. It was really kind of stupid to have to keep zigging and zagging back and forth across the city when she could have just gone back to the wedding venue after getting into the dress she'd bought for the ceremony.

But brides got what brides wanted, so Delia pulled into the garage, hurried inside her house, and went straight to the master suite. Since she wasn't part of the wedding party, she didn't have to worry about an elaborate hairstyle or anything too fancy. She'd bought a pretty sleeveless silk sheath in a becoming shade of celery green, and she brushed out her long red hair and pulled it up into a simple twist at the back of her head. A pair of green tourmaline drops that matched the silver ring she wore more often than not, and she figured she was as ready as she'd ever be.

The drive to Anthem took around twenty minutes, giving her time to center herself and reinforce the mental barriers that had kept the worst of the psychic interference at bay over the past few hours. She needed to be fully present for her family, to play the role of supportive cousin and dutiful daughter while also doing her best to secretly monitor the supernatural crisis unfolding across the valley.

The resort's lobby was all polished travertine and moody lighting, with floor-to-ceiling windows that offered spectacular views of the mountains to the east. Delia spotted her family immediately—her parents talking with an attractive couple who looked a few years older than they and who had to be Alec's parents, while Olivia stood nearby in a strapless white dress that was all about perfect tailoring rather than any fussy beading or lace.

"Delia!" Olivia's face lit up, and she hurried over for a hug. "How did everything look at the chapel?"

"Absolutely perfect," Delia replied, knowing she could be truthful about that even when there were so many other things she had to keep to herself. "The florists outdid themselves."

"I can't wait to see it." Olivia's dark eyes shone

with excitement, and for a moment, Delia allowed herself to forget about demons and rituals so she could focus on the simple fun of watching a family member prepare for one of the most important days of her life.

"You look beautiful," she said, which was only the truth. The gown was perfect for Olivia's tall, willowy frame, and her dark hair had been styled in an elegant updo that showed off a pair of delicate pearl and diamond earrings that looked like antiques.

There was her cousin's "something old," Delia supposed.

"Thank you," Olivia replied. "I know it's silly, but I keep waiting for something to go wrong. Like this whole thing has been too easy."

If only she knew how much effort had gone into making it look "easy."

"Nothing's going to go wrong," Delia assured her. "This is your day, and it's going to be perfect."

Aunt Vicky appeared at Delia's elbow. "We need to head over to the chapel. The photographer is waiting for us."

Right. Olivia and Alec obviously weren't worried about seeing each other before the ceremony, and they'd scheduled a photo session to precede the main event, taking advantage of the warm, golden-hour lighting in the chapel's gardens.

Everyone hustled out to their cars. Soon

enough, Delia was back at the chapel, standing off to one side as the photographer posed the happy couple and the small wedding party in various locations around the garden. The sunset had turned out to be spectacular, with beams of gold and amber breaking through the heavy clouds, and Delia guessed the lighting was just perfect.

But as they were just finishing up and getting ready to head inside the chapel, another massive energy surge hit the city, strong enough that the photographer and Alec's one groomsman, a tall, sandy-haired guy named Nick, paused and looked around as if they'd heard something.

"Did you feel that?" asked Alec's sister Abby, a petite brunette. "Like the whole grounds shook or something?"

"Probably just a truck going by," Alec said easily, but Delia caught the worried glance he sent toward Olivia.

Her cousin, meanwhile, had gone pale. "I felt it, too. Like a vibration, but not quite."

The psychically sensitive members of the wedding party were picking up on the ley line activation. Delia realized she needed to get everyone inside and through the ceremony as quickly as possible, before the supernatural interference became too obvious to ignore.

"I'm sure it was nothing," she said. "The

chapel grounds back up to a main street, and there's a lot of truck traffic around here."

To her relief, everyone appeared to accept this explanation, and they headed inside.

The chapel had looked beautiful when Delia checked the flowers earlier, but now it had been transformed. Candles flickered on every surface, their warm light making the white peonies and orchids and hydrangeas seem to glow. Soft music played from hidden speakers, and the atmosphere seemed to be exactly what Olivia had dreamed of... lush and romantic, and utterly peaceful.

Or at least, it was peaceful if you couldn't sense the supernatural storm building across the city.

Delia took her seat in the third row, between her parents and Alec's grandmother, a sharp-eyed woman in her eighties who'd flown in from Phoenix for the occasion. As the chapel filled with guests and the ceremony began, she allowed herself to be drawn into the moment—the processional music, Olivia's radiant smile as she walked down the aisle on her father's arm, the traditional vows that somehow felt fresh and meaningful.

But underneath her enjoyment of the wedding, Delia's psychic senses couldn't stop detecting ripples and shifts in the supernatural situation downtown. The energy felt as if it was building toward something massive, something that would reach its peak in just a few hours. And even though her bond with Caleb was tenuous at best, she had a feeling that, whatever he was planning, he was running out of time.

"Do you, Olivia Marie Gunderson, take Alec Robert Donohue to be your lawfully wedded husband?"

"I do."

The words rang out clear and strong, and for a moment, the simple power of the marriage ceremony seemed to push back against the darkness that threatened the city. Could love be a force of protection...commitment a shield against chaos?

Right then, Delia thought that kind of energy could be exactly what they needed. Not only Delia's growing psychic abilities or Ty's angelic powers or even Pru's dogged pursuit of the truth, but the combined strength of everyone who cared about protecting this place and the people in it.

As Olivia and Alec embraced, sealing their union, another energy surge rolled across Las Vegas. This time, though, instead of hunkering down in the bunker of her psychic defenses, Delia reached out through her connection to Caleb and sent everything she had—her love for him, her determination to make sure he was safe, her absolute refusal to let Vinea's plan succeed.

For just a moment, she felt him receive the message. And in that moment, she sensed his surprise at the strength of what she was able to send, followed by something that seemed almost like hope.

The connection was severed almost as quickly as it had formed, but it was enough. She knew Caleb had gotten her message.

And she knew he was alive. They still had time.

The reception line formed right after the ceremony. As Delia waited her turn to congratulate the happy couple, the small evening bag she'd hung over one shoulder vibrated. Quickly, she pulled out her phone, thinking that was probably Pru telling her to hurry things along, even though Delia had told her friend that there was no chance of her getting away from all the wedding festivities until nine o'clock at the absolute earliest.

But no, the text was from an unknown number.

The ritual begins now. Come to Angel's Dream alone, or watch your cousin's new husband join her in widowhood before the night is over.

Her body stiffened, although it didn't seem as if anyone waiting on either side of her noticed anything wrong. That didn't matter, though.

No, what mattered was that Vinea knew exactly where she was...and knew which of her family members would be the most vulnerable to threats.

She looked down the receiving line to Olivia and Alec, both of them glowing with happiness as they accepted congratulations from their guests. Her parents, her aunt and uncle, all of Alec's family —none of them had any defenses against the kind of destruction Vinea was planning to rain down on the city.

Another text appeared on her phone.

You have one hour. After that, the newlyweds die, followed by everyone else you care about.

Delia's hands shook as she typed a quick message to Ty and Pru.

He's threatening my family. I have to go.

Ty's reply came back immediately.

Don't. It's a trap. We're close to finding another way in.

No time. He says one hour, or they die.

Delia, wait —

She turned off her phone and slipped it into her purse, then made her way through the crowd to the spot where her parents stood talking with some of Alec's relatives.

"Mom, Dad, I have to go," she said, having already manufactured an excuse as she headed over to talk to them. "Client emergency. Tell Olivia I'm sorry I'll miss the reception, but something has come up that I have to handle personally."

Her mother frowned. "Tonight? Did you tell your client that you were at a family wedding?"

"I did, but they're insisting. I need to go, or I'm going to lose this client." She gave them each a quick hug, breathing in the familiar scent of her mother's Dior perfume, trying to memorize the moment in case it was the last time she saw them. "I love you both."

"We love you too, Delia," her father said, although his expression was almost puzzled. While they were all secure in their love for one another, her family wasn't the most demonstrative one in the world. "Is everything all right?"

"It will be," she said, and hoped she was telling the truth. "But I have to go."

The drive from Little Chapel of Hearts to downtown Las Vegas would give her about fifteen minutes to figure out how to confront a lord of Hell and somehow rescue Caleb without getting them both killed in the process. Easy peasy.

Saturday night traffic was thick, and she found herself gritting her teeth as she lurched from one red light to another. But no...stressing about her slow progress was only going to make her that much more off balance.

Instead, she let her psychic abilities expand beyond the protective walls she'd built, allowing the full force of the ley line energy to flow through her body. The sensation nearly overwhelmed her— she became the center of a vast circuit connected to every supernatural site in the city, every person with even the smallest bit of psychic ability, every line of power that crisscrossed the valley.

But instead of trying to shut it out, she embraced it and let it fill her until her entire being hummed with borrowed power. If Vinea wanted to use the ley line network to fuel his ritual, then she would tap into that same network to stop him.

She could see the transformation of Angel's Dream Wedding Chapel from three blocks away. What had once been a simple white building with a kind of homegrown charm now seemed to exist partially in normal reality and partially in some other dimension altogether. Shadows moved across its surface in patterns that made her want to blink and look away, and the air around it shimmered with heat distortion despite the cool evening air.

Did it appear that way to everyone, or were her enhanced senses picking up on something that wouldn't be visible to most people?

She parked her little Kona what she hoped was a safe distance down the street and sat in the car for a moment, doing her best to gather her admittedly shaky courage. Her bond with Caleb hung on just enough that she could sense he was still alive. But she could also feel Vinea's overwhelming presence, a darkness so ancient and powerful that it made every instinct scream at her to run.

Instead, she calmly got out of the car and walked down the street, the heels of her dressy nude sandals clicking on the sidewalk, the supernatural energy of the city flowing through her like a river of light. Whatever happened next, she wouldn't let fear stop her from trying to save the man she loved.

The front door of Angel's Dream stood open, revealing an interior that definitely hadn't existed when she and Caleb had first visited the chapel. Beyond the threshold lay a vast space that seemed to stretch much farther than the building's exterior dimensions should have allowed, filled with malevolent shadows.

Delia pulled in a deep breath.

Hang on, Caleb, she thought.

I'm coming for you.

Chapter Fifteen

— ·(((·◉·)))· —

THE CEREMONIAL ROBES FELT HEAVIER with each step as the demons escorted Caleb through corridors that definitely hadn't existed when Angel's Dream was just a simple wedding chapel. The walls around him pulsed with a life of their own, black stone veined with lines of sickly red light that glowed like sullen magma, marble carved from the depths of Hell. Every so often, the architecture would shift slightly, angles rearranging themselves in ways that made his inner ear protest and his stomach lurch.

He'd been walking for what felt like hours, although Caleb suspected time moved differently in whatever pocket dimension Vinea had carved out of reality. The demon lord himself had vanished after delivering his final threats, leaving Caleb in the custody of six lesser demons who radiated the kind of casual menace that told him they'd be all too thrilled if he gave them an excuse to get violent.

Not that he was planning to.

Not yet, anyway.

The sabotage he'd sown in the ritual framework over the past day was still in place, tiny flaws and instabilities that would hopefully blossom into something much larger when the time came. But triggering those failsafes would require perfect timing, and Caleb still wasn't entirely sure when that moment would arrive.

His psychic bond with Delia had strengthened briefly during what he assumed was Olivia's wedding ceremony, a burst of warmth and love and resolve that had made his eyes burn with tears he didn't dare shed. She was alive, she was fighting, and somehow, she'd managed to tap into power sources he hadn't even known existed. That brief connection had also told him something else— she was planning something desperate, something that would put her directly in harm's way.

Be careful, he thought, projecting the mental message toward wherever she was, even though he knew she probably couldn't hear him through the supernatural static that filled the air around and under Angel's Dream. *I can't lose you.*

"Move faster," one of his guards growled at him, its voice a grind of metal over stone. The thing looked vaguely humanoid, but its skin had the texture of charcoal, and its eyes reminded him of embers glowing in a dying fire. "Lord Vinea grows impatient."

As much as Caleb would have liked to tell the demon what his lordship could do with his impatience, instead he picked up his pace, even though the heavy ceremonial robes made it difficult to move quickly. The fabric absorbed light, creating the illusion that he was wearing a hole cut out of reality itself. Symbols worked into the weave shivered at the edge of his peripheral vision and seemed to disappear if he tried to look at them directly, but he'd managed to introduce several subtle modifications into the garment's mystical circuitry. When the ritual energy really started flowing, those little alterations should create some interesting resonance patterns.

Assuming, of course, that he lived long enough to see them activated.

The corridor ended abruptly at a set of massive double doors carved from black stone with an oil-slick surface, possibly obsidian. As they approached, the doors swung open without any visible mechanism, revealing a chamber beyond that made Caleb's breath catch in his throat.

They weren't in Angel's Dream anymore. Hell, they weren't even in Las Vegas.

The space that stretched out before him was

vast and circular, carved directly into living red rock under an open desert sky. Stars wheeled overhead, and the air tasted of sage and dust and something else—something old and powerful that made his demon blood respond with unwelcome heat.

"Welcome to the true heart of the operation," Vinea said as he materialized from the shadows at the edge of the circle. The demon lord had abandoned his human guise again, and he wore dark robes similar to Caleb's, although they didn't do nearly enough to conceal his reptilian form. He offered his captive a smile full of razor-sharp teeth. "I trust the journey wasn't too arduous?"

Caleb forced himself to survey his surroundings with what he hoped looked like casual interest rather than growing horror. The circular space was easily a hundred feet across and had intricate symbols carved into every surface. But it wasn't the arcane geometry that made his skin crawl.

No, it was the physical evidence of how long this place must have been in use.

The rock walls were stained with what could only be centuries of accumulated blood. Bones had been embedded in the stone itself, as if previous sacrifices had been absorbed into the very structure of the chamber. And at the center of it all stood an altar that looked like it had been hewn from a single massive meteorite, its surface polished smooth by ages of use.

"This is where it all began," Vinea continued, beginning a slow transit of the chamber's perimeter, his black robes dragging on the equally ebony-hued stone floor. "Long before humans learned to build cities or write their little stories, this place was already ancient. The first demons to walk this plane used it as an anchor point, a way to stabilize their presence in this reality."

The history lesson was interesting, but Caleb was more focused on figuring out the chamber's supernatural defenses. The ley lines that had criss-crossed Las Vegas now seemed to converge here rather than at Angel's Dream, and he wondered how Vinea—or those he was working with—had managed to make it seem as if the wedding chapel had been their only focus.

Something he'd have to worry about later, though, since this convergence of currents had created a nexus of power that made the air shimmer with barely contained energy. But more than that, he could sense other presences somehow near... entities that felt old beyond measure, things that had been sleeping in the deep places of the earth and were now beginning to stir.

"I thought you said you'd only been planning this for the past few years," Caleb said, still trying to project an air of reluctant cooperation. Anything to make the demon lord think he was still on board with his hideous plans.

Also, he was curious. This chamber had been here for eons, not just a couple of years.

"Planning?" Vinea's laugh echoed strangely in the circular chamber. "My dear nephew, this was never about *planning*. This was about waiting for the ideal confluence of energies that would allow us to finally complete what was begun millennia ago."

The demon lord gestured toward the altar, and Caleb noticed for the first time that channels had been carved into its surface—channels that led to a complex network of grooves cut into the chamber floor, all of them leading toward points around the circle's perimeter where other, smaller altars stood. Seven of them, he counted, each one positioned at what had to be a critical node in the chamber's mystical architecture.

"Your blood will flow through these channels," Vinea explained casually. "Each drop will carry a piece of your essence, your connection to both planes, your ability to serve as a bridge between the mortal realm and the domains below. As the life drains from your body, the portals will stabilize, creating permanent gateways that can never be closed."

The mental image of his blood literally flowing through carved stone channels made Caleb fight hard against his gag reflex, but he managed to keep his expression neutral. "And then what? You bring through a few hundred demons and call it a successful invasion?"

"Oh, nephew." Vinea's burning eyes glittered with anticipation...and something else.

Scorn? Possibly. Good thing that Caleb didn't give a rat's ass what the demon lord thought of him.

"You're still thinking far too small," Vinea continued. "This isn't about a few hundred demons. This is about opening the floodgates, allowing every entity that's been trapped below to finally claim their rightful place in this reality. Demons, fallen angels, corrupted spirits, entities that predate your species by eons—all of them finally free to walk under an open sky."

This description sent ice flooding through Caleb's veins. He'd caught glimpses of some of the entities that lurked in Hell's deepest circles, things so ancient and powerful that even regular demons gave them a wide berth. If creatures like that crossed over to Earth....

Well, it would make H.P. Lovecraft's worst nightmare look like a walk in the park.

"How many are we talking about?" Caleb asked. He sounded steady enough, which could only be a good thing. Or maybe it was simply that his brain wouldn't allow itself to absorb all the horrors that lay ahead if the ritual was successful.

"Hundreds of thousands," Vinea replied with

obvious satisfaction. "Perhaps millions, once word spreads that the barriers between planes have finally fallen. Your precious mortal civilization will adapt, or it will be swept aside."

Millions. The casual way Vinea spoke of essentially ending human civilization made white-hot rage flare in Caleb's chest, his demon blood responding with heat that made the air around him shimmer slightly. For just a moment, small flames danced between his fingers before he wrestled them back under control.

"I see the fire is still there," the demon lord remarked. He looked pleased, although trying to assign human emotions to a being such as he was always problematic. "Excellent. That passion will make the ritual far more effective."

Caleb flexed his fingers, feeling the bonds that held his powers in check respond to his emotional state. The mystical cables were sophisticated, but they weren't perfect. And anger, he had begun to discover, seemed to create fluctuations in their effectiveness.

"When do we start?" he asked, figuring there wasn't much point in delaying the inevitable.

"Soon." Vinea gestured toward the western edge of the chamber, where Caleb could see the last dregs of sunset painting a mountain range in hues of blood and umber. "The alignment reaches its peak in approximately four hours. We'll begin the preparatory phase as soon as the sun has finished setting, which is only a few moments from now."

Four hours. That wasn't much time for his team to mount a rescue, especially when they had no real idea where he was being held. Yes, they could always converge on Angel's Dream, since that was where they thought the ritual would take place, but they would arrive there and find absolutely nothing. For all he knew, now that Vinea had removed him to this horror of a ritual chamber somewhere out in the desert, the demon lord would have allowed the wedding chapel to return to its usual state.

And sure, the psychic bond with Delia was still there, that gossamer-thin thread of connection that told him she was still alive and moving, but he couldn't send clear messages through the supernatural static that filled this place. He couldn't tell her that he'd been moved somewhere far outside the city.

Which meant he needed to be ready to trigger his sabotage on his own, without backup.

The thought should have been terrifying. Instead, Caleb found it oddly liberating. Having to act alone simplified things in a way. No one else to worry about, no one else to protect. Just him and a plan that had maybe a ten-percent chance of working on a good day.

He liked those odds better than he probably should have.

"There is one more thing," Vinea said, his tone shifting to something that might have been regret if it had come from anyone else. "I'm afraid your lovely Ms. Dunne decided to involve herself in tonight's activities."

At once, Caleb straightened. His demon blood wanted to flare with fire again, but he somehow managed to hold it in check. "What do you mean?"

"She's currently attempting to breach the defenses at Angel's Dream," the demon lord replied, obvious satisfaction glinting in his fiery eyes. "Walked right up to the front door, bless her brave little heart. I do so admire mortals who are willing to sacrifice themselves for love."

No. No, no, no. Delia was supposed to be safe, supposed to be with her family at the wedding reception, as far from this nightmare as possible. The idea of her trapped in that supernatural maze, facing creatures that could snuff out her life without a second thought, made something primal and furious rise within him.

"You said you wouldn't touch her if I cooperated," he said, and this time he didn't bother to hide the rage in his voice.

"I said she would be safe as long as you fulfilled your role," Vinea corrected him, voice smooth as the basalt floor beneath their feet. "But when she chose to come looking for you, well...that rather changed the parameters of our agreement, didn't it?"

Flames erupted from Caleb's fists, white-hot fire that made the air around him shimmer. The bonds holding his powers strained, mystical cables smoking as supernatural heat met whatever materials they'd been crafted from.

"Easy, nephew," Vinea said, although he sounded more amused than concerned. "Your anger is delicious, but you won't be going anywhere. The chamber's defenses will hold you here until the ritual begins."

The casual dismissal of his fury made Caleb want to launch himself at the demon lord, bonds or no bonds. But beneath the rage, a cold part of his mind was calculating distances and angles, searching for weaknesses in the chamber's defenses, looking for any advantage he could exploit.

The sabotage he'd woven into the ritual framework was still in place. And now, with his emotions running high, he could feel cracks forming in the mystical bonds that held his powers in check.

"I won't let you hurt her," Caleb said.

"You won't have a choice," Vinea replied. Then his reptilian features arranged themselves into something like concern. "Though I confess, I'm curious to see how she fares against the defenses. Her psychic abilities have grown remarkably in recent weeks. She might even survive long enough for you to say goodbye." With that parting shot, the demon lord's form began to shimmer and fade. "I must attend to our uninvited guest. Don't worry —I'll leave you with guards to keep you company. Wouldn't want you getting lonely before the main event."

As Vinea vanished completely, the six demon guards moved to surround the altar, their burning eyes fixed on Caleb.

He looked up at the stars wheeling overhead and reached out to Delia. She was there, blazing with determination and fear and a love so powerful it made him ache for her that much more. She was fighting her way through Angel's Dream's twisted corridors, facing horrors that would break most people.

Hold on, he thought, projecting the message with everything he had. *I'm coming for you. Just hold on.*

But even as he sent the thought, he knew the truth. He was trapped here, bound by mystical chains in a ritual chamber carved from ancient stone. The only way out was through the ritual itself—and that meant triggering his sabotage early, before Vinea could complete the preparations.

It was time to stop playing along.

Caleb closed his eyes and reached deep into himself, past the human shell that made him vulnerable, past the fear and doubt that whispered he wasn't strong enough. He touched the core of his dual nature, the place where mortal determination met demonic fire.

The mystical bonds began to smoke and crack.

"Bring me to the altar," Caleb said, making sure he sounded resigned rather than grimly determined. "Let's get this over with."

The demon guards exchanged glances, as though they weren't quite sure they should do anything with their master gone. After that brief hesitation, however, they moved to comply. As they escorted him toward the meteorite altar at the chamber's center, each step made the carved symbols on the floor pulse brighter in response to his presence. By the time he reached the altar itself, the entire chamber was alive with sickly red light.

"Lie down," one of the guards commanded, and Caleb complied, settling himself on the chilly stone surface. The meteorite felt wrong against his back, too smooth and too cold, as if it was actively draining heat from his body.

The largest of the demon guards produced what looked like a ceremonial dagger, its blade carved from the same black stone as the chamber walls. But when it held the weapon up to the starlight, Caleb could see that it wasn't entirely black—threads of silver ran through the obsidian, forming patterns that didn't follow any earthly geometry.

"Lord Vinea said to begin the preparatory bloodletting," the demon growled. "You are to remain conscious throughout."

Caleb stared up at the stars above him and tried to center himself. The sabotage he'd planted throughout the ritual framework was ready to trigger, and the bonds holding his powers in check were weakening with every surge of emotion.

All he needed was the right moment.

"Any last words?" the demon asked as it positioned the dagger over Caleb's chest.

"Yeah," Caleb said, making sure he met the creature's burning gaze without flinching. "You really should have done your homework on quarter demons."

Before the demon could ask what he meant, Caleb let the fury he'd been holding in finally explode outward. White-hot flames erupted from his body, fueled by every ounce of anger and determination and love he possessed. The mystical bonds holding his powers vaporized, and the ceremonial robes he wore began to smoke as the modifications he'd worked into their fabric activated.

The demon guard stumbled backward, surprise flickering across its inhuman features. "Impossible. The containment field should have—"

"Should have been designed by someone who

actually understood how mixed blood works," Caleb broke in as he rolled off the altar, flames wreathing his entire body. "See, the thing about quarter demons is that we don't follow the same rules as full demons. Our power doesn't come only from Hell—it comes from the connection between planes. And you just brought me to the most powerful nexus point on the continent."

The chamber's mystical architecture was responding to his presence, ley lines blazing brighter as his unleashed power fed back into the network. But instead of stabilizing the ritual frame-work, his energy created cascading failures throughout the system, turning Vinea's carefully balanced equations into chaos.

The six demon guards rushed him, but Caleb was ready. Two years in Hell had taught him that sometimes the best defense was an overwhelming offense. He met their charge with a wall of fire that sent all but one of them scrambling backward, their forms beginning to dissolve as the flames ate away at their ability to maintain a physical form on this plane.

The remaining guard—larger and more substantial than the others — managed to get close enough to rake claws across Caleb's ribs. Pain flared through his side, but the injury only fed his anger, making his flames burn that much hotter. He grabbed the creature by what passed for its throat and channeled every ounce of heat he could muster directly into its core.

The demon's death scream echoed off the chamber walls as it crumbled to ash.

Around him, the ritual framework continued to unravel. Mystical conduits sparked and failed as his sabotage spread through the chamber's architecture. Each failure sent tremors through the stone, and the careful patterns of the summoning circle began to warp.

But something was wrong. He could feel it in the way the ley line energy was responding to his interference. Instead of simply disrupting the ritual, his actions had created a feedback loop, and raw power was beginning to flow back through the network directly into him.

Caleb tried to shut it down, to stop drawing from the nexus, but the energy had momentum now. It poured into him like water through a broken dam, more raw power than he'd ever channeled before. The pain from his injuries faded to nothing as supernatural fire raced through his veins.

It was incredible. Intoxicating. He could feel his human limitations beginning to burn away, replaced by something vast and terrible and utterly without mercy.

More, something whispered in the back of his

mind. *Take more. You can end this. You can end everything.*

The chamber walls began to crack under the strain of so much uncontrolled energy. Chunks of ancient stone crashed down around him, but Caleb barely noticed. The power kept flowing, kept building, kept changing him into something that could contain forces no mortal was meant to touch.

His human side screamed warnings he ignored, too drunk on the rush of absolute power to care about any of the possible consequences of what he was doing.

Silver flames erupted from his body, no longer the controlled fire he'd learned to wield, but something primal and chaotic. The temperature in the chamber spiked, ancient stone beginning to bubble and melt under the assault.

Delia, he thought desperately, trying to hold onto some shred of his humanity. *Have to save Delia.*

But the power was too much. It was burning away the human parts that made him who he was and replacing them with pure demonic essence.

The fire consumed everything. His thoughts fragmented, scattering like ash on the wind. The last coherent image in his mind was Delia's face, the way she'd smiled at him the last time they'd been together, the love in her eyes when she'd said she believed in him.

Then even that was gone, swallowed by silver flames.

Somewhere distant, he sensed Vinea returning, could feel the demon lord's shock at finding the ritual chamber in ruins and the sacrificial victim transformed into something wild and dangerous. But by then, Caleb was too far gone to care.

The thing that had been Caleb Lockwood lay motionless on the cracked floor, wreathed in silver fire, suspended between transformation and destruction. The power still flowed through him, but without conscious direction, it had nowhere to go. His body trembled with the strain of containing forces that should have torn him apart.

All he could do was wait—for death, for completion of the transformation, or for something else entirely.

He waited for Delia.

Chapter Sixteen

—·«‹‹‹·◉·›››·»—

THE INTERIOR OF WHAT HAD ONCE BEEN Angel's Dream Wedding Chapel defied every law of physics Delia thought she understood. The space stretched impossibly far in all directions, with walls that seemed to curve and shift the moment she looked away from them. Gothic arches soared over-head, carved from black stone that pulsed with veins of sickly red light, while shadows moved with deliberate purpose across surfaces that seemed to crawl with oil-slick darkness.

But none of that mattered compared to the figure materializing at the center of it all.

Vinea was something that belonged in mankind's oldest nightmares. He stood nearly eight feet tall, all black scaly skin and burning eyes, and the dark robes he wore dragged on the floor. "Ms. Dunne," he said, odd, shifting tones underlying his voice and making her ears ache. His tone sounded almost jovial. "How delightful that you chose to join us. I was beginning to think you'd lost your nerve."

Willing herself not to react, Delia stepped farther into the cathedral of horrors, the psychic energy flowing through her making every supernatural symbol carved into the walls flicker and pulse in response to her presence. The protective barriers she'd built around her consciousness held firm, but she could feel the sheer wrongness of this place pressing against them like a tide of dark sludge.

"Where is he?" she demanded, surprised by how steady her voice sounded.

She knew she'd never been this frightened. Not ever, even when waking from the worst nightmares.

Maybe it was because she knew she couldn't wake up from this.

The demon lord's fiery eyes glittered with amusement. "Straight to the point. I do admire directness in mortals. It's so refreshingly honest compared to the labyrinthine machinations my own kind prefer."

Before she could even begin to think of how she should respond to that remark, he gestured toward the far end of the chapel. The air there began to shimmer, and Delia's breath caught in her throat.

Through the rippling space, she could see a vast circular chamber carved from red desert rock under an open sky. And there, lying motionless on the cracked floor, was Caleb.

Silver flames wreathed his form, flickering weakly, as if they didn't have enough fuel to sustain them. His eyes were closed, his body rigid, and she could sense through their psychic bond that something was terribly wrong. The energy signature that was uniquely his felt fractured, as if something was trying to overwrite his essential nature from within.

"As you can see, your lover has encountered some...difficulties," Vinea continued, his tone still far too casual. "The boy tried to disrupt my work, and in the process, he drew far more power to himself than his mixed heritage could safely contain. The transformation has begun."

The transformation. The thing Caleb feared most—his demon blood overwhelming his humanity, taking away everything that made him who he was.

"What did you do to him?" The words came out sharp as the crack of a whip, and she watched Vinea's smile widen in response to her obvious fury.

"I did nothing," the demon lord said, and the worst part was that she could sense he was telling the truth. "He did this to himself. In his desperation to sabotage the ritual and protect you, he accessed power sources beyond his capacity to control. Now the demonic essence is consuming what remains of his human soul."

Through their psychic bond, Delia could feel Caleb's consciousness flickering like a guttering candle. He was still in there, still fighting, but the transformation was pulling him deeper with each passing moment. Soon there would be nothing left but demon, and the man she loved would be gone forever.

"I have to reach him," she said, and took a step toward the shimmering portal.

"I'm afraid that won't be possible," Vinea replied as he moved to block her path. "The ritual chamber is collapsing due to your lover's interference. Even if you could reach him, you'd both be crushed when the pocket dimension implodes."

Another wave of ley line power flooded through the city, and Delia felt it flow through her as well, its wild, sparking energy reminding her of downed electrical lines. Instead of fighting the sensation, she embraced it, drawing strength from every psychically sensitive person in Las Vegas, from every connection of love and loyalty and pure grit that bound the city's residents together.

"You're not stopping me," she said, and this time her voice resonated with determined undertones that made the carved symbols on the walls flicker uncertainly.

Vinea's unearthly features shifted from amusement to genuine interest. Or at least, she thought that might be the cause of that flare of red in his flame-hued eyes. "Fascinating. The reports of your growing abilities were accurate, it seems. But raw power without training is like a loaded gun in the hands of a child—dangerous to everyone, especially the wielder."

The demon lord raised one clawed hand, and the air around Delia thickened, pressing against her from all sides like invisible quicksand. She tried to move and found her limbs responding sluggishly, as if she was trying to run underwater.

But the psychic energy flowing through her reacted to the attack, automatically creating barriers of compressed will and determination. The crushing pressure lessened, then disappeared entirely as she pushed back against the demon lord's assault.

"Interesting," Vinea murmured, genuine surprise flickering across his inhuman features. "Raw talent combined with instinctive defense mechanisms. You really are quite remarkable."

"Thanks," Delia said dryly, even as she reached out with her newfound abilities. The ley line network responded to her will like an extension of her nervous system, power flowing wherever she directed it. "I've always been kind of an over-achiever."

The demon lord's laughter echoed strangely in the transformed space. "Confidence in the face of overwhelming odds. Another admirable human trait. But I'm afraid enthusiasm is no substitute for experience."

This time, when Vinea attacked, it wasn't with supernatural pressure, but something far more insidious. Tendrils of darkness reached out from the walls, wrapping around her arms and legs like living chains. The moment they touched her skin, they began to drain away the psychic energy she'd been accumulating, siphoning her power into the chapel's twisted architecture, making it even stronger, even stranger.

Panic flared as she realized her abilities were being systematically stripped away. The protective barriers around her consciousness wavered, and suddenly she could sense the full horror of what Vinea had created here — not just a ritual site, but a vast machine designed to harvest and process human suffering on an enormous scale.

Focus, she told herself, forcing down the terror that threatened to overwhelm her rational mind. *You're not helpless. You've already come farther than you ever thought you could. But you need to fight on your own terms...not his.*

Instead of trying to break free from the

draining tendrils, Delia stopped fighting them entirely, letting herself go still and calm. The darkness rushed into her, clearly expecting to find a helpless victim. Instead, it encountered something it wasn't prepared for—the combined love and determination of all the people she was fighting to protect.

Her parents, safe at the wedding reception. Olivia and Alec, now married and beginning their new life together. Caleb, trapped in transformation but still alive, still fighting. Pru and Ty, racing across the city to mount a rescue that might already be too late.

The darkness that had been draining her energy found itself overwhelmed by something it couldn't process or contain. Love was a force that connected everything in the universe, that underlaid everything ever imagined or felt, everything ever created or shared. And when that energy was focused and directed by someone with the will and the desperation to wield it....

The tendrils holding her burst into white flames that made the demon lord stumble backward, his unnatural features twisted with actual pain as the light seared his unholy form.

"Impossible," he snarled, his composure finally cracking. "You're nothing more than a human. You don't have access to that kind of power."

"You're right," Delia said as she stepped

forward, white light beginning to radiate from her skin in pulses that matched her heartbeat. "I don't. But they do."

She gestured around them, and at once, the chapel was filled with the presence of everyone in Las Vegas who'd ever fought to protect something they loved. Not physically—she wasn't summoning ghosts or spirits — but their combined will, their shared determination to stand against a darkness that threatened everything they cared about.

The demon lord's burning eyes widened as he seemed to realize what Delia had just summoned. "A lattice. You've created a psychic lattice."

"I didn't create anything," Delia corrected him, even as she focused on drawing still more power from the connections that bound the city together. If someone had asked, she couldn't even have said how she was doing any of this. It had come to her out of pure instinct, like knowing how to breathe. "I just realized I could use what was already there."

Vinea raised both hands, dark energy crackling between his claws. "Clever. But cleverness alone won't save you from what's coming."

His assault began as a whisper in the back of her mind—*you're not strong enough*—but within seconds, the doubt exploded into a cacophony of self-hatred that made her stagger backward. Her knees buckled as wave after wave of despair crashed over her, each one bearing the weight of every failure she'd ever experienced, every moment of weakness, every time she'd let someone down.

The psychic lattice she was drawing on began to fray at the edges as Vinea's attack found its target. The connections that had seemed so strong moments before now might as well have been spider silk, ready to snap at the slightest pressure. She could feel the people of Las Vegas—*her* people — slipping away from her one by one as their own buried fears and doubts were dragged to the surface.

Caleb will die because you're not good enough to save him.

Your family will suffer because you thought you could play hero.

Everyone you love will pay for your arrogance.

The voices weren't coming from outside her head—they were her own thoughts, twisted and amplified until they became weapons turned against her. Delia gasped, hands clutching at her temples as the assault intensified.

For a moment, she wavered. What if she wasn't strong enough? What if all this power wasn't enough to save Caleb, to stop the portal network... to protect all the people she loved?

But then she felt it—a familiar warmth pushing through the otherworldly static that filled the chapel. Caleb was reaching out to her, and what she sensed in that contact made her gasp.

He was still there. Even consumed by transformation, even burning from within, some core part of him was holding on. Waiting for her.

Together, came his mental voice, faint and fractured but unmistakably his. *We do this together.*

Delia reached back through their connection, sending everything she had—her love, her resolve, her absolute refusal to let the darkness win. The psychic lattice she'd tapped into exploded outward like a supernova, encompassing not just Las Vegas but stretching out across the desert to the desolate place where Caleb lay in his silver cocoon of fire.

The moment their powers merged, reality shuddered.

The walls of Angel's Dream began to crack, competing forces tearing at the pocket dimension Vinea had created. Through the portal, Delia could see the ritual chamber collapsing, ancient stones crumbling as Caleb's sabotage finally reached its full effect.

"No!" The demon lord's roar shook the entire structure, but his voice was weaker now. "You cannot disrupt work that will take centuries to repair!"

"Watch us," Delia said, and poured everything she had into her psychic link with Caleb.

It was like creating some kind of supernatural feedback loop. The power Vinea had been accumulating for his ritual suddenly had nowhere to go as

Caleb's sabotage cascaded through the network. Energy that should have opened permanent gateways to Hell instead began to collapse back on itself, creating a chain reaction that spread across the entire Las Vegas valley.

Through her strange new senses, Delia could see the demon lord's carefully constructed network failing node by node. Wedding chapels and event venues across the city suddenly found their supernatural infestations simply...gone. The ley line energy that had been building toward critical mass began to dissipate, flowing back into natural patterns that had existed for millennia.

But Vinea wasn't finished. As his grand design crumbled around him, the demon lord gathered his remaining power for one final assault—not against Delia or the lattice she'd been using to bolster her strength, but against the pocket dimension itself.

"If I cannot have this plane," he snarled, his form beginning to blur and shift as reality bent around him, "then I'll make sure you lose everything as well."

The walls of the chapel began to collapse inward as Vinea tried to fold the entire space in on itself.

Delia sensed Caleb's flash of alarm, followed immediately by his desperate attempt to break free from the transformation that held him. But he was still too far away, still too consumed by the changes ravaging his body.

That was when the front door of the chapel exploded inward in a shower of splinters and light as bright as an atomic blast.

Ty burst through the opening with brilliant white light blazing around him like armor, and when he spread his arms, silver flames erupted from his fingertips to race along the chapel's walls, stabilizing the collapsing dimensional structure.

"Delia!" His voice traveled across the chaos as Pru appeared behind him, her laptop bag slung over her shoulder. "Go to him! We'll hold this place together!"

Delia thought she understood what Ty meant. The meteorite altar where Caleb lay wasn't just a focus for the ritual—it was the physical anchor that allowed Vinea's pocket dimension to exist. If she could reach Caleb, if she could use their combined power to disrupt the anchor....

The demon lord realized the same thing. With a roar of rage, Vinea launched himself toward the dimensional gateway that showed the ritual chamber, clawed hands reaching forward.

Delia didn't think. She simply moved, drawing on every ounce of power she could access and hurling herself through the shimmering portal after him.

The transition was nauseating, like being

turned inside out while riding a roller coaster through a blender. But then she was there, in the vast circular chamber where the real ritual had been taking place, and she could see Caleb clearly for the first time since this nightmare began.

He was alive, but changed. Silver flames wreathed his form, and when his eyes snapped open at her arrival, they blazed with a terrible light that made her think of volcanic glass—beautiful and dangerous and not at all human. The ceremonial robes he wore had burned away completely, leaving him surrounded by a corona of supernatural fire.

But Vinea was there, too, his massive form bearing down on Caleb with murderous intent.

"Stay away from him!" Delia shouted, and white light erupted from her hands to strike the demon lord square in the chest.

The impact sent Vinea staggering backward, black ichor spilling from the wounds she'd just inflicted. Even injured and weakened, though, the ancient being was still a lord of Hell.

"Two for the price of one," Vinea panted, his terrible red gaze fixed on both of them now, his reptilian features twisted with pain and rage. "How convenient. I can drain you both and still have enough energy to complete the ritual."

The demon lord raised his hands, and darkness began to pour from the carved symbols that covered the chamber walls. This wasn't the mere absence of light, but something actively malevolent that devoured hope and love and everything good in the world.

It washed over Delia in a tide of despair, threatening to drown everything she was in an ocean of suffering. But then Caleb's hand closed around hers—his skin fever-hot but solid, real, somehow still him despite the transformation—and their combined power flared outward like a star being born.

"Together," he said, and his voice was different, deeper, with harmonics that made the very air seem to vibrate. But underneath the otherworldly intonation, she could still hear the man she loved. "Just like you said."

They stood in the maelstrom, their fingers intertwined, facing down a wounded but still dangerous lord of Hell with nothing to aid them but their love for each other and their refusal to let the darkness win.

It should have been suicide.

And yet....

The power that flowed between them was something that existed at the very core of reality itself—the force that bound atoms together, that lit the stars, that connected every living thing in an invisible web of shared existence.

Vinea's ferocious attack smashed into that

combined radiance and simply...stopped. The darkness that should have consumed them found itself unable to comprehend what it was facing. Love was a law of physics, as basic as gravity or electromagnetism.

And when that law was violated, reality itself pushed back.

"Impossible," Vinea whispered, his ancient eyes wide with something that might have been fear. Black, smoking blood poured from his wounds now and pooled at his feet. "This plane...the barriers between worlds...they're not supposed to...."

His words cut off as silver flames began to race along his form, not the hellfire he commanded but something purer, brighter. The light was coming from the chamber itself, from the ley line network, from every person in the city whose psychic gifts had been sparked by the unbridled energy flowing around them.

"The portals," Delia breathed as understanding struck. "We're—we're reversing them."

Instead of allowing entities from Hell to cross over to Earth, the dimensional gateways had begun to pull in the opposite direction. And Vinea, as the primary architect of the network, was caught in the backflow.

"No!" The demon lord's roar shook the entire chamber as his form began to fade despite his desperate struggles. "This isn't over! I'll return! I'll—"

His words were cut off when he vanished entirely, pulled back to Hell by the very network he'd created to escape it.

The chamber shuddered as the ancient stones began to crack and crumble in earnest now. With Vinea gone and the ritual framework completely sabotaged, the pocket dimension was collapsing, reality snapping back to normal.

"We need to get out of here," Caleb said, his voice strained, and she could tell he was struggling to maintain control. The silver flames wreathing his body flickered dangerously. "This whole place is coming down."

But even as he spoke, Delia could see the real problem. The energy Caleb had channeled earlier —and the power still flowing through him now— was threatening to complete the transformation. His human side couldn't handle that much raw demonic essence indefinitely.

"Not without you," she said firmly, then reached out through their bond to share not just her psychic abilities but her essential humanity— the core of herself that would always be mortal, grounded.

Real.

The effect was immediate. The silver flames that surrounded Caleb's form began to fade as his dual nature found its balance again. He was still changed—she had a feeling the experience he'd just suffered through had awakened parts of his demon heritage that could never be put back to sleep—but he was still himself.

Still the man she loved.

Hand in hand, they ran through the collapsing chamber while chunks of meteorite and ancient basalt crashed down around them. The portal back to Angel's Dream was still there, but it was shrinking rapidly as the dimensional anchor failed.

They dove through the shimmering gateway just as it snapped shut behind them, tumbling onto the floor of what was once again simply a wedding chapel.

Ty and Pru rushed over to help them up, both of them looking relieved...but also as if they weren't quite sure what had just happened.

"Is it over?" Pru asked, the satchel that carried her laptop and other odds and ends threatening to slip off her shoulder. She yanked it back up with an impatient gesture, as if she couldn't believe she had to waste time on something so trivial.

Caleb pushed himself to his feet, then helped Delia stand. The silver flames were gone, but she could still sense the change in him—power held in perfect balance, no longer fighting his dual nature but embracing it.

"It's over," he said, and his voice was his own again, warm and human and wonderfully familiar.

Through the chapel's windows, Delia caught a glimpse of the city she loved returning to its normal, neon-lit self. The supernatural storm that had hovered overhead for more than a day was dissipating, ley line energy flowing back into its natural patterns. She could sense that the network of psychically sensitive individuals was still there, but it was no longer being drained or controlled by an outside force.

"What about Vinea?" Ty asked as he looked around the chapel, his angelic senses apparently still detecting residual traces of the demon lord's presence.

"Banished," Delia replied. "But not destroyed, unfortunately. I suppose he'll probably try again at some point."

"They generally do," Ty remarked, his expression deadpan.

"Let him," Caleb said, his arm slipping around Delia's waist as if he never intended to let go of her again. "We'll be ready."

They walked out of Angel's Dream Wedding Chapel and back into the normal world, and Delia pulled in a deep breath. She'd just been through something no ordinary human should ever experience, and yet she knew she needed to forget as much of it as possible, needed to find a way back to herself.

They walked Pru and Ty over to his truck, which was the sole vehicle in the chapel's parking lot.

"Mine's just down the street," she told them.

"Maybe we should go with you," Pru said, and Ty glanced up into the night sky, now free of clouds, with a glorious full moon shining down on the street.

"It's safe," he said, and Caleb nodded.

"We're fine." A pause, and he added, "Thanks."

Ty shrugged. "No problem. You two did most of the heavy lifting anyway."

And he went around to open the passenger door for Prudence.

After waving goodbye, Delia and Caleb continued down the block to the spot where her little white Kona waited for them. It felt as if she'd parked it there a hundred years ago, but it seemed just fine.

"So," she said, as Caleb climbed into the passenger seat and she reached over to fasten her seatbelt, "want to go crash a wedding reception?"

His smile was warm and real and utterly human, despite everything he'd just been through. "Thought you'd never ask."

Chapter Seventeen

—‹‹‹‹‹·◎·›››·—

THE DRIVE TO ANTHEM TOOK ALMOST twenty-five minutes...mostly because it felt as if every single person in Las Vegas had somehow sensed the change in atmosphere and had decided to get out and party...and every mile of it gave Caleb time to take stock of the changes that had occurred in his body during his confrontation with Vinea. The silver flames were gone, and the demonic energy that had threatened to consume him completely had settled into something more manageable, but it still felt as if a cell-deep shift had taken place. The barriers between his human and demon natures had dissolved entirely, leaving him something new—neither fully human nor purely demonic, but a perfect synthesis of both.

This new normal should have been terrifying. Instead, he found it oddly liberating.

"You're awfully quiet," Delia observed from the driver's seat of her Kona. She'd insisted on playing chauffeur, claiming he looked like he was about to fall over, and Caleb hadn't bothered to argue. The adrenaline crash from their battle with Vinea was hitting him harder than he'd expected, making him glad that all he had to do for now was sit there and watch the lights of Las Vegas pass by outside the little SUV's window.

"Just thinking," he replied, and gave an experimental flex of his fingers. Small sparks of silver fire danced between them before disappearing, although he noted the silvery hue was beginning to fade and turn warmer, more the color of the fire he was used to summoning. That reassured him, made him think that, even if he might never return to what he'd once been, he'd still be able to figure out a way to live with this new normal. "How are you holding up?"

Delia sent him a quick glance, her expression thoughtful, before she returned her attention to the crowded streets around them. "I feel like I should be a wreck. Instead, I feel almost stronger, which I know must sound weird." She paused, then added with a rueful smile, "And I'm starving. I guess saving the world works up quite an appetite."

The casual way she referred to what they'd just accomplished made Caleb's chest tighten with an emotion he couldn't quite identify. Pride, he thought. Or maybe love.

All right, definitely love, if he was going to be honest with himself.

"Good thing we're heading to a reception, then," he said as he settled back in his seat. "It sounded like your cousin was planning a pretty good party."

The Anthem Country Club sat nestled in the foothills southeast of Las Vegas, its Mediterranean-style architecture and manicured grounds a stark contrast to the desert landscape that surrounded it. As they pulled into the circular drive, Caleb caught a glimpse of a warm glow of lights from the private dining room where the wedding reception was being held. Through the room's floor-to-ceiling windows, he saw people talking and laughing, celebrating the beginning of Olivia and Alec's new life together.

It looked so normal. Beautifully, blessedly normal.

And damn, he was ready for some normal.

No, scratch that. A whole *hell* of a lot of normal.

"Are you sure we should be crashing the party like this?" he asked as they approached the entrance. "I mean, we're not exactly dressed for a country club reception."

Delia glanced down at her wrinkled green

sheath dress, which had somehow survived their interdimensional adventure without any major stains but still looked a little worse for wear, then over at his jeans and rumpled black shirt—luckily, he'd kept them on beneath the ceremonial robes, or he would have been wandering around in his underwear—before she gave a philosophical shrug. "We look like we've been through hell and back. Which, I suppose, we have. Anyway," she added with a grin, "I'm family. They have to let me in, right?"

He sure hoped so.

The reception was in full swing when they entered the dining room. Olivia and Alec were on the small dance floor that had been laid out in the middle of the space, swaying to a jazz standard that Caleb thought he recognized but couldn't quite place. The bride's slim white dress had its train bustled up and out of the way, and her face was radiant with happiness as she gazed up at her new husband. Around them, guests mingled with drinks in hand, sharing stories and laughter, completely unaware of how close they'd all come to disaster just a short while earlier.

"Delia!" Linda Dunne spotted them first, hurrying over and looking relieved. Caleb didn't know what story Delia had given her mother to explain her absence, but it had clearly been enough to make Linda worry that she wouldn't show up for the reception at all. "I'm so glad you could finally make it. How did everything go with your client?"

"It worked out fine," Delia replied smoothly as she gave her mother a quick hug. "Sorry I had to duck out like that. But you remember Caleb, right?"

"Of course," Linda said, then turned to him and offered him a friendly smile. "It's wonderful that you could join us."

His answering smile felt rusty when he slapped it on, as if his face wasn't sure what to do with such an expression. However, Linda didn't seem to notice anything odd as he replied, "I'm glad to be here. It's beautiful."

And it was. The private dining room overlooked the golf course, and the city lights of Las Vegas twinkled in the distance. With the white linens on the round tables scattered around the room, crystal stemware, and arrangements of white hydrangea and peonies everywhere, everything looked elegant and understated...and a good deal more elaborate than the simple dinner for friends and family that Delia had first mentioned to him.

Well, like a lot of other things, weddings often got kind of out of control.

"Have you eaten?" Linda asked, now looking a little concerned. "The kitchen here did an amazing job with dinner, but there's still plenty left."

He supposed that was one thing most mothers had in common. No one would have ever nominated Blair Lockwood for a Mother of the Year award, but even she'd always wanted to make sure her son had plenty to eat.

"We're starving," Delia admitted, and her mother immediately began steering them toward a buffet that had been set up along one wall.

As they made their way across the room, Caleb could sense the subtle shift in the supernatural landscape around him. The ley line energy that had been building toward critical mass all day now flowed in natural patterns again, no longer twisted into the hellish network Vinea had created. But he could also sense something else—other psychically sensitive individuals scattered throughout the reception, their abilities awakened by the night's events but now settling into a new equilibrium.

"You feel it, too," Delia murmured beside him, and he realized she must have been sensing the energy flows as well.

"Yes," he replied quietly, grateful that Vinea's meddling didn't appear to have wreaked any permanent damage. "It's like the whole city just took a deep breath and relaxed."

And that meant he and Delia could, too.

They filled their plates with prime rib and salmon, roasted vegetables, and the most succulent potatoes au gratin he'd ever eaten. The food was excellent, but Caleb found himself more interested in watching Delia interact with her extended family. She moved through the room with easy grace, accepting congratulations on her cousin's behalf, sharing stories about the wedding preparations that made it sound as if the change of venue had been an amusing lark rather than a desperate attempt to keep everyone from getting sucked into a hellmouth, and waving off her rumpled dress with a kind of natural ease that made him more in love with her than ever.

He knew this was what he'd been fighting to protect. Not just Delia herself, but everything she represented—everything this family gathering represented. Watching her laugh at something her uncle said, seeing the way her face lit up when Olivia came over to thank her for all her help, Caleb understood on a visceral level why the demons' plan had been so fundamentally terrible.

It wasn't just about the potential body count of such a demonic takeover, although that would have been horrific enough. No, even worse would have been the destruction of everything that made life worth living in the first place.

That made being mortal so wonderfully fragile and perfect.

"Penny for your thoughts," Delia said as she slid up beside him where he stood near the windows overlooking the golf course.

"Just thinking about how differently this night could have gone," he replied as he accepted the glass of champagne she offered him. "If we hadn't stopped Vinea...."

"But we *did* stop him," she broke in, her voice firm. "And Olivia and Alec got to have their perfect wedding reception, Pru's definitely leveled up in terms of leveraging her connections, and Ty gets to go back to...well, whatever mysterious angel business he's usually involved in."

The casual way she mentioned Ty's angelic nature made Caleb raise an eyebrow. "Still processing that last display from him?"

"I'm processing a lot of things," Delia said with a smile, then sipped some champagne. "Like the fact that I can apparently tap into a citywide network of psychic energy without any training whatsoever. Or that you can channel enough demonic power to go toe-to-toe with a lord of Hell and come out the other side still essentially yourself."

Something in her tone made him look at her more closely. Her expression was serene enough, but he thought he saw a certain shadow in her eyes. "Is that what's bothering you? The changes?"

"Not 'bothering,' exactly," she said, then paused as she seemed to search for the right words. "It's just...we're different now, aren't we? Both of us. The things we can do, the way we're connected to all this supernatural energy. None of it is going away."

"Maybe not going away," he replied, then hesitated for a moment. Everything was raw and new, and he was still trying to process what had happened. At the same time, though, he wasn't as worried as he'd been even a half hour ago. "But I think it's calming down. Don't you feel it?"

She was quiet for a long moment, her gaze tracking from the window to the small wooden floor where her cousin was dancing with Alec, dark head lying against his chest. "I think I do," she said after a long pause. "I mean, I still feel different. But not quite as different as I did when all that was happening."

"Same here," he said. "Maybe those powers will surge if we need them, but I don't think you have to worry about them consuming every aspect of your life."

She was quiet again. When she spoke, her tone was more musing than troubled, despite her next words. "I keep thinking about what happens next, though. I mean, are we going to spend the rest of our lives fighting demons and investigating supernatural conspiracies? Because after all that, the real estate business is looking pretty tame by comparison."

Despite everything they'd been through, Caleb found himself chuckling. "I don't know about the rest of our lives, but I think we might have earned ourselves some breathing space. And that's no small thing."

She reached over and took his hand, twining her fingers with his. They were warm and strong and just what he needed to feel then.

"No," she said, "I suppose it isn't."

Before Caleb could respond, Olivia appeared beside them, glowing with happiness and maybe a little too much champagne.

"There you are!" she exclaimed, throwing her arms around both of them in an enthusiastic, if slightly tipsy, hug. "Delia, I can't thank you enough for everything you did. The chapel was absolutely perfect, and the flowers were gorgeous. Everything went off without a hitch."

Somehow, Caleb kept his mouth from twitching at the "without a hitch" comment. "Your cousin is kind of a miracle worker," he said. "The reception is really beautiful."

"Thank you." Olivia beamed at him, then turned to Delia. "And thank you for insisting we change venues. I know Alec and I were being difficult about it, but you were absolutely right. Angel's Dream would have been all wrong for us."

"I'm just glad everything worked out," Delia replied, and Caleb admired her ability to keep her expression perfectly neutral. But then again, she had plenty of experience working with difficult clients and maintaining her cool no matter what the circumstances. Smiling, she added, "Sometimes you have to trust your instincts."

"Exactly!" Olivia agreed, then lowered her voice to a conspiratorial whisper. "Actually, I heard something interesting from one of Alec's golf buddies, who also lives here in Henderson. He's a fire chief with the city of Las Vegas. Apparently, there was some kind of electrical fire at Angel's Dream earlier tonight. The building had to be evacuated."

Caleb and Delia exchanged a significant glance. He guessed that the chapel's return to normal reality must have involved some kind of physical manifestation that required an official explanation, even though it had seemed intact enough as they left the building.

"That's terrible," Delia said, just the right amount of concern coloring her tone. "I hope no one was hurt."

"No, not from what I heard," Olivia replied. "But I guess I really must have some kind of psychic powers after all, since I kept having those dreams about fire."

"Or just good instincts," Caleb murmured, and caught the flash of wry amusement in Delia's eyes.

They spent another hour at the reception, making polite conversation with Delia's relatives and Alec's family, dancing to the music that Alec's sister Abby, who appeared to have taken on the role of DJ, was playing from her iPad and beaming to a decent sound system...pretending to be nothing more than an ordinary couple enjoying a lovely evening out. But Caleb could feel the exhaustion building in both of them, the delayed reaction to the night's supernatural battle finally catching up.

"Ready to get out of here?" Delia asked quietly as "The Way You Look Tonight" began to play and people moved toward the dance floor, glad of the chance to slow dance as the evening wore down.

"More than ready," he replied.

They paused to say goodbye to family members and offer final congratulations to the happy couple. Olivia hugged them both again, offering more thanks for all of Delia's help, while Alec shook Caleb's hand.

"Just let me know if you find a good flip that you're not sure you want to take on," he said. "I've been thinking about branching out into that kind of investment."

"Sure," Caleb replied, trying not to grin. He wouldn't have been able to pick Alec Donohue out of a lineup before this evening, but he could already tell that the guy seemed like the type who'd much rather ride someone else's coattails than do any of the hard work himself.

Delia was also looking amused, but she managed to refrain from comment. Just as they were about to leave the room, they bumped into her mother.

"You need to take better care of yourself," Linda Dunne told her daughter. "You look exhausted."

"It's been a long day," Delia agreed, then gave her mother a tired but genuine smile. "A good one, though."

The drive back to her house took them through the heart of Las Vegas, past neon-lit casinos and hotels, past clubs with music pounding loud enough Caleb could hear it even with all the Kona's windows rolled up tight. Everything looked utterly, perfectly normal—tourists walking the Strip, traffic moving in its usual sluggish fits and starts, the eternal carnival of lights and sound that never quite slept. If not for the lingering sensitivity to supernatural energy that remained from their earlier battle, he might have been able to convince himself that the night's events had been nothing more than an extremely vivid dream.

"It feels so weird," Delia said as they turned into her neighborhood of large, Mediterranean-inspired homes. "Looking at all of this, knowing what almost happened, and having it all seem exactly the same. All those people going out to have fun on a Saturday night, completely unaware that reality almost got rewritten around them."

"It's better that way," Caleb told her, knowing

this was the simple truth. "The last thing anyone needs is to start second-guessing every weird shadow or electrical malfunction."

"True." She pulled into her driveway and touched the remote for the garage door, then waited until it opened fully before she pulled inside and closed it behind them. She shut off the engine but made no move to get out of the car. "Caleb?"

"Yes?"

"What we did tonight—the way our abilities worked together, the connection we shared—that's not going away, is it?"

Something vulnerable in her voice made him want to reach out and take her in his arms, but that would have been awkward, thanks to the console that separated the passenger and driver's seats. Instead, he settled for shifting so he could face her better. "No," he said, realizing he needed to be utterly honest about all this. "I don't think it is. Not completely, anyway. Does that scare you?"

"A little," she admitted. "Not because I don't trust you, but because I've never been connected to another person like that before. It's intense."

That was putting it mildly. During their battle with Vinea, their psychic bond had deepened to the point where Caleb could feel her emotions as clearly as his own, could sense her thoughts and intentions without any need for words. It was intimacy on a level that went far beyond anything physical.

The intensity had faded, but, as he'd just told her, he didn't think it would ever disappear entirely.

"We don't have to figure it all out tonight," he said. "We can take this one day at a time."

Delia nodded, then was silent for a moment, as if wrestling with how to phrase her next words. "You know there's a reason why we came here instead of me just taking you home."

Yes, he'd already guessed that, had understood why she wanted to take this next step at her house. His home was bigger and more impressive, but she needed to be someplace where she felt utterly safe.

"And you're okay with that?"

Her eyes met his, clear and unhaunted.

"I wouldn't have brought you here if I weren't."

His hand reached out to touch hers. "Then let's go in."

Chapter Eighteen

—·«((•◦○◦•))»·—

HER HOUSE FELT DIFFERENT THE SECOND she and Caleb went through the door that connected the garage to the kitchen. Not physically...everything looked just the same, from the white cabinets to the black granite countertops and the cheerful little philodendron that sat on the small table in the nook to one side...but energetically. The protective barriers she'd built around her consciousness during the day's supernatural chaos appeared to have been extended to her home as well, creating a sanctuary that seemed completely separate from the otherworldly events they'd just survived.

"Wine?" she asked as she headed toward the rack that sat on the kitchen counter. She was doing her best to sound utterly casual, but she wasn't sure whether she'd succeeded.

Was this a stupid idea? They were both dog tired, and....

No. Her brain shut down that line of thought at once. They loved each other, and they'd just been connected in a way two people probably never had been before. Where else could they end up except here?

"Sure," he replied, and followed her over to the place where the wine rack waited for them.

Delia handed him a bottle of pinot noir and a corkscrew—she'd never been all that great at opening wine bottles in the first place, and her hands were just shaky enough now that she knew better than to attempt it—while she went over to one of the cupboards to get out a couple of stemless wine glasses. The cork came out with ease, and she guessed he'd used the barest flicker of his demon powers to remove the thing. Her fingers brushed his as she gave him one of the glasses she held.

Even that simple contact sent a spark of heat through her.

Okay, maybe she wasn't as tired as she'd feared.

Neither of them said anything. Instead, they took their glasses of wine into the living room, where they sat down on the sofa.

"So," Delia said, figuring there wasn't much point in dancing around either their immediate future...or the one that loomed off in the distance, dark with its own possibilities. "What happens now?"

It was a loaded question, and they both knew it. The question could have referred to their expanding supernatural abilities...or the chances of another demonic incursion.

Or it could have simply referred to the two of them sitting in her living room at nearly midnight after saving Las Vegas from an interdimensional invasion.

"I don't know," Caleb said, expression frank as he sat down beside her. "For the first time in a long while, I actually don't have a plan."

"That might not be such a bad thing," Delia replied, then sipped some of her wine. "Plans seem to go out the window when demons get involved anyway."

He chuckled and drank some wine as well. "They do tend to be chaos agents," he said. "Even the higher-ups like Vinea."

Delia held back a shudder. Yes, she'd had to face down demons before, but neither Calach nor the creature inhabiting August Sellers' body had been a demon lord.

She'd be extremely happy to never have to repeat that experience.

"Can I ask you something?" she said at last.

The question had been weighing on her, and she knew she couldn't ignore it.

Besides, Caleb had always said that he wanted them to be completely honest with each other.

He didn't hesitate. "Anything."

Delia allowed herself a breath, although she didn't take a fortifying sip of wine. "When you were channeling all that power during the fight with Vinea...when you were changing...were you afraid you'd lose yourself completely?"

Dark eyes met hers. Those were the eyes of the man she loved. Whatever he'd been during that moment, he seemed to have come back to himself.

"I was scared shitless," he admitted.

Would he have ever confessed such a weakness to anyone else?

Probably not. That he was comfortable saying such a thing to her told her all she needed to know.

He went on, "For a few minutes there, I wasn't sure there'd be anything left of the person you knew."

"But there was," Delia said. Her voice caught, and she paused to gather herself. No matter how much it had hurt to see him like that, no matter how terrifying it had been to watch his transformation, she'd still somehow known he would come back to her. She went on, "Even when you were more demon than human, I could still sense you underneath all that power."

She set down her wine glass and shifted closer to him on the couch, close enough that she could feel his body heat. Nothing supernatural, just the reassurance of a human body, a human heart.

Caleb set his glass down as well and reached over to cup her face in his hands, and she wanted to weep at the gentle strength in his touch. "I love you," he said simply. "Not just the part of you that can channel ley line energy or see through dimensional barriers. All of you. Even the part that hogs the last piece of garlic bread at dinner."

"I do not—" she began to protest...even though she knew he was right about the garlic bread.

But he grinned and cut her off with another kiss, and this time Delia lost herself completely in the touch of his mouth against hers, the way he tasted of wine and something else, something that was uniquely him.

Because of their connection, she could sense his emotions as clearly as her own—love and desire and relief all tangled together into something as complex as the lattice she'd connected to, a pattern alive with the psychic energies of Las Vegas. But underneath those emotions was a deeper feeling, a recognition of one another that transcended the physical or even the emotional.

When they finally broke apart, Delia was

surprised to realize her lashes were damp with unshed tears.

"I love you, too," she whispered. "I was so afraid I'd lost you. When Vinea had you trapped in that ritual chamber, when I could feel you changing...."

"You didn't lose me," Caleb said as he brushed a strand of hair away from her face. It had come loose from its twist as they kissed, but somehow that felt right. Soon, she hoped, it would be completely free. "You found me. The connection between us—that's what brought me back from the edge."

This time, she was the one who moved toward him, and they lost themselves in another kiss, softer this time but no less meaningful. When she pulled back, the heat building low in her belly and the wicked curve she felt forming on her mouth made her pulse quicken.

"Stay tonight," she said.

It wasn't a question.

"Are you sure?" he asked, even though she guessed he'd known all along that this was the reason why they'd come here in the first place.

Still, he wanted her to be certain. The consideration in that simple question made her heart skip.

"I've never been more sure of anything in my life," Delia replied, knowing there was no reason to hold back.

Honesty. Always honesty.

"We almost lost everything tonight," she added. "I don't want to waste any more time pretending we don't both want this."

She got up from the couch, then took his hand and led him toward the hallway that connected to her bedroom.

Her bedroom was familiar and safe, decorated in shades of soft blue and warm cream, a relaxing space she always enjoyed returning to at the end of the day. Now moonlight streamed through the windows, casting everything in silver relief.

She turned to face him beside the bed, suddenly almost shy despite everything they'd shared. "I should probably mention that I've never done this with someone who's part demon before."

"And I've never done this with someone who can read my mind," Caleb replied with a smile that looked reassuring rather than nervous. "I guess we'll figure it out together."

He reached for the zipper of her dress and pulled it down slowly, and Delia shivered at the way his fingertips brushed against her spine as the silk was peeled away. Underneath the sheath was a set of lacy underwear in pale green, a gorgeous little secret she'd chosen that morning without really understanding why.

Now she was glad she'd listened to that inexplicable instinct.

He laid the dress carefully on the upholstered bench at the foot of her bed. Maybe she'd never want to wear it again, but she appreciated that he treated it with respect anyway.

Had she ever felt as beautiful as she did standing there in the moonlight, watching the way his dark eyes took her in?

She doubted it.

Her fingers found the buttons of his shirt, working them free with hands that trembled only slightly. Soon, the wrinkled black cotton lay on the bench next to her dress, and she reached out to touch him, her fingertips tracing the scars Vinea's claws had left on his ribs, wounds she hadn't even realized he'd received, she'd been so caught up in the heat of battle.

Had he always healed this quickly, or was this something new, an ability he'd gained after that transforming fire burned through him?

Regret and relief warred in her chest in equal measure—regret that he'd been hurt, relief that he'd survived. And when he pressed his lips to the pulse point at her throat, she could feel the way her entire being responded to his touch, the way their connection amplified every sensation until it became almost overwhelming.

There was magic in this, she realized as they sank onto the bed in the silvered darkness. Not the supernatural power that had fueled their battle against the forces of Hell, but something much deeper—the alchemy that occurred when two people chose to trust one other completely.

His hands moved over her with a reverence that made her throat tight, as if he was memorizing every curve of her body, every place where her breath would catch as he touched her. When his fingers traced the line of her collarbone, then drifted lower, she gasped against his mouth, her own hands sliding down the planes of his chest to explore the lean strength of him. He was already hard against her thigh, and the knowledge that he wanted her this much sent another flush of heat through her.

"Delia." Her name on his lips sounded like a prayer, like something sacred.

She answered by finding the strong line of his throat with her mouth, tasting salt and heat. His response was immediate—a low sound that vibrated through his chest as his fingers slid between her thighs, stroking until the pleasure built and built and she shattered against his hand, crying out his name.

For a moment, she could only breathe, trembling in the aftermath. But then she felt him shift above her, his weight settling between her legs, and when their eyes met in the moonlight, she saw everything she felt reflected back at her. Love... trust...the simple knowledge that this was where they both belonged.

When they finally joined, it was physical, of course, and yet she also felt something far more profound, a completion that went beyond bodies, beyond the moment itself. She felt it in the way he held her gaze, in the catch of his breath that matched her own, in the slow, deliberate rhythm that built between them until there was no separation between his pleasure and hers.

The release that followed left them both breathless, clinging to each other as if they'd survived something far more intense than any supernatural battle. And in a way, Delia thought as Caleb pressed his forehead to hers, they had. They'd survived the journey to this moment—all the fear and doubt and danger—and emerged on the other side, whole and together.

This was what she would treasure forever. Not just the physical intimacy, but the absolute certainty that Caleb Lockwood loved her.

Before, when she'd been with other men, she'd thought she loved them, or at least cared for them. She'd never been one to become intimate until her heart was engaged. Now, though...now she realized it could be so much more, was all about her soul flowing into his and somehow, inexplicably, finding herself healed in return.

Afterward, they lay tangled together in the moonlight, Delia's head pillowed on his chest while his fingers played with her loose hair. His breaths were deep and slow, and she could sense his contentment, the feeling of finally being exactly where he belonged.

"No regrets?" she asked softly.

"None," he replied, then pressed a kiss to the top of her head. "You?"

"Only that it took us this long to get here," she said before she settled more deeply into his arms.

They slept then, slept for so long that the room was flooded with sunlight when Delia finally awoke. The clock on the nightstand told her it was nearly ten.

Well, she supposed they'd earned a good sleep.

Next to her, Caleb shifted, and she allowed herself a moment of wonder at the sight of him in her bed, that this incredible man had trusted her enough to be vulnerable with her.

Then his eyes opened, and he propped himself up on one pillow.

"Good morning," he said, and she smiled.

"Good morning."

They leaned in and kissed one another. Her

body stirred, but she thought she was content for the moment. Later, though....

"Do you think it'll be easier now?" she asked. "Living with what we are, I mean."

"Honestly?" Caleb responded as his shoulders lifted ever so slightly. "I don't really know. But I do know it'll be easier doing it together."

She tilted her head as she gazed at him, studying the handsome planes of his face in the bright morning light. "Even if it means more supernatural crises? More demons or angels or whatever else is out there?"

"We'll deal with it when it happens...*if* it happens," he said, then pressed a soft kiss on the top of her head. "For now, let's just enjoy the fact that we're both alive and that Las Vegas is still standing."

"Fair point," she agreed. "But maybe we should have Pru check to make sure everything really is fine."

"Later," Caleb said firmly. "Right now, the only thing I want to check on is this."

He demonstrated what "this" entailed by rolling her beneath him and kissing her with the kind of thorough attention that successfully derailed any further discussion about demons or angels or the otherworldly currents that had flowed through Las Vegas.

For the first time since this whole supernatural mess had begun, she felt like she was exactly where she belonged.

They'd both fallen asleep again after that round of lovemaking, and when Delia woke once more, the sun was even higher in the sky, and she was alone in bed. For a moment, disorientation made her wonder if the events of the night before and earlier this morning had been nothing more than an elaborate dream, but then she caught the rich scent of coffee drifting in from the kitchen and smiled.

She pulled on her silk robe—she'd have to suggest that Caleb leave a few things here, as long as he was amenable to that—and padded barefoot down the hallway, her loose hair falling around her shoulders. She found him standing at the counter, dressed in his jeans from the day before, muscular torso gloriously bare, looking utterly at home in her kitchen as he sipped from a big mug of coffee.

The sight of him made something warm and contented unfurl in her chest.

Or maybe somewhere a bit lower down.

She was just reaching for a mug for herself when her phone rang. It had been sitting in the kitchen all this time, since she'd left it on the counter the night before. The caller ID showed Pru's name, and Delia sighed.

"Good morning, Pru," she said after she put the phone to her ear.

"Oh, good, you're alive," her friend said without wasting time on a greeting. "I was starting to worry when you didn't answer my texts last night."

Delia pulled her phone far enough away so she could see the unread messages that had piled up overnight. Apparently, she'd been more thoroughly distracted than she'd realized. "Sorry, it was a long night."

"So, are you and demon boy finally together? Because your voice has that 'I got some' quality to it."

Heat flooded Delia's cheeks, and she was grateful Caleb was focused on pouring some more coffee into his mug and couldn't see her face. "Pru...."

"I'm taking that as a yes," her friend said cheerfully. "Good for you. Anyway, everything in Vegas seems to have settled down to its usual dull roar, but Ty still thinks we need to remain vigilant."

"Oh, he does?" Delia returned. "Were you two also staying up past your bedtimes?"

"We went out for some coffee afterward," Pru replied, her tone now overly severe. "And then he dropped me off at home. Anyway, while things seem okay for now, he's still worried that we might not be totally out of the woods yet."

Delia rolled her eyes, and Caleb tilted his head at her. "Pru and Ty think we shouldn't be breaking out the bubbly quite yet," she told him.

"We don't need to worry about that right now," he said as he moved closer to her. "In fact, I think we've earned a little downtime."

"Have we?" she asked, but she knew there was a hint of a smile in her voice. "Because it feels like every time we think we're done with the supernatural world, it finds another way to drag us back in. It's worse than the Mob."

"Hey, I'm still on the phone here," Pru pointed out. "But I have to say, I agree with Mr. Tall, Dark, and Demonic over there. You two just saved Las Vegas from an interdimensional invasion. You've earned at least a day off."

Delia couldn't help but laugh. "Since when are you all about taking breaks?"

"Since my best friend started dating a guy who can apparently channel enough power to take on a demon lord," Pru replied. "Look, I'm not saying you two should drop everything and jet off to the Bahamas for the next six months, but I think you're probably fine with taking a day...or maybe two or three...before you get back on the horse."

Six months in the Bahamas with Caleb sounded absolutely heavenly. But, setting all supernatural concerns aside, Delia knew she had clients and responsibilities here. The crew at the flip house had continued to work through all the drama, probably blissfully unaware of how close Las Vegas had been to getting overrun with demons, but she still needed to stop by and check on their progress before too much more time had elapsed.

"Okay," she said, "we'll think about it."

"I figured you would."

After she ended the call, Delia set down her phone and looked over at Caleb. "So...what do you think?"

"I think," he said, as he put down his coffee and reached over to twine his fingers with hers, "that right now, Las Vegas is safe, the ley lines are flowing normally, and Vinea is stuck in Hell for the time being. We can take a few days to just be normal people."

"Normal people who can channel demonic energy and tap into citywide psychic networks?" she asked, raising one eyebrow.

"Normal-ish people," he amended, and she chuckled.

"I like the sound of that," she said, then moved closer until she was standing within the circle of his arms. "Normal-ish people who can handle whatever comes next. Besides," she continued with a grin, "it's not like either of us can go back to being completely normal now. Might as well embrace the weirdness."

"'Embrace the weirdness,'" Caleb repeated, a warm light in his cola-brown eyes and an answering grin of his own on that oh-so-kissable mouth.

"I like that."

The Vegas Slayers series continues in Devil to Pay.

Also by Christine Pope

LEGENDARY

(Urban Fantasy/Paranormal Romance)

Silver Linings

Lion's Share

Trial by Fire (February 2026)

Here Be Dragons (May 2026)

VEGAS SLAYERS

(Urban Fantasy/Paranormal Romance)

Speak of the Devil

Devil in the Details

The Devil Went Down to Laughlin

Devil May Care

Devil to Pay

The Devil's Due (August 2026)

The Devil Next Door (December 2026)

THE WITCHES OF MINGUS MOUNTAIN

(Paranormal Romance)

Stolen Time

Borrowed Time

Killing Time

Wind Called

Demon Loved

Christmas Past

Season of Magic

Healer's Heart (June 2026)

PROJECT DEMON HUNTERS*

(Paranormal Romance)

Unquiet Souls

Unbound Spirits

Unholy Ground

Unseen Voices

Unmarked Graves

Unbroken Vows

Unholy Night

THE DJINN WARS*

(Paranormal Romance)

Chosen

Taken

Fallen

Broken

Forsaken

Forbidden

Awoken

Illuminated

Stolen

Forgotten

Driven

Unspoken

Hidden

Written

Given

Mistaken

FAMILIAR SPIRITS*

(Cozy Mystery/Paranormal Romance)

Spells and Spaniels

Cauldrons and Cats

Hexes and Hedgehogs

Charms and Chihuahuas

Runes and Ravens

LATTES AND LEVITATION*

(Cozy Mystery/Paranormal Romance)

Caffeine Before Curses

Muffins After Magic

Pastries and Prophecies

Eclairs and Ectoplasm

Sugar Skulls and Specters

Wedding Cakes and Wishes

HEDGEWITCH FOR HIRE*

(Cozy Mystery/Paranormal Romance)

Grave Mistake

Social Medium

Household Demons

Perpetual Potion

Jingle Spells

Wandering Monsters

Uninvited Ghosts

Prophet Motive

Ballroom Bits

Spell Check

Brew Confessions

Charm School

UNEXPECTED MAGIC*

(Urban Fantasy/Paranormal Romance)

Found Objects

Finders, Keepers

Lost and Found

Finding Destiny

THE WITCHES OF WHEELER PARK*

(Paranormal Romance)

Storm Born

Thunder Road

Winds of Change

Mind Games

A Wheeler Park Christmas

Blood Ties

Healing Hands

Wishful Thinking

Smoke and Mirrors

MISS PRIMM'S ACADEMY FOR WAYWARD
WITCHES*

(Fantasy/Academy Romance)

Misspelled

Dispelled

Expelled

THE DEVIL YOU KNOW*

(Paranormal Romance)

Sympathy for the Devil

Charmed, I'm Sure

A Wing and a Prayer

Wish Upon a Star

THE WITCHES OF CANYON ROAD*

(Paranormal Romance)

Hidden Gifts

Darker Paths

Mysterious Ways

A Canyon Road Christmas

Demon Born

An Ill Wind

Higher Ground

Haunted Hearts

THE WITCHES OF CLEOPATRA HILL*

(Paranormal Romance)

Darkangel

Darknight

Darkmoon

Sympathetic Magic

Protector

Spellbound

A Cleopatra Hill Christmas

Impractical Magic

Strange Magic

The Arrangement

Defender

Bad Blood

Deep Magic

Darktide

Star Bright

THE WATCHERS TRILOGY*

(Paranormal Romance)

Falling Dark

Dead of Night

Rising Dawn

THE SEDONA FILES*

(Paranormal/Science Fiction Romance)

Bad Vibrations

Desert Hearts

Angel Fire

Star Crossed

Falling Angels

Enemy Mine

TALES OF THE LATTER KINGDOMS*

(Fantasy Romance)

Dragon Rose

Ashes of Roses

One Thousand Nights

Threads of Gold

The Wolf of Harrow Hall

Moon Dance

The Song of the Thrush

———

THE GAIAN CONSORTIUM SERIES*

(Science Fiction Romance)

Beast (free prequel novella)

Blood Will Tell

Breath of Life

The Gaia Gambit

The Mandala Maneuver

The Titan Trap

The Zhore Deception

The Refugee Ruse

———

STANDALONE TITLES

Hearts on Fire (Paranormal Romance)

Taking Dictation (Contemporary Romance)

Golden Heart (Gaslamp Fantasy Romance)

Night Music: A Modern Reimagining of The Phantom of the Opera (Contemporary Romance)

Ghost Dance: A Sequel to Gaston Leroux's The Phantom of the Opera (Historical Mystery/Romance)

Flight Before Christmas (Fantasy Romance)

* Indicates a completed series

About the Author

USA Today bestselling author Christine Pope has been writing stories ever since she commandeered her family's Smith-Corona typewriter back in grade school. Her work includes paranormal romance, fantasy romance, and science fiction/space opera romance. She makes her home in Arizona.

Christine Pope on the Web:
www.christinepope.com

facebook.com/ChristinePopeAuthor

youtube.com/@ChristinePopeAuthor